Trisha

Hope yo

and maybe Sarah will

enjoy the ride.

Martin W. Petry

MW01602722

Hard Justice

The Violation

by

Martin H. Petry

Bloomington, IN  Milton Keynes, UK

authorHOUSE®

AuthorHouse™
1663 Liberty Drive, Suite 200
Bloomington, IN 47403
www.authorhouse.com
Phone: 1-800-839-8640

AuthorHouse™ UK Ltd.
500 Avebury Boulevard
Central Milton Keynes, MK9 2BE
www.authorhouse.co.uk
Phone: 08001974150

First published by AuthorHouse 12/11/2006

ISBN: 1-4259-6051-0 (sc)

Printed in the United States of America
Bloomington, Indiana

This book is printed on acid-free paper.

Acknowledgements

There are many more friends who have endured this 3 -year effort than can be named. However, I would like to thank my creator for shutting one door and opening another.

When one possibility ends there are many more to undertake if such a gift can be accepted...

PART ONE

Chapter 1

Sam was feeling exceptionally well. He was recalling his lunchtime conversation with his wife, Monica. She was giving him the evening's schedule; they were celebrating his son Timothy's birthday. While Sam went over the conversation, he performed the end of the day rituals. He was grinning widely, thinking of how detailed his wife's arranging of the evening would be. The whole evening sounded great. He mulled over how the whole family enjoyed these moments, as a family. Sam removed his work gloves as he made his way back to his truck. The kids would be smiling, hugging and kissing. The girls made such a fuss over Tim. Sam got into his truck and rested from the day's aches and pains. He thought about Monica and himself. How after the celebrating with the kids, they would sweetly love each other, a finish to another special evening. He started the truck and began his drive home.

Traffic seemed heavier than usual. Sam grumbled a bit while he smacked the steering wheel. Sam's frustration was evident. Out of habit, he lit a cigarette, had a few drags, _____ then realized he was trying to quit. Sam shook his head, had a last drag, and flipped the butt out the window. Sam gazed over the hood, through the windshield. Traffic was becoming downright unreasonable.

Sam noticed the time on his watch; he switched the radio tuner to his first selection. The weather report was broadcasting; he went to a second choice, receiving the end of a traffic report. Something about roads being closed due to a manhunt...Sam's gut went sour; he nervously reached for a cigarette. He had forgotten about quitting. He sat motionless with building frustration in his truck while it was running, going nowhere. Sam thought, "Why today?" After his first deep drag, he expelled the calming feeling in his lungs. Sam was indignant about the commercial broadcasting. Sonny's Hardware was on his list. He thought of how the commercial was interrupting vital news. He was making a mental note, to avoid Sonny's Hardware to avenge this nuisance. Time lost in arriving at the agreed upon schedule was Sam's greatest concern. Breaking news was back on, and Sam finished his smoke. There was a reporter on seen, this reporter was waiting on information to come via a police report. Sam thought he heard his road mentioned. As the regular programming broadcasted, Sam reached for another smoke. His fingers fumbled with the pack until he extracted another, second nature, bad habit he hadn't quit, and lit it.

Impatiently Sam checked his watch again. 4:38 P.M. Monica should be running into the same traffic he found himself in, on her own way home, he relaxed realizing they'd both be late. By the clock, they were 8 minutes passed the pre-arranged meeting time they had agreed to during their earlier conversation. Sam dragged some more on the cigarette. He tilted his head back as he exhaled the calming smoke. The traffic began to move, so slowly. Sam swore to himself. At the very first opportunity, he was going to get some cell phones. He had always detested the thought of paying for them, somehow the value, now made sense. The fact that this was happening close to home was un-nerving enough. Again, he shook his head. He raised his smoke to realize it had burned out. He flicked it and lit another.

The broadcast went back to the on scene reporter. A few words, as the police spokesperson addressed the microphone and crowd of reporters. *Today at approximately 4 p.m., one woman and three children were discovered. They were murdered. A witness, one Ginny Holman residing at 1472 Home Ave. called to the station reporting two men fleeing from a neighbors' house....* Sam hit the brakes. The lit cigarette fell out of his mouth between his legs. He parked the truck opening the door, and jumped from truck. He began running home. His mind was the only part of his body moving faster than his legs. He was processing what he had heard. *How could this be??? They weren't supposed to be*

5

home! Sam passed the cars, which had previously been his impediment. His lungs were burning, not just from the running, but for the needed breath exchange for the emotional shock he just absorbed. Sweat broke on his forehead, as it found its way into his eyes; he wiped them with the back of his arms in a panicked stride. He arrived at the first roadblock. The police on duty looked skeptically at Sam; he was winded and disheveled as the police saw him. They assumed an offensive posture. Sam hadn't realized how he looked, with labored breath; Sam identified himself, the posture of offense immediately shifted. One of them, got on the radio, the other came to Sam. By the time, Sam was catching his breath; an unmarked cruiser skidded to a halt from a lesser busy road. The detectives spoke to the officers and then lead Sam to the car. Once in the vehicle the siren yelped as it made emergency progress through traffic. As the car arrived at Sam's house, the detectives broke the cold silence. "Mr. Murphy, this might be a good time to call a friend… The scene is bad!!! Might there be someone we may call for you?" Sam replied, "No, but thanks."

They got out of the car and proceeded passed other parked cars. Sam walked passed the Medical Examiner's Wagon. The cargo area's doors were open…. his throat grew tight, his knees weakened slightly. The detectives must have noticed as they both shored him up by grabbing his arms. When they sensed his coming around they relieved their support just as quickly as they had offered it. As they had reached the threshold of the entry, the detectives stopped Sam. They once again tried to feel him out. Sam stood silently… considering what they were preparing him for. He imagined it must be bad. His throat swallowed, and he seemed to find some ease. And, he then reminded them; the phone he'd be using… was inside the house. They allowed Sam to pass.

Sam saw the threshold differently; he was never entering his happy life again…. Whatever lay beyond the entry was his ever-living nightmare. He thanked them again and proceeded on weakening legs. When he entered, his body felt as though it been struck. He lost his breath. His two children lay lifeless, in an un-natural position. His hand went to support himself on the buffet. The very one he and the children had refinished. Sam sucked in air just in time to prevent passing out. His memories shifted to that of his wife. He realized the beginning of this crime started here and ended elsewhere, this grim loss was just unfolding. Tears were now flowing from his eyes; his sleeves were soaked from wiping tears he was unaware of. As Sam reached for them, the detectives retrieved him. "Mr. Murphy, this is a crime scene." Sam understood the need as he retracted his reach. His gut shuddered more. They lead him into the bathroom. More horror! His eldest daughter, Tracy, she was only 17 and brutally exposed, wounds upon her for nothing more than sick pleasure. He was at a total loss, he felt physically ill. His swallowing increased as the metallic taste grew in his mouth. A deluge of tears swelled from his eyes dropping to a wet chest. Emotional escape forced him to back out of the bathroom. The horror seemed to crush him. The sound of the zippers closing on the body bags reminded him of the others. Instantly Sam asked pitifully. *Where's my wife?* They lead Sam to the bedroom. The devastation he was about to see was far worse than what he had already seen. This room was so special for them; it was the place where their whole dream started… Their bedroom was the altar to their life. Everything was destroyed, violated. Monica was not in clear sight. She was on the floor, behind the bed. The M.E. personnel had finished their jobs; they had been packing up as Sam arrived.

Sam looked at their bed…. It had been the source of all their pleasure, dream building and living, now a horrible scene seen as a slab of sacrifice. Sam moved passed the bed, as his eyes fell on his beloved, he buckled, ____ howling a bone chilling agony. Those remaining in the room winced. He embraced his wife seeking all that she could no longer give him. He held her, realizing she could never hold him as she had. All of those present had sensed the loss of love in what they saw and heard. Sam kissed his wife, her lips were cold, and he released her and rose from his lost life. Everyone in the room was surprised at Sam's sudden motion. The suddenness of the move forced all to wipe their tears. The two detectives asked, "Mr. Murphy, if you don't mind, there are some questions…"

Unexpectedly Sam changed up. Coldly Sam asked to be called by his first name. They returned to the kitchen, it was the clearest part of the house. Tracy was being brought out in the ghastly body bag. A while later… Monica. Sam said nothing until his family was removed. As Sam sat, he again thought of how this once familiar place would never be the same. "Mr. Murp__ Sam? We have to ask you some questions, if you are able?" Sam indicated he'd need a minute to make some calls. Sam dialed and spoke very few words to those he spoke to. He returned a bit later and apologized. Sam was looking for a cigarette he left in the truck; a detective had retrieved his own and offered them up to Sam. Sam's trembling hand showed his distress as he reached for the offered cigarettes. He placed the smoke into the corner of his mouth and lit it. He had a large drag and thanked the detective who offered. He then asked them if they would mind if he had a drink. Their response didn't matter; Sam was only being polite. He asked them if they wanted anything. Both offered nods, Sam poured a drink for himself and then made coffee, just the same.

The questioning had begun and Sam answered as best as he could. He realized the coffee was done as he finished his drink. The detectives did have some coffee. Both gave their flavor to Sam. Hendricks had his coffee black and sweet. Jameson had a light. After Sam had fixed the two officers beverages, he went back to the bottle he left open and poured once again. It was a heavy drink. When Sam took his seat, the detectives had changed from questions to comments. They went over what they thought had happened. The mention of possible rapes was taxing to Sam.

Over an hour had passed. Sam was not a heavy drinker. By the end of the interview, however, Sam was on his fifth drink. The detectives had finished the coffee and had left their business cards, letting Sam know they would be in touch. They would know more after they had the M.E.'s report. While they exited, a patrol officer entered who had Sam's keys; he had retrieved Sam's truck. They all left Sam alone.

The drinks were catching up with him. He welcomed it. He had another tall drink and lit a smoke. He staggered to his backyard furniture. This drinking was serving as intended. He passed out facing a rising moon.

Chapter 2

Sam woke to dry mouth. The sun shone through his eyelids leaving blood red hues in his eyes. His head felt as though it was in a vise with an axe centered squarely in it. The pain was crippling, the pounding in his head had left him unsure of the horror from yesterday as being real, or just a terrible nightmare. The hangover he was experiencing told him the horror was real. Sam raised himself up, his head responded disagreeably. He felt like crying, he could produce no tears in his dehydrated state. As he gained his footing, he faced his house. His thirst drove him to the garden hose.

The valve to the hose was to the left of the sliding glass door. The water in the hose went cool after he turned the petcock; the sun had not yet heated the water in it. He was thankful, although he would have drunk it warm. He raised the hose to the back of his neck, instantaneously reducing the pounding at the base of his head. He lifted the hose; the water flowing from the hose cascaded over his head. The water whisked away the heat, slight relief. After some time Sam turned off the water, and turned back to his nightmare. Forward motion did not come easily; his effort was moving his feet forward.

The hose's water had provided an immediate thirst relief, it also made for a cold sweat as Sam moved forward. His stomach had not received the water as he thought it might have. His sense of balance was lacking. His left hand reached up searching for the exterior wall of the house. He found a blurred line along the wall. His eyes followed his hand, he noticed spattered blood on his hand, and it was the last straw. His physiology responded violently with a vomiting episode, it worsened only when Sam developed dry heaves. Sam had never been so vulnerable or lost. Sam thought of the detectives from the night before… he remembered his calmness. He shook his head and wanted to whimper.

If his family could see him now, is all Sam could think of. He was always hard on himself. Now the hardness became more than a condition, it was a receptacle for his grief and misery. And, in realizing this, Sam's vulnerability diminished. His loss remained.

He stood again and turned the petcock valve, which produced a flow of water once again. Sam thought to himself, in his previous life… anger motivated him to succeed in his business. He rinsed the illness away in front of him, and his loss crystallized. *Never again would life be as it was.* The vomit rinsed away only a small portion of the unwanted pain. Sam rinsed himself off and washed out his mouth. After he turned the water off, he proceeded to the slider and entered his nightmare.

Sam sensed the horror diminishing, while the loss remained. He started to become angry, he did try to avoid the flood of emotions he was experiencing. In his previous life, anger motivated him to provide a comfortable living for his family. Anger was containable. Today it abided none of the barriers Sam had built for containment. The anger he had today, had no transferable purpose. He was cautious. He knew, here at the sight of his life's disposal, there was a direction to take. He also knew the wrong direction would be worse than the condition he now found himself in.

Sam thought about having a shower. He considered the work and decided a shower would only have to be repeated. Before beginning the grim duty of cleaning up, he decided to make some coffee. While he waited on the brewing, he decided on a process of salvage in this ruin. He thought about the complete destruction his home and family had endured. He compared it to his own ability in being diligent in his own business. So complete! The phone rang; the noise of the appliance gave Sam a need to end the ringing. He tripped on some debris reaching for the phone. Sam answered the phone, but didn't speak into the mouthpiece. It was one of the detectives from the night before; he informed Sam the autopsies were being done as they spoke. He further mentioned Ginny Holman would be coming to the office to view mug shots. He closed the conversation by stating Sam could expect reports as information warranted. Sam thanked the detective, and hung up.

He wondered; were these detectives up to the challenge? Sam was masterful at observing circumstances. He could size operational diligence, and make decisions according to forward progress. Sam saw the obvious destruction. He also saw a pattern… *Those responsible for all of this have demonstrated hardcore tendencies. Capture would not come easily. They, in fact, had escaped.*

The coffee had finished brewing. Sam poured himself a cup. After a sip, he fumbled for a smoke and lit up. While he formulated an attack plan, the doorbell rang. Sam barked, "Door's open come on in." Jake opened the door and presented himself. Jake and Sam were primary partners of Sam-Jak Inc. These two were brotherly in their relationship; they didn't have familial bonds. Jake wasn't much for small talk. He noticed Sam's effort. He walked over to the coffee and poured himself a cup. He had a sip, and looked at his friend. He noticed Sam was smoking in the house. It was a change from before. Jake reached into his pocket and produced a cigar. After he ignited the cigar, he evened the burn. A massive cloud of bluish smoke seemed to envelope Jake where he stood. Jake was deliberate in all things he did, this was one of the strongest attributes of both men's relationship. Jake finally spoke.

"Wasting no time, are ya?" Sam spent a moment. He tried to summon the words, all he could manage was, and "Things have changed." Jake took some more from the cigar, he moved closer to Sam. Jake's approach was likened to someone moving towards a wounded animal, he didn't really know what to expect. "I've noticed." Jake moved about the house, inspecting the destruction, working the coffee and cigar handily. Jake turned to Sam and looked in his eyes. He couldn't manage the words. Sam knew what Jake was thinking without him having to say much. Sam watched Jake as he finished the coffee. Jake spoke again, "I guess I'll start here."

Sam was glad Jake showed up when he did. Sam knew Jake was not a man capable of much sensitivity. He also knew that was one of the reasons they got on so well. Sam could trust Jake. Sam had been busy before Jake had gotten there. He had picked up anything worth saving from the death chamber of Tim and Ashley. He deliberated going into the bedroom, he wavered, recalling last night, he realized he was still raw. His sanctuary had been violated. The altar of family worship he and Monica had so carefully constructed was gone.

Jake had seen Sam thinking of something. He knew it wasn't good. He thought of something he could do while he continued to clean up the debris. After Jake had added to the pile of debris from the bathroom to the pile Sam had already started, he poured two more coffees. He brought Sam his coffee and took a seat. "Hey pal, take a load off. Have a sip of coffee." Sam reached for the coffee, and Jake lit a cigarette for his friend. Both men sat in silence, finding comfort in drinking the coffee and smoking their own materials. Some time had passed; Sam was dashing his cigarette and finishing the last of his coffee. "You ought to clean up Sam; you look terrible, almost like what the cat dragged in." Sam looked at Jake. He considered what Jake had just said, and realized his friend wasn't kidding. Jake always told it like it was, and any resistance would just fire him up. The only choice he had was to take the shower. Sam responded like he always did. He took a moment, "Jake, I think I'll go take that shower!"

Jake was accustomed to agreement when he offered advice. "Make sure you lose the fur, while you're in there!" Sam made his way to the bathroom. He entered and was amazed by Jake's effectiveness. The bathroom looked nothing like it was the night before. The snapshot of violation Sam had had in his mind was no- where to be seen. The image would haunt Sam for quite some time. Thanks to Jake, only the image remained, not the reality. Sam disrobed and entered the shower. The water seemed to force Sam to the tub floor. The pulsating water relieved Sam of tension he was unaware he had. Relaxing under the flow of water, Sam felt his throat tightening up and the tears came again.

Sam had faced loss. But he had faced it with a remarkable strength from his family. When his parents had been killed in an auto accident, Monica and Tracy were his support. Tim and Ashley were not born yet.

As he focused on his family, he realized only memories were left. The tears compounded into sobs... The howling once again had begun.

Jake was glad Sam was facing himself. He jumped into high gear, knowing how Sam and Monica had worshiped the bedroom. Jake recalled many stories Sam had told him during the slower times at work. He deemed any activity Sam would engage in cleaning the bedroom would be dangerous to his friend. He prioritized the need to protect his partner. The howling sobs coming from the shower were evidence enough for Jake.

Jake was a hardcore type. He had always been that way. This nature of his was not conducive to having a wife and family. Jake understood his own condition. The fact that he couldn't have a foundation in a family did not exclude him from seeing the value others placed in having one. Jake liked himself. His actions seemed to speak for the words he couldn't bring himself to verbalize. While he had always been happy for Sam and his family, he was very worried for his friend now. Jake was not pitiful. He was confidant in who he was.

He likened marriage to the old saying: *In for a penny, in for a pound.* Jake liked his pennies! While Jake was going through Sam's bedroom cleaning up, he felt a tremendous bitterness. Jake utilized this bitter feeling to apply more energy to his process. He desperately wanted to save his friend from a place, which might leave him suicidal.

Sam's sobs had lessened as Jake broke a sweat. The items worthy of salvage found a new home in a box. The debris went into plastic bags. Jake worked with machine-like effectiveness. As the sobbing ceased, Jake's classification process had been accomplished. Those guilty of this devastation, if they could see Jake working, would be in awe. What they accomplished in the time they had, paled in results, compared to Jake's efforts.

Jake wasn't sure of when Sam would be finishing up, but he knew it wouldn't be too much longer. He doubled his effort as he removed the bagged trash from the room. All the salvage, which had been sorted, was also removed. Jake had heard the water being shut off... He made a beeline towards the bedroom and fetched some clothes. He laid them in front of the bathroom door. Jake found a towel and wiped the sweat from his face and neck. He poured another coffee and re-fired his cigar. When the bath door had opened a cloud of steam poured out of the room. Sam had seen the cloths on the floor and grabbed them. He dressed and joined Jake.

Sam found Jake grinning a bit. Jake was reflecting on his earlier visit to the job sight. Sam said nothing. Jake would reveal his grinning when he was ready. They both sat a bit. Jake had that cigar in his mouth. He loved to roll it off his tongue between chewing it and smoking it.

"The boys have sent their deepest wishes for your comfort." Sam nodded in affirmation to what Jake had told him. As Jake reviewed the meeting this morning in his mind, he considered if Sam needed to know the details. "Stan and George were a little uncomfortable with running the job…. I told them, 'fire up the machines and follow the week's goals as best as you can.' You should have seen them Sam, they all wanted to shut the job down and come to you for support."

Sam knew how Jake took time to formulate his words. He remained silent, waiting for Jake to deliver the rest of his ideas. "They were, let's say disappointed. They wanted to convince me their efforts would be better spent in your support." Jake took a pause. He was figuring his words. "I had to gather them all and pacify those babies. Sam you would have laughed if you could have, they wouldn't give up on their idea to help you out. I had to remind them there would be plenty of time to offer condolences. Right now, it was time to earn their pay. I told them to, 'Suck it up!' They were speechless and they fumed a bit. They all wanted to know what might be happening…. Were we closing the business? How would it affect them? The usual grumbling, when there was little left to say, I told them, "fire up these machines and get to work." Jake giggled a bit, "As they were walking to their respective equipment, I told George and Stan… No bullshit interruptions!" Sam shook his head. Jake was not an easy fella to get on with. Sam imagined Stan and George wanting to fight more, but he knew they wouldn't cross Jake, that was an un-winning position. Jake cleared his throat. "I guess they got my message when I told them their partnership was on the line. So my friend, I see you got rid of the fur…. Are ya hungry?"

Sam hadn't thought about food, he was still thinking of all he thought he needed to do. Jake read his mind and laughed. Sam knew that laugh. It usually accompanied thinking that was no longer required. The men collected themselves and headed to Jake's truck. Sam was not going to be doing much thinking today, and he was grateful for his friend Jake and his company.

Chapter 3

The men were in Jake's truck; Sam had no idea of their destination. Jake was doing the driving, and he had an idea of a favorite little eatery of theirs. Sam hadn't realized how hungry he was. He knew Jake had a good idea, as his hunger became evident. Sam noticed there were tunes on the radio. He figured Jake had already decided to spare Sam of the news reports leaving him so unbalanced. Sam appreciated his friend's efforts. The ride wasn't long; there was no discussion. Jake knew Sam would speak when he was ready. As Jake pulled up to his destination he found some satisfaction with the timing... most of the morning crew had already finished breakfast and left. The eatery was less than half-full. As the men exited the truck, Jake moved into a lead position, he figured he could be a better bodyguard for Sam if he were in front. Sympathy offerings were not going to be allowed today, there would be plenty of time for that later.

Most of the folks in this place knew Jake and Sam. Most of them liked Sam more than Jake. As Jake entered, he flashed a look at Mike. Mike was the owner of *Babes Diner*. Mike had no problem understanding what that glare meant. Mike had called over the counter girl. Brenda went to Mike. He told her, "No flirting with those two, get the order and leave them be." She didn't like what Mike had to say, but she agreed. Mike was aware of Brenda's affection towards Sam. While Mike was setting Brenda straight, the men went to the corner booth at the far end of the dining area. Mike knew Brenda. He knew her well. She was worth having around. She did good work, but had a propensity to flirt. Mike knew the flirtatious way was helpful to business at times, but when it went too far, those involved chose another place to eat. This circumstance was a heavy consideration of his. He hoped she would do as he said, and let them be.

Brenda's heart melted around Sam. She fantasized of a time where she would serve him in whatever way he wanted, her fantasy provided her hours of pleasure, she did respect that Sam was married and that he loved his wife. Mike looked at Brenda's eyes. He felt a need to repeat what he said. Brenda seemed disturbed by Mike's nagging. She looked at Mike realizing how serious he was. She confirmed that she understood what he meant, and was off to her work.

Brenda went to the coffee maker and poured two cups. She placed them on the tray she used, and moved to the station. When she had arrived at the table, she placed the coffees in front of the men. She was minding what she promised to Mike, as she scribbled the orders. She thanked them for the orders and left the table. Mike had been scrutinizing her mannerisms while she took the order. She wasn't happy about Mike's directions. She showed her disapproval in the manner she handed off the order. She went back to the table where the men had been sitting, and started setting places on the table. She sensed an opportunity and seized upon it. "Sam, I hope you know how sorry we all are..." Before she could say anything else, Jake indicated he needed a glass of ice water. She looked at Jake with a scowl. She never liked Jake much. Sam cleared his throat, "Thanks Brenda, Thanks so much." Anything that Sam said seemed to fuel her fantasy. She beamed when Sam addressed her. Jake quickly mentioned the ice water again; she looked at Jake much the same way he was looking at her. She left the table, and retrieved the water, with less ice than Jake wanted. Jake held his tongue; He didn't want to make his diversion more than what it was supposed to be. Jake had realized Sam was only ready to respond, rather than act or speak. "Sam, this is a shitty deal. I'm beyond being sorry. I'm not sure why it happened, but I'm sure we'll see it to the end." Sam just nodded. After some thought Sam remembered the phone call he got from the detective. Sam watched Jake's hands grab the glass. Sam reached for his cigarettes and produced two. He lit them both and handed one to Jake. Sam was hurrying because he had seen Jake crush a glass in his hands. He wanted to avoid a repeat of that fiasco.

Jake grabbed the smoke and thanked Sam. The two men sat silently smoking while they sipped coffee.

Mike had rung the pick-up bell. So, Brenda collected the orders from him and was making her way towards the men. She arrived and placed Jake's plate down. She used a more delicate motion in placing Sam's plate. She asked the men if there was anything else she could get for them. Secretly, she hoped Sam would require something else from her. Jake spoke up. "I'll have some more water... And, don't be so damn stingy with the ice this time!" Sam looked at his food while Jake chastised Brenda. She grabbed Jake's glass and went to fill his glass. If Mike were not so observant she might have flipped Jake the finger... she did as Jake demanded and returned with his water. In a split second, she decided spilling it on Jake wouldn't be a good move...

The men began eating. Sam lacked enthusiasm about his choice, but he obeyed his hunger. In short order, the plates were left empty, some yolk from the toast wiping was all the evidence that remained. Brenda had noticed the men were finished. She totaled their bill and left it on the table. Before she had totaled the bill, she managed to scribble her number on another piece of paper. When she felt confident, she placed the paper in front of Sam. "Sam, if you ever need to talk, here is my number." Jake glared at her, and then passed one to Mike. "Brenda that is kind of you Thanks very much," Sam replied. He pocketed the number. She beamed a smile. Jake grabbed the bill with a disapproving gesture. Jake left a $10 for a $9.50 breakfast. He almost felt like asking for the change. Before he could request the change, he realized, the interaction, which just occurred, was why he was in business with Sam. Where Sam was considerate and smooth, Jake was rough and without demeanor. Jake marveled at how Sam was suffering, and how he could be smooth even under this awful burden of loss. Jake's disgust of Brenda diminished. Sam had always been a leveling influence in Jake's life. As the men left the table, Sam dropped $2 dollars on the table to cover the tip Jake wouldn't leave. Jake could only shake his head.

Chapter 4

The clock in the truck indicated the time as 10:51 a.m. Jake started the motor and drove. He decided on a destination, keeping it a secret. He headed towards *The Buried Treasure*. This was Jake's pride and joy. While Sam and other guys had gotten married and had families, Jake had invested his time into his own love. *The Buried Treasure* was Jake's idea of home. She was a large sloop, a 45' Pearson. Jake, Sam, Monica and the kids had sailed many times together. Jake felt as though the freedom of the water would minimize the assault of memories flooding Sam.

Once Sam had an idea of their destination, he spoke of other needs. "There is so much to do…" Jake shrugged, and continued driving to the marina. Sam thought of how Jake lacked caring for others opinions. Sometimes it bothered Sam. It was the one thing about Jake Sam wished he could change. Wished…. What a waste. Sam understood all of his cares came from a place, which no longer existed. He lit a cigarette and exhaled the smoke. "Jake, we should go back to my place; I have to finish the work." Jake rolled the cigar he had in his mouth over his tongue. "Sam, do you think anyone else will do it before you can?" Jake realized he just dropped a bomb! Jake was hardly apologetic, but he found an apology for what he just asked. "I'm sorry Sam that was an inconsiderate thing to say, let's just go to **The Buried Treasure** and just sit. We'll come up with a plan out there."

Even when Jake was cold, he still made sense. Monica's parents wouldn't be there for a couple of days. Neither of them had brother's or sister's. All that could be done was done. Jake was right. The truck wheeled into the marina, Jake parked in his usual spot. The men walked silently past Jake's neighbors. The marina was not busy. It was not desolate either.

Jake slowed his pace as they approached. He scanned **The Buried Treasure,** as his field of vision grew smaller. He loved the silhouette she left to the eye. Sam always felt great seeing Jake approaching *The Buried Treasure.* He was truly enjoying his ritual. Today, his enthusiasm lacked. Sam wasn't selfish by nature; even in his deep agony Sam tried to appreciate Jake's wisdom. The men had reached the vessel, Jake boarded first. He checked all the mechanical parts; the winches, lines, blocks, cockpit instrumentation, and finally he started the auxiliary power. Sam was well versed in why the motor was called auxiliary power. Sam's mind went to a time when he asked Jake the reason it was called, auxiliary power. Sam smiled as he recalled the time...

"Hey Captain Jake! Why would you call a fine looking diesel engine like that one, auxiliary power?" Jake had been coiling some rope when he heard the question. Before Jake could formulate a response, his hands fouled his coil. Jake was literally shaking with disbelieve. "God Damn it Sam! They call it an auxiliary power plant because it is a sailboat!" Jake was further mollified after Sam made another comment. Sam had pointed to the engine... "That right there Captain Jake, is a primary power plant for this boat." The coil Jake was working on was looking like a bird's nest. Jake shook his head, looking at the fouled coil; he dropped the rope, turned and walked away. Sam and the guys were snickering with each other. They all loved it when Sam started to work over Jake. Sam wouldn't cease his humorous roast of Jake. He repeated Jake's first comment, "God Damn it Sam! They call it auxiliary power because this is a sailboat!" The rest of the crew howled in laughter.

After everyone settled down, the auxiliary fired up,

and Jake proceeded to show all, the difference. Most of the sailing was never even keeled. The Buried Treasure was listed over, most of the day. Jake put full sails out and trimmed them for maximum speed. The previous joviality had suddenly been far from anyone's consideration. Sam had sailed with Jake like this so he was still cracking off the jokes. Everyone who laughed before was far from laughter then. Fear and panic tax a body, far greater than one might expect. They were cold, wet and tired, one of them was even heaving over the high side of the boat. Sam's grin grew wider, recalling how those fellows looked. Jake was muttering auxiliary power while he brought the boat to the slip....

Jake had noticed Sam's grin. Jake inquired. "Auxiliary Power?" Sam nodded, Jake grinned then shook his head and asked Sam to cast off. In short order, Jake was motoring past the first buoy. Jake was a great sailor, and his ability allowed him to raise sails long before any other captain might have. Shortly, the auxiliary power was shut off. Jake and Sam were sailing. They tacked frequently passing four more buoys. Both men worked with synchronicity, the result was smooth sailing. When they reached open water, they relaxed a bit. Jake had automatic pilot, and he rigged it. A cigar was procured as well as a beer from the cooler. Sam still felt green from the morning. He opted for water. The wind was moderate and the sun was out, both men paused before a needed discussion. Jake broke the ice.

"Sam, my heart is broken up over all of this for you… I know how important they are to ya, in time we'll figure their importance for ya…" Sam realized Jakes subtlety, he was glad to be in his company. Sam responded to Jake's comment. "Jake, as much as it hurts, I can't figure… WHY? It wasn't like any of this was owed to us!" Jake listened… "It makes no sense Jake!"

Jake realized Sam was not going to breakdown; he wasn't amazed or even surprised. What Jake was witnessing from Sam, Jake called, *Sam's Resolutin' Format.* Jake had seen Sam's *Resolutin' Format* make losing jobs, winning propositions. Where other companies had suffered, their own company pushed through. Sam's ingenuity was awesome, and Jake knew one thing, whoever had done this to Sam, had far greater worries than John Q. Law. Jake spoke up, "Sam, I do think you are Resolutin'…" Sam looked at Jake, and nodded in agreement. "Indeed I am. I'll tell ya something else Jake, those cops are spinning their wheels."

Jake decided it was time to come about; he disconnected the autopilot and made adjustments with Sam. When the turn was completed and when Jake had reset the autopilot, he spoke to Sam. "You know how it goes Sam…counting on them is a certain gamble!" Jake finished off his beer, tossed the can overboard and retrieved another. After he opened it, he began with his thinking. "This whole thing is gonna be like a sail. We may get there on one tack, or it may take a few." Jake had a pull on the beer. "The journey might be accelerated, it might be delayed, none-the-less we will arrive"

Sam was looking at his water. He poured it out, and went below. He ascended with a drink in his glass. Jake was lighting his cigar again, Sam pulled out a butt. Both men savored their respective smokes. Jake asked Sam, "So what's the plan?" Sam sat back and stretched himself out in the cockpit. He looked at Jake. "When I'm done Resolutin' I'll have a plan." Jake figured that was good enough.

Both men enjoyed **The Buried Treasure** as she pushed through the sound. They sat quietly and finished their drinks. Sam had since lost his cigarette. He must have felt that drink. He stood up and went below again. On his way, he told Jake he needed a nap. Jake winked and disengaged the autopilot. He finished his beer and too began some of his own figuring.

Jake looked at his watch, ___12:45. He thought about work, he wondered of the digging being done.

Chapter 5

Sam, deeply in his heart, and secretly, loved Jake's boat. Not only did he love what it did for Jake, he loved that he was a resident mate. Sam got to his familiar berth. When Monica was along it had been their berth; the recollection drew him into the berth. Sam might have convinced himself that Monica's essence would be here waiting… maybe in a smell? Sam's eyes welled tears, no convulsing released his pain. He fell to the bunk and stretched out receiving the cradled motion of this great hole in the water. Maybe her scent was within a pillow? He grabbed the extra pillow and hugged it up to his chest. He took an inhalation and held it, almost as if he was holding it, for memory selection. Sam was flooded with recollections of being in this berth. He no longer needed any cues from senses; his mind was recalling the sound of the water tickling the hull, the drink, and the self-medicating was working for Sam. He had selected his memories, and the tears had ceased flowing. Sam was entering a good place.

Jake was holding a straight course, and a light trim. He used the autopilot when conversation was a consideration. He manned the helm, navigating from his hands. Jake figured, if he died sailing, he'd be one lucky fella. He enjoyed the solitude of sailing. The weather never really mattered to Jake. He was enjoying the calm of the water, mostly for Sam. Considering everything.… he was very glad, to be on **The Buried Treasure.** Jake had been thinking of the course he could hold; Sam might get an hour or so if the wind held. He figured he could get the best of his tack before Sam's nap would be ending. He was doing what he could. The stuff to come, would sort itself out.

Sam was drifting off, the gentle rocking of the boat lent him, and the memory of Monica nestled on him. How they both abided the laws of physics and gravity. This comforting thought grew as Sam's head itched. Maybe it wasn't an itch, maybe part of the time Sam spent here with Monica, was providing sensual cues. Sam's hand responded, by rubbing the itch, it was coming from the scar his head owned. More memories flooded Sam's subconscious. Sam recalled the time of injury. He smiled a bit as his breath rate slowed. He was dreaming. The touch of the scar brought him to the loving he and Monica made during one of Jake's hard sails. He was in the bunk under Monica, the boat was smashing through the water, the rise and fall was extreme. It was not consistent, which provided them frustration in achieving, simultaneous orgasms. They were both feeling fatigue, and were ready to cease. Jake let off on a tack, enough to sway them from abandoning mutual satisfaction. The boat still had the rise and fall; just without the smashing through the water, it tended to roll. They both found their rhythms in unison. Just after they climaxed... the boat rolled high, Sam's head was forced into the built aspect of the bunk. Monica hadn't realized what had happened. When she looked into Sam's eyes she noticed a tear. Her focus shifted to her Sam, she reached under his beautiful head and discovered her love was bleeding.... She offered another type of loving. Sam drifted between that and other times when sailing was less injurious to both himself and his bride. His recollection of how they harmoniously yielded to the motion of the water, allowed them a loving to die for. Sam was in the glory of his love's essence. This vessel, **The Buried Treasure,** she was kind to Sam.

His conscious nightmare wasn't there. Jake was coming to his first leg sooner than he thought, he hoped Sam was resting easy. The next tack was going to be a reach; she would be lurching into the bow. He wondered if Sam might want to take the wheel, after he woke up. In Jake's eyes, Sam was a first rate mate. Jake wasn't too keen on Sam at the helm, he sometimes wondered if Sam lost a tack just to watch him have a temper tantrum. Jake always thought **The Buried Treasure** was a magnificent vessel. And, such a vessel should be sailed without error, certainly not a blown tack. As much of a purist that Jake was, he couldn't fault Sam for pulling his leg. Honestly, Jake never minded being the tyrannical captain, as long as Sam was feigning being a numbskull. Somehow, they always ended up laughing about it. Jake recognized the need to come about; the numbskull would be here soon enough... he turned the wheel. The bow cut starboard. **The Buried Treasure** rolled port, as the stern turned over. The wind took the boom across the cockpit, while Jake released the sheet, allowing a smooth loose of the boom stopping at a reach. The wind now pushed the mast, the stern sat higher on the water, as the bow cut deeper. **The Buried Treasure** lurched forward, over the water, bow pushed.

Sam woke to the new motion of the boat. The new direction no longer served as a lullaby. Sam blinked, his nap was a pleasant one, and he guessed he was thankful. Monica's essence was gone. Sam raised himself up, and exited the bunk. He was thirsty, needing water. He took the glass he used before, and poured some for himself. Sam drank it, the taste hinted of whiskey. When he finished, he poured another. He emptied half the glass and topped it off with whiskey. Sam peered through the cabin windows before he made his way to the cockpit.

Jake seemed to be waiting on Sam, as he ascended to the helm Jake nodded. He took one of his hands off the wheel and removed his cigar from his mouth. "How'd yaw sleep?" Sam took a seat. He sipped on his newly poured drink and fumbled for a cigarette and lit it. "I dreamed of her." Jake grimaced a bit. He engaged the autopilot again and sat across from Sam. He grabbed another beer, and had a pull. "I didn't dream of her as you might have, but I thought about her..." "Sam, you know this boat has class, right?" Sam nodded. "When Monica was on this boat, the boat never looked better. And, when the boat had the family, well, __ then she was a proud vessel. She never sailed more proudly." Sam raised his glass. Jake matched his salute. They drank the toast and enjoyed the sail. Jake's mind drifted back to the digging, he stressed himself in searching for a reason as to why this might have happened. Something wasn't settled. Jake was figuring it out; he knew it was there. Sam had said, "This was not deserved." Jake was checking the list, he wasn't sure if Sam had that right. The earlier statement gave him concern. Jake was like that, he always reserved judgment until he was as sure as he could be. If he decided, there was value to his consideration; Sam would be the first to know. Otherwise, Sam needed ambiguity, like another crime scene. Jake was content to sail. Sam seemed to be too, so they sailed, and drank.

The men had sailed themselves to the limit of intoxication. As they sailed passed the slippage area, Jake turned the boat about and released the main sheet, while Sam furrowed the jib. Jake engaged the auxiliary, and brought the boat to the dock as gently as you could have stone cold sober. Once Sam had the docking lines fastened, Jake shut the power down on the boat. The men were busy in stowing the vessel. The two detectives had noticed them return while they waited.

Jake had the bead on them first, and let Sam know they were having some company. When Sam looked there was a third figure. He had not seen her before now. They finished securing **The Buried Treasure.** As they did, the detectives waved. Sam waved back. "Looks like company, Captain Jake." Jake started laughing. "The short one looks like she could be company, the other 2 well, there's another boat leaving later…" He cackled on, laughing at his own humor. The appearance of the detective's and this mystery guess gave Sam a leveling and sober focus of reality. The change in Sam's attitude was noticeable to Jake. Maybe not to anyone else who was present, but Jake had taken notice. Jake was wearing two hats he was attempting to keep Sam in distraction, while running blocking for him. He knew the cops had a job to do, but the job had better be done with respect for Sam's loss, even for his, as secondary as it was.

Jake was the kind of guy, who was highly critical of ineptitude; he never had difficulty in pointing out incompetence. There was never a misunderstanding about Jake's criticism, if you had it coming, you'd be mistaken to think Jake would embrace diplomacy in delivering it. Jake had a way of showing one side. Many people underestimated a first impression of Jake. While they would be correct assuming that he was a joker, they would get a devastating and pointed tongue thrashing, if they got out of line. One they likely would not forget. If the individual enduring the abuse had a problem with Jake's assault, they'd be suffering, from the same wrongly held perception, which invited the berating. Jake was a very handy guy with an ability to punctuate his words. If you were hard of hearing, Jake delivered a rudimentary form of 'Signing.' That usually got the audio-challenged understanding.

Jake had sized up the two detectives before he actually met them. The jury was out on the more likeable third party. Jake didn't get any read from her yet, but he'd have that figured soon enough. The older detective had the walk of a serious cop. Jake's estimation put him close to retirement. The younger cop was no less serious. He just had *a hungry look* to him. Jake decided to be observant. He just hoped they would play sensibly, for his friend's sake. Jake also realized that he and Sam were a little loose. The law enforcement crew might not be so appreciative knowing they were drunk. Jake knew the game. He just wondered what hand they were playing... Truth be told, both Sam and Jake had always been skeptical of everything, which is why they understood each other so well, and why they were as successful as they were. As the trio approached, Jake noticed a gleam in the younger cop's eye. He was drooling.... **The Buried Treasure** had that effect on people. Jake knew, this kid was alright, one down, two more to know...

Sam raised his hand to shake with the detectives. "Mr. Mur.... Uh, Sam, this is Special Agent Sabina Cooper. Agent Cooper this is Sam Murphy." Hendricks, the older detective allowed the exchange.

Sam reciprocated. "Detectives' Hendricks and Jameson, Special Agent Cooper, this is my friend and partner... Jake Blaques." While the handshaking was completed, Jake sized up Hendrick some more. He thought of Hendrick as professional, but to Jake, Hendrick didn't appear to be invested. He wondered if Hendrick was putting in his time. Detective Hendrick had attempted an explanation for Special Agent Cooper's presence. Jake thought he might have done better by her, until she filled in.

"Thank you, Detective Hendrick. I think I can be more precise, so I'll take it from here." Upon hearing this, Jake had whistled. It smacked of meaning. Kind of like, *did you see that?* He watched Hendrick's eyes squint a bit towards Cooper. Hendrick had been outdone, as if Jake had been ripping him up. Jake knew he'd like Special Agent Cooper. She wasn't too hard on the eyes either, now that Jake thought on it, she was a Federal Hottie. She was about to stipulate her presence. But before she could, Jake set a different priority. "If you'll allow for our present condition, we might make better progress over some vittles, cause I'm pretty hungry." The mention of the idea, forced a glance at worn timepieces. "What do ya say Sam, __ Surf & Turf?" Sam shrugged as he looked at the others. Hendrick opted out. He was heading home. Cooper and Jameson had a glance at each other. Both of them indicated they could eat. Jake took it from there. "Detective Jameson, you're with me, Sam, you catch up with Special Agent Cooper." Jake was moving towards his truck, Jameson asked Cooper if she could see him home, she nodded affirmatively. Jameson told Hendrick he'd see him in the morning.

Chapter 6

Jake waited in the passenger side of his truck; Jameson was a little confused by the fact that he was driving. Jake was cackling a bit about driving after he'd been drinking. He was wondering how Jameson might talk them out of an accident once Jake had driven the truck into a fixed object. Jameson had yet to realize that Jake was a boisterous man while he was drinking, and more so when he wasn't drinking.

Agent Cooper opened the door for Sam as they made it back to the car. Jake was yapping as to why Jameson wasn't quick enough to do the same as Agent Cooper had done for Sam. The thing that floored Sam was Jameson's response. "Well Mr. Black, I guess the Federal Government has a more conscientious training program than us one-sheriff local types." Sam snickered to himself, while he got into Agent Cooper's car; she smiled when she heard Jameson's response. She shut the door after Sam was seated. While she got around to the driver side, Jake was telling Jameson how the next time he would be voting; he would consider the deplorable training practices of this one-sheriff town. When she finally did get into the car, she was chuckling. She looked at Sam and asked him. "Your best friend and partner, huh?" Sam smiled at Agent Cooper and responded to her question. "Oh yes Agent Cooper, Jake is very colorful." They all started the drive to one of the favorite eateries of Jake and Sam. It didn't take long, barely enough to share small talk. As they pulled into the restaurant's parking area, Sam indicated to Agent Cooper that the place didn't offer much ambiance, but the food made up for it. Jake and Jameson were already waiting at the entry as Sam and Agent Cooper had caught up. Jake was mumbling something about the food getting cold. Sam took opportunity to toss some ribbing Jake's way. *"Jesus, Jake, if ya wait any longer, I might be thinking the restroom would have a line…. waiting on you and one of your magnificent discussions of shit-house philosophy."* The party laughed a bit, as Jake had to think through Sam's excuse. Then Jake retorted as he waited on the hostess. "Just remember this Sam. My shithouse philosophy gives many folks plenty to think on, after they waited so long to hear it." Once again the party laughed. Agent Cooper was enjoying the show between the two men. Jameson was like a kid in a locker room with older gym-students, watching their exploits as a youngster would. When the hostess returned and saw the party, she offered to Sam her deepest condolences. Sam thanked her accordingly. Before it could go any further Jake mentioned they were here on business with law enforcement. She understood what Jake was saying and obliged in calling for her best waiter.

The waiter saw his party, he knew Jake well. He knew Sam, but not like Jake. He sat them and asked about drinks. Jake ordered double-single malt bourbon, Sam had the same Cooper ordered a scotch and soda; Jameson opted for a Samuel Adams. He had the order and was off. There was a silence. Jameson started off. "Sam, Agent Cooper is here because she had noticed your case and thought ... well Agent Cooper you might as well tell it right the first time...."Cooper took it from Jameson. "Yes, Mr. Murphy and Mr. Blaques," Sam interrupted, "Call us Jake and Sam, Agent Cooper." "Very well, Sam and Jake, this murder produced a hit on a program I designed. This program seeks case similarities of an investigation the FBI is currently examining. This case has reached the threshold of criteria the program was designed for." The waiter had returned with the drinks and menus, he also had a bus boy bring plates and bread. The waiter had given menus after the drinks were placed. "I'll give you a few minutes to decide." The table remained quiet considering what Agent Cooper had said. Sam took a sip of his drink, and fetched a smoke. Jake already had his cigar in mouth. He had struck a match to pull a long draw on it. Agent Cooper had noticed how Jake had held that cigar in his mouth. She was thinking of something, she just couldn't put a finger on it. Sam picked up on what Cooper had said. "Agent Cooper what…" Cooper interrupted, "Please Sam, as you have requested, call me Bina…" Sam nodded affirmatively. "Could you be more specific of these similarities between this investigation and my case?" Agent Cooper took a sip of her drink, and placed it back down. She looked at the men surrounding her. "No Sam, I'm sorry I can't." Sam seemed to be a little confused. Jake was in disbelief. Agent Cooper knew Jake was formulating something in a retort, she continued. "What I can tell you is that this whole investigation falls under the auspices of Homeland Security. And, as it goes, we in the FBI determine what falls to homeland security, and what gets greater scrutiny from the Justice Department."

Jake rolled that cigar in his mouth as he spoke up. "As long as I'm not in trouble, and as long as you're representing whatever agency to be doing the investigating, that is fine by me… Imagine having to sit here with 2 of him." Jake nodded in Jameson's way. Jake looked at Jameson. "No hard feelings there Detective Jameson, she looks better than you and your partner, and that goes a long way in my book." Jameson couldn't blame Jake for what he said because it was the truth. Cooper was definitely better looking company than he was. Jameson raised his glass to match Jake's. Sam didn't toast with the other two. "Why thank you gentlemen!" Cooper played along.

Sam was busy thinking on what it was Bina was supposed to be doing there. He was still not sure of his thinking. Agent Cooper noticed Sam's concern and confusion. She thought Sam was still in shell shock. Maybe the shell shock had progressed to P.T.S.D., she wasn't sure, but the evidence was observable.

"Sam, my being here is really only a in a review process. We are really only connecting the dots. We'll lend assistance as we can to the Lyme Police Investigation."

Jameson already knew the score, his department was getting wind of this as Sam and Jake were sailing the sound. Jake and Sam finished off their drinks. They were well ahead of their guests. Jake caught the eye of the waiter and shook his glass indicating more drinks. The explanation Agent Cooper gave didn't seem to do anything for Sam. Jake was holding back a comment, which seemed to be burning his tongue. Instead of saying what he was thinking, he looked at Jameson. "This is okay with you Detective Jameson?" Jameson was caught by surprise as he finished sipping his Samuel Adams. He lowered the beer and replied, "Uh Jake, Sam, allow me the time to say that this investigation from the FBI doesn't sit so well with the old- timers, but as I am new to the Detective Division, well…. I welcome the help."

Jake slipped further into disbelief. Sam dashed his cigarette. Obviously, this conversation wasn't doing anything for the men's confidence in resolving the horror Sam was enduring. Agent Cooper had immediately noticed the shift in the credibility the men had for law enforcement. Fortunately, the waiter was back to break the flow of conversation. The waiter was placing the drinks down for Sam and Jake. He knew his customers. Jake asked the waiter, "Are you ready for the orders?" The waiter nodded affirmatively. Jake gave his order, as did Sam. Agent Cooper ordered a queen cut of prime rib with a lobster tail. Her appetite surprised the men. She was a smaller woman. When it came time for Jameson to order he stumbled through it like he hadn't been in an eatery like this for some time. Jake had to let him have it. "Jameson, this isn't a place that only has donuts on the menu, live it up a bit." Jameson couldn't help but smile at Jake. Much like his welcoming of FBI oversight, Jameson felt good about taking some grief from Jake. The table chuckled, as did the waiter. Jameson gave his selection to the waiter. Jake also had to rib Agent Cooper a bit. "Bina, don't they feed your skinny little backside over there at justice? I'd have some difficulty finishing your meal. I don't know where the hell you are gonna be putting that." Agent Cooper smiled. "Care to wake up and find out Jake?" Jake smiled widely… Sam's head fell to look at the carpet, his head started to shake. Jake cleared his throat, and rolled the cigar around on his tongue as he spoke. "Bina, I don't think I'd be in an agreeable mood to your idea of physical fitness. My idea would be to work it off before we went to sleep!" Agent Cooper was no stranger to sexist and chauvinistic commentary. She looked at Jake as she leaned forward; she posed as a sultry female objective and played Jake's chess game. "Jake, my, my, aren't you just the stud! The only problem with your thinking... is that you'd never survive that type of physical training..." The table was silent for a priceless second and then erupted with laughter. Jake was so amused by Bina's banter, and impressed. He half thought she'd be taking offense to what he had just said.

Sam was smiling, but he was still distracted in considering the reality. Agent Cooper sipped her drink. She kept an eye on Sam and winked off at Jake. Jake was part of the equation. Sam was part of the answer. The two came together. She really did admire Jake's way of warming up to folks. He was real. But, she was more interested in getting some *one on one* with Sam. He would be the only one able to provide her with what she was looking for. He was the survivor. She sat back and sipped at her drink until it was empty. Jameson was giggling with Jake. He was now like the younger gym student high-fiving the older student; just glad he was being noticed. Jake was also caught up in his own jocularity. Sam was mildly amused. He was enduring his friend's attempts at humor. As far as Cooper saw it Sam was still skeptical. She could convince him later. He had about all that he could absorb anyhow. There was no telling how much hoisting of the drink the two did while out on **The Buried Treasure.** They were hard at it here. She decided to let it be. Sam had lit another smoke. He had a few drags on it. The meals were being delivered. The waiter had noticed everyone save the beer drinker were in need of new drinks. He asked if they'd all like another round. Every-one including the beer drinker acknowledged they did, and Jake added ice water. The waiter left them to their meals. The men were sizing up Cooper's order, then her. They couldn't figure where she was going to put all of it. They wondered if she always ate this way. At least Jake and Jameson did. Sam was kinda off, still drawing on his smoke. He looked at Bina. She had similarities to Monica on some level. He just couldn't make it out. He was getting a little bombed. He decided it wasn't that important as he finished off his cigarette, and dashed it out. Jake and Jameson were already eating. When Cooper saw Sam proceed at his eating, she did so too. As the table began the conversation dropped off. The waiter returned with the drinks. He questioned how everything was, verbal responses were offered only after swallows. The overall impression was great to good. The waiter nodded and departed for his other stations. The four had made inroads they needed to and ate. As the meal finished up the waters were used to wash the food down. Agent Cooper was the last done, completely. The two men, Jake and Jameson couldn't believe their eyes. Sam had little interest in the diet of Bina. He was alone in his thinking.

When Agent Cooper offered what Jake had seen as a concerned eye, he interjected once again. To Cooper's amazement he did so while holding the unlit cigar in his mouth. "Agent Cooper, uh Bina, don't mind Sam. When we see Sam like this we all know he is Resolutin'.

"When he has something to say, we'll give a listen." He cackled some and sipped his bourbon. Cooper thought Jake was a little insensitive, but she held her tongue. There was more than meets the eye between these two. They were like brothers. She did ask about one thing Jake had said. *Resolutin'?* Jake lit his cigar again and did some tossing of it around in his mouth as though it was effortless. "Resolutin' is what Sam does lots." "It is why our company Sam-Jak Inc. was so successful." Jake leaned forward a bit, "You see, we all think Sam could be committed when he gets to Resolutin', we always think he goes daft on us, _____ then, suddenly, he blurts out something really smart." "It is the only reason we keep him around." Jake's hand reached up behind Sam and lightly patted his back. "We try to let him out occasionally." The waiter returned. He started collecting the plates. "Will there be any desert?" Jake looked at Bina. "No chance for a pre-slumber work out Bina?" She laughed and Jameson couldn't believe his ears. Sam seemed to ignore Jake's Tom Foolery. "I think I'll pass on the invite Jake, I'd really like to proceed after you have a physical fitness work-up." "It is no fun explaining to the medical examiner how I didn't get my pleasure even after you had and died." The waiter about fell over laughing, Jameson was giggling like an idiot, and Sam finally smiled. Jake had the biggest grin Sam had ever recalled seeing. Maybe it wasn't as desperate as he had thought. Jake looked at the waiter. "Hey there son, if she's likely to kill me, what do ya think your chances are?" More laughter. He looked up at the waiter and said, "No thanks, just the bill." Again, he was gone. Sam lit another cigarette as his focus waned from the table.

Agent Cooper had asked Jameson some things about seeing the crime scene. They had decided to see it again in the morning. The waiter had dropped the bill at Jake's place. Jake looked up at him again, "It isn't enough that she wanted to kill me, now you wanna soak me with the bill?" Jake was muttering to himself about how the young today are only good for disrespect. He pulled out a significant amount of cash and threw more than enough to cover the bill. "The meal and service was A-1 kid keep it!" The waiter knew the play; Jake was always a good tipper as long as the service was good. The cash seemed to get the law enforcements attention. Jake looked at the cash he was holding and their reaction. He folded it up and put it back in his pocket as he stood up. Sam wasn't a second behind him. Jameson was left out as Cooper had read the men's play. They were all heading away while Jameson finished the last of his beer. He motivated movement once he returned the bottle to the table. Once they were in the parking lot, Jake looked at the detective and agent. "So, we'll see you tomorrow?" They both nodded. Jameson headed towards Cooper's car, she didn't get the door for him and Jake whistled to Sam. "You must be special buddy, seems that Bina only gets the door for mutts like you." "Hey Jameson what do you think about that?" "Well, Jake, I think you had better not get into any accident making your way home...." Jake sneered at Jameson. "You can take the day off tomorrow Jameson, just send your partner over, he has less to say than you…" "Jake," *Jameson* couldn't resist. "We'll be over tomorrow at Sam's house… after roll call and maybe some physical fitness training…" He got into the car laughing as did Cooper. Jake was and had been played, Sam laughed briefly. They departed.

As they pulled up to Sam's house, Jake was concerned for his friend. "Are ya sure, you want to be here Sam?" Sam nodded affirmatively at Jake. "Want any company?" Sam shook his head. "What I want, I can't have Jake." "I'm just gonna go hit the sack." "See ya in the morning?" Jake nodded back. Sam got out of the truck and closed the door. Jake waited a second, and left Sam at his house, worrying as he drove away. Sam walked up the path to the doorway. He hated this place. He knew this would be his last night here. He opened the door walked into the house and pushed it closed without completely closing the door. He staggered a bit through the room where his young ones were left. He continued moving into the kitchen as he grabbed the bottle left from yesterday. The bottle had no cap to it. He took a pull on it getting out to his lawn furniture. Sam dumped himself onto the lounge he spent the previous night on; he didn't realize the moon was less bright than last evening. These conditions of the world held no more interest for Sam. Sam lit a cigarette, and managed another swallow of the anesthetizing liquid. Sam had a feeling. He wasn't sure what it was. He lacked clarity. His reference point, his reason for being was gone. Worse yet, they had been taken from him. Sam didn't want this kind of freedom. He wanted what he had, and all it would offer. All Sam could do was focus on getting by this onslaught of emotional terror.

Sam sat on his lounge chair and smoked down his cigarette. He was a portrait, awaiting the artist, unable to come and render a masterpiece. **Man Separated** might be the name of the artist's strokes yielding Sam's moonlight agony. Sam took another shot of the whiskey. His body shuddered when it accepted the drink. Sam tossed the bottle down on the lawn, it rolled along the grass in silence yielding to friction and gravity about 15' away. Sam broke the pose and reclined on the lounge. A last puff off the smoke and he dashed the butt on the patio. He eased back, closing his eyes. Sam's body wanted to howl, his mind allowed a sigh. Sam faced his emotional terror here at the threshold of his subconscious. He allowed the whiskey to guide him passage through his nightmares.

Chapter 7

Mornings began early for Agent Cooper. She didn't need a wake-up call; she favored the morning, finding time for herself and her needed rituals of balance between the mind and body. Her focus was overcoming a recent gunshot wound, as in two years ago. The injury was devastating. Her right shoulder was badly damaged. Her rehabilitation was miraculous. She confounded the doctors.

The powers that be, had not restored her to full duty, they had not thought she would be returning to work at all. She was still under psychological review. FBI shooting investigators had determined Agent Cooper was contributory to herself being shot. She took risks that didn't always pay off in the wisdom of The Bureau. She wasn't wrong in her actions preceding the shooting, but she wasn't right either. The blip on the radar screen occurred when Cooper had been shot. Therefore she was being scrutinized as an aberration. In observing Cooper's future, investigating eyes would be likely to recognize a similar blip. Agent Cooper had some breathing room. Her instincts lead her here. The FBI hadn't deemed this to be active duty of an ongoing investigation involving an Agent shooting. Agent Cooper's hunch was closer than they had thought. She knew it, and Sam was about to know it.

She considered how a possible conversation with Sam might flow as she made her way to the exercise room. When she had begun her routine, the consideration she had for Sam faded. Her mind needed to overcome the pain she fought in her repetitions of fitness. As she finished one activity and moved to another, she wondered how much support she'd be able to gain from Sam. After all of her routines had been served, she looked forward to a couple of laps to cool off. She gathered her towel and robe and walked through the partition to the pool area. She placed her towel on a chair near a table and reached into her robe pocket for a pair of swimming goggles. She placed them on the table so she could remove her robe and sweat attire revealing a bathing suit. Her left hand rubbed her scarring on her right shoulder. She hated the wound she had. She was thankful she still had her arm. She wondered if her paradox would compare to Sam's. She entered the water and began her laps. Her right arm strained through her pace... she ignored the pain, even gained some strength from it. By the time, she finished her routine; other guests had begun their own fitness rituals. She was also thankful she could conceal her scars from others.

She exited the pool and donned her robe allowing it to dry her. The towel became a hair wrap. She pocketed her goggles and returned to her room. She removed the robe once in the room. She peeled off the bathing suit. She stood naked looking at herself in the mirror. This was the most detestable part of the ritual. She had to face her altered body. No doctor had told her this was a necessary part of rehab. She was balancing her mind and body. She figured her new reality needed to be faced everyday. Otherwise, she could never overcome the scarring of the mind. The body responded because it had too, the mind needed training. The cost associated to her job had a different perception. Injury from being in the line of fire always did. So the Doc's said.

She cried, not in futility, but in sorrow for loss, and gain of pain. She moved into the bath to take a shower. Her morning ritual was complete. She could face the day. When she finished rinsing down, she left the shower. She dried off quickly, and combed her hair back she wasn't preoccupied with how she looked. She performed minimal preparations in dressing for the day's activities. She was a driven woman; she packed and checked out of the hotel. She got to the squad and entered it. Once in the squad she leafed through Sam's file. The FBI didn't have anything interesting on Sam, just the particular law abiding records of any citizen they needed to know about. Agent Cooper smiled a bit. Sam's file raised no flags in the eyes of The Bureau. Cooper saw a flag. Sam had survived… Agent Cooper had gotten places because she championed

Victim Analysis Profile. This was not recognized within The Bureau. She had found that utilizing resources from the victim or survivor of the victims, like Sam's case, was more expedient in discovery of material fact. Other agents arrived at credibility flaws in the victim, she turned these so called credibility flaws into clues, and her results had done well in closure statistics used in job performance analysis. She wasn't doing anything other than what had been deemed necessary in investigation practices. She just used the information gained from the investigation differently. Her exploitation of the information went unrealized in the Justice Department Policy. Some might have considered Agent Cooper lucky. They might have resented that about her. They hoped she didn't come back to The Bureau. They were giving her all the time she needed. She knew it was a limited and fleeting opportunity.

She looked up Sam's address and started her car. She experienced a little nervousness on the drive to Sam's. She was looking forward to talking with Sam before the detectives would arrive. She hoped Jake wasn't an early fella. She needed one-on-one time, with Sam. Although Jake was a comical man, he would have presented a distraction, she was hoping his arrival would be later than hers. She pulled up to Sam's house. One truck was there, the plate matched to Sam Murphy. She had accomplished an early arrival. She parked the squad roadside, rather than in the driveway. She left her copy of Sam's file in the squad. She was counting on either Hendrick or Jameson for the Crime Scene

Report. That would be here soon enough. As she walked up to the door, she noticed the door was ajar. She changed up her approach, as something might have been wrong. She didn't draw her weapon, but she did proceed as though she might need it. She knocked on the door. No one had seemed to hear the knocking. She pushed the door open with her foot, and peered into the house. All seemed cleared. She entered the house, as she did, she relaxed a bit. The shower was running. Further examination revealed the coffee pot was brewing some coffee. She walked past it out to the backyard. It was evident Sam had slept on the lounge. There was a bottle on the lawn, which would have otherwise been disposed. Sam's shoes were at the side of the lounge. Agent Cooper wondered why the bottle didn't end up shattered. She heard the shower being turned off. She would wait here in case Sam thought he was alone. She didn't want to see Sam in a compromised position.

A minute or two later Sam emerged from the bathroom, wrapped in a towel. His first stop was the coffee maker, he noticed Agent Cooper outside where he had slept. He poured his coffee, and surprised Agent Cooper. "How do you take it Bina?" She turned to Sam. "Good morning Sam, black will be fine, Thank you." She waited. Sam brought her the cup. He handed her the beverage, then he excused himself to get properly dressed. He wasn't but a minute, he exchanged the towel for a pair of jeans, he added a T-shirt, and appeared barefoot to enjoy his coffee with earlier than expected company. Cooper found a seat near the adjacent furniture located near the picnic table. When Sam sat down, Cooper had noticed Sam's eyes were puffy. She thought he might have been crying in the shower. He hadn't mentioned it. She sipped on the coffee and sat back. Sam did the same, but additionally, he lit a smoke. "How was your rest Sam?" Cooper asked. "Well Bina, I suppose I am somewhat refreshed. And, your sleep, How was yours?" Cooper nodded affirmatively. "That is not why you are here though?" Sam asked plainly. His response gave Cooper a pause. She knew Sam was sizing her up, she hadn't anticipated his abruptness. "That is correct Sam; it is not why I am here." She took another sip of coffee as she considered her next statement. "Sam, I told you and the detectives how I came to be here… through a computer program. It uses a net the justice department constructed and implemented post 911. The mechanics of this program are classified. I can't address them anyway. I have tweaked this computer to serve my own ends." She leaned forward to have another sip of coffee. Sam was listening. He was propped back in the chair smoking his cigarette. He held his coffee unlike Bina. She realized she was still a guest. As she sat back, she began again. "My own end is not outside Bureau observation." She paused and sipped her coffee. "This investigation is directly related to an Agent Shooting." Cooper wanted to be very careful here. She leaned forward and had another sip. She returned the cup to the table.

Sam noticed a warmer would be helpful. Sam got out of his chair and retrieved the pot, he filled her cup when he returned and placed the pot on the table. He sat down once again. Cooper thanked him. Sam realized the equalization that had been traded. Agent Cooper was very smooth. Sam appreciated it. She had removed her need to continue without thought; Sam's curiosity was tickled. "You were saying something of an agent shooting???" "Oh yes. I was about to tell you, I was the agent..." She let that hang out, by sipping her coffee again. She stood up and went to the bottle Sam had discarded the night before. "There is something else you should know..." she bent down to pick up his leftovers. She brought it back to the table. Sam was expecting the other shoe to drop. Bina was surprising this morning. "The truth of it is that The Bureau doesn't want to know. The Bureau is overwhelmed with obvious threats. If they did know my intentions, I would likely not be an Agent. So, there it is." Sam was surprised at Bina's candor. He knew there was more, he figured she was waiting to expound. Sam stood up and poured himself a coffee. She was still good. He grabbed the bottle she recovered and went to the kitchen. He did so silently. He needed a minute to realize all she meant to say. Cooper waited patiently. Sometimes that's what was needed. Sam was returning. He seemed to have made his mind up. "Bina, I'll assume what you have just told me requires a modicum of discretion. I'll further assume this is selective information. Based upon these assumptions I gather you'll tell me more of what you need from me?" Sam lit another cigarette as he sat down. Cooper breathed easier. She had gained Sam's initial trust and offering of cooperation. "When I was shot Sam... I was following a lead on a serial killer. I must have startled my mark, he got the clean drop on me. Thankfully, my vest tested well." Cooper stood up. "This might give you a better understanding. The wounds almost left me without an arm." She unbuttoned her blouse and pushed the collar exposing her shoulder. She even got her thumb under her bra-strap, revealing a truly impressive wound.

She waited for Sam to get a mental picture, then she re-covered. She sat back down and sipped her coffee. She had Sam's undivided attention. "When did that happen?" Sam had another drag. "It happened 18 months ago." Sam sipped his coffee again; he considered how such an injury would leave him... "Only 18 months?" Cooper nodded. Sam shook his head. He wondered if he would be so proficient in 18 months, he looked back at Bina with a newly required respect. "Okay Agent Bina... What is the play?" "Patience Sam, patience is what we need for now." Sam considered 18 months of rehab. He understood that he might not capable of such healing in the face of the same injury. But Bina's injury, as terrible as it was, _____ couldn't match the loss of his family. He fully understood the implications of what she just said. He hoped she understood his sensibility of justice, and how it was to be served, at least according to Sam. Sam considered

60

she had paced herself with great thought and revealed herself plainly, but she was still the law. She hadn't won him over completely, but she had gained more trust than the detectives had. That was something. "What is the result of patience, Bina?" "Well Sam, for one, I have yet to see the crime scene report. So, we wait on that from the local law enforcement community." Sam finished off his butt and dashed it out. Sam looked at his watch, still too early to answer the phone calls from yesterday. "Does it hurt much Bina?" She didn't expect the question, but she considered it. "Hurt is a relative thing Sam. Sure it hurts, mostly when I exercise it. The difference between pain of the body and pain of the heart is remarkable." Bina looked at Sam. "You are finding this to be true right now. Bodily pain can be willed away. It is much more difficult to provide avenues of healing for the mental and emotional scarring of loss. Wouldn't you agree?" Sam took a pause, he perceived her reach for him; he was tentative in giving a response. "Yes, I suppose you are right about that Bina." Silence had befallen them as they considered all that had been said. It ended when they heard Jake turn off his motor. Bina was satisfied, she had accomplished the first part of her plan and she felt good about it. Besides, the party was just about to begin. Jake was vocalizing his entry as soon as he exited the truck. They both shared an understanding of loss, and this is what she needed to move on in the investigation.

Chapter 8

Jake entered into the house. He thought he might be the first to greet Sam. He was glad to see Sam's visitor was Bina. "Guess I'm not the early bird today." He looked at Agent Cooper. "You look mighty chipper Bina." Cooper smiled. She thought how her smile might have not been so genuine if Sam were more standoffish. Jake was a pretty quick study; he knew something had gone down before he got here. He was sure he would be brought into the loop. "And, how is it with you Sam?" Sam waved at Jake and pointed to the coffee. When Jake had looked at the pot of coffee, he frowned. "Now ya see? This is exactly why I hate not being the early bird." "Well Jake, ya can't be dragging your ass to parties all night and expect to be the early-bird..." Cooper smiled. She thought it was good for Sam to get a little ribbing in with Jake. She thought Jake appreciated it the same way she had. Jake smiled at Sam. "Shit Sam, why don't you own up to the fact... You're just jealous!" Jake looked at Bina and winked. Jake poured the last of the pot into a mug. He went to work making another pot.

"So Jake?" Cooper asked. "Did you and Jameson have a good time last night, and will he be ready for work?" Jake turned around, and he sipped his mug of coffee. He pulled a cigar out and popped it into his mouth. "Bina, I doubt the boy will ever see life in the same way! As far as work? We'll see how good a partner Hendrick is, Ha Ha Ha!"

As soon as Jake settled down, Sam brought up why Jake wasn't the early bird. "Jake, I'm glad you got here before the detectives. Bina was just informing me of her motivation regarding my case. Bina, why don't you fill Jake in?" Once again, Cooper was surprised. She hadn't known Jake had a need to know classification. She didn't know why she didn't make the connection. Sam had just removed any doubt as to Jake, being in the know. "Well Jake, in short; I showed Sam a wound I received hunting down a serial killer. A lead went bad and the perp got the drop on me. We were discussing how I thought the two connected. Ah, let me see… I am not supposed to be investigating the crime involving my shooting. The Bureau doesn't see a connection that I do. So, my efforts are not on the radar screen. I'm kinda…" Jake helped her out. "Playing the middle against 2 sides???" "Hmmm, yes Jake, that is appropriate. Thank you." "Anytime there Bina…."

Jake took a sip of his coffee, and lit his cigar. He looked at Bina. He was working up to a question. "Do I get to see?" Jake laughed. "Sorry

Jake, not while you are smoking that cigar." Jake pouted…in jest. "Oh, hey! Sam I stopped at the job sight. The guys, they are really moving some earth. They said to say hello. George and Stan looked like they were a panic." Sam nodded at Jake.

Jake looked at Sam. "Hey Sam is everything okay?" "Yeah, as good as they can be. I am interested in what else Bina has to say." Cooper responded. "Business records would be helpful. Short of that, I am waiting on the crime scene reports, as well as the autopsies. We can formulate a course of action at that time." Jake looked at Sam; he was in a daze as far as Jake could see. Jake walked to the phone and dialed the lawyer's number. As the phone rang, Jake explained his actions. "I'll have those business records by the end of today…'" Someone answered the phone. "Yes, hello… This is Jake Blaques, is Stephan available? He's not? What a shame. Can I leave a message young lady? The moment you see Stephan, you tell him to call Jake Blaques at Sam Murphy's house." Jake waited "Is that so? What is your name? Charlene? Okay Charlene. Tell Stephan if I don't hear from him in the hour, I'm going to stop the job sight I'm on, and I'm going to start one on his parking lot. Yes. That is it. Okay thanks Charlene." Jake cradled the phone while he laughed. Sam just shook his head. It was obvious to Cooper this was inside humor. Jake realized how Cooper might have been feeling like a fifth wheel. Jake looked over at Sam. Sam shrugged. Jake looked back at Cooper. He had a huge smile on his face. Jake looked like a big kid with a secret he couldn't wait to reveal. Cooper anticipated what was coming.

"Back when we were getting started, we didn't know the ropes of business. You know the paper work and such. We were getting killed on a job, our lawyer had dropped the ball or didn't pick it up, one way or the other we were getting killed. I think Sam and me were more upset with each other than we had ever been. I was breathing hard on Sam because that was his end. Here we were ready to dig, we had overcome all kinds of variances. We made adjustments, absorbed expense… you get the idea. We both had thought we were ready to work. Just as we are firing up the machines, this little pencil pusher shows up with some more paperwork. We would have laughed him off the job sight, but, he had the law there. I was cursing at Sam he was cursing back telling me Stephan assured me we were good. When I had settled down, I heard Stephan was to blame… Well, now that I knew who was to blame I lost my mind." Bina looked at Sam for verification; he was nodding with the craziest smile.

"Anyhow I told that pencil pusher to stay right where he was. I was bringing the lawyer back, even if I had to drag him. I left the job sight in a front-end loader." Jake rolled his cigar; his enthusiasm in telling the tale was energized. "I drove it down the street right to his office. His brand new foreign sports car was right in the parking lot, the very lot we had just worked on. The work we did was not paid for; it was a retainer of sorts. I drive this front-end loader right behind his little car I think it was the brand new. I started lowering the bucket onto his car. When I stopped, it was inches off his windshield." Jake had a sip of his coffee. "I parked the machine right there and matted the diesel: clouds of dark smoke start pouring out of the machine. The torque of the engine is loosing material on the bucket all over this brand new ride... Stephan comes running out of his office, looking like his world was on the brink, screaming 'what the hell are you doing?????' "

Jake started busting out laughing, Sam was less enthused, but none the less entertained. "Get this! The more he screams the more I let the engine have it." I hold my hand up to my ear as he screams. He gets infuriated, just then, the cops roll in. They are laughing; waving me down." Cooper noticed how Jake was crying from laughing so hard. He was losing the ability to continue the story. Sam picked it up. "Jake salutes the cops. He gets off the accelerator and tells the cops, he's got to park the machine. Jake backs the machine up, stopping just short of the guy's client's car. Now everyone is out of the building. Jake raises the bucket and turns it half way open. He lowers the blade to rest on Stephan's bumper and depresses the rear shocks so the car is almost off its own front tires. Jake shuts the machine down and climbs down. Stephan is hyperventilating while he is trying to swear at Jake. He's running around like a lunatic, trying to get the cops to have Jake move the machine. To see Stephan then, you would have hardly thought he was a lawyer. The same cop backing up the pencil pusher was now looking at Jake and this lawyer. Jake looks at the cop and asks, 'weren't you the cop who just shut my job down?'"

Sam stopped to have a sip of coffee, and to light a smoke. He continued as soon as he was set. Jake was laughing, and laughing hard. "The cop nods at Jake. Jake goes, 'Well which job are you gonna hold up, this one or that one?' Stephan say's, 'There is no job here, it is a brand new parking lot.' Jake turns to Stephan and says, 'Well Stephan, my machines are tearing up something today, might as well be started here. Right on this car.' Jake turned around and started walking back to the machine. Stephan chases Jake down, 'What other job?' 'What other job??' Jake looks at Stephan. 'The job you were supposed to smooth over, one of the jobs this parking lot paid for, that job. If we can't start there, here, sure would relieve my sense of un-needed aggravation.'"

"Bina, the cops were laughing so hard, the guy behind the machine was nearly crying, and Stephan was screaming at Jake to get that machine off his car." Sam was laughing as he told the story to Bina. Jake picked it up from there. "The best part Bina…" Both men were having difficulty at this point, but Jake forced himself to finish. "The best part was when the cop started writing out the ticket. I was no further than 5 feet from Stephan. The cop comes over and gets ready to hand off the ticket…We all thought the cop was gonna lay the ticket on me… turns out he gives it to Stephan for creating a public nuisance." Both of the men broke out in huge belly laughs. It was hard for Cooper to imagine just how funny all of this was, she yielded to the contagious nature of a good laugh and joined in. Before anyone could stop, the phone rang! Laughter was replaced by silence; everyone looked at the others surprised.

The phone rang, as it would, until the connection was made. Another more boisterous laugh occurred simultaneously, just as they realized Stephan was on the other end. The phone rang another 2-3 times before Jake could collect himself to answer the phone. Sam seemed to have settled down before Jake. He was anxious to keep things moving along. Jake was aware of Sam's anxiousness to answer the phone, he was just finishing a laugh. Jake held his fingers to his lips, indicating Stephan was going to get more…. When Jake answered, he spoke into the phone as a woman. "Hello, this is the Murphy residence?" Jake was listening to Stephan. He let the others know by nodding his head. "This is Stephan!" "Oh thank you soooooo much, I am so glad you called. Yes, Jake is very upset… yes! Yes! Oh no Stephan, _____ no… You might want to know ah_____ there is an FBI Agent here wanting to see company documents…. What's that??? You say I don't need to get Jake? Oh, you say, just tell Jake you'll see him in a couple of hours… Oh, okay, yes, _____ Ah Stephan? Did you want to talk to

Sam? Not right now? No, okay, _____ when you get here? Very Good Stephan, Yes, I'll tell Jake. Bye."

Jake was teeming with hysteria; Sam looked as if he might have been crying. His head was dropped. To look at him, you might have thought he was avoiding eye contact. When Sam raised his head, his hands grabbed his belly. He was holding back laughter, while crying. Cooper's body was shuddering. Jake hung up the phone, they all busted out in hysterical laughter. The place, the being of the place, and the spirit in the place was heavy and the laughter ended much sooner than it's potential.

Agent Cooper had mad a mental note... These fella's found fun in life and expoited it even at their own expense, even now. She considered their pasts. These men were wealthy, not in a material sense, but more of a living sense. Sam's family had been the fountain of their lives. She thought of it to be a first for her, she couldn't recall when this had ever happened to her. Cooper realized just how lucky this girl, Monica, must have been. Her absence would be deeply felt! Cooper's eyes welled up, tears slowly rolled down her cheeks. The men focused on her, just as they would have if she were Monica, she reeled them in.

"I'm so sorry, _____" Sam retrieved a box of tissue. "It's just that, _____ oh!" She nervously fumbled the tissue, "I see bad things like this all the time, _____you can't let it get to you." She was crying because it was all she could do... she blew her nose and cleaned up a bit. "This is so sad, when it hits folks you can identify with. I'm sorry, this is so nonprofessional."

Within a few seconds, she had regained her composure. Her tears were genuine, she felt awful for Sam and his friend, Jake. She didn't miss the opportunity she seized just then, she could have manufactured the tears, she was glad they fell without prompt. The men had heard all that Cooper said. She looked to them to be slightly emabarrased. Jake nodded and winked back to her. Sam remained stoic. Cooper read it as she stood up to excuse herself to the bathroom. Sam was *Iron Clad*. Cooper made several mental notes as she made her way, so as to regain her composure. After she disappeared, Jake cleared his throat. "Ahem, Sam, she is right, it is sad, and that was as close to sincere as it gets buddy, ya might think of thanking her." Sam looked at Jake with the same face as she got. His eyes fell to the floor in the direction of Jake's feet. "You're right, Jake. Thanks!"

Jake blurted out, "Oh yeah, couple of hours, huh?" Both men started laughing. Cooper rejoined them and asked, "Stephan?" Both men nodded. Cooper joined the nodding, "That was really good. I guess Stephan wished he had paid for that parking lot, huh?" Everyone started the laughter again. A new alliance had been formed. To what ends? Whatever the ends, it started from the loss, and as the fingers lace the boots, the walking begins after the knot has been tied. These three started the walk, while realizing great loss in a moment of living. Overcoming that loss meant settling Justice, which seemed a long way off. After a bit, Sam stood up, he stretched and asked, "What's next?"

Chapter 9

Jake was the last one to settle back down. Cooper had already had some ideas. She wanted Sam investing himself in this process. Not only would his involvement allow Sam a needed grieving; it would streamline the investigation. "Sam, it would be helpful to involve a funeral director. When a mortician contacts the Coroner's Office, an application of urgency is apparent. This means an autopsy, or in this case, autopsies would then have an added priority."

Sam thought about what Cooper had just said. He seemed to be thinking it through. Cooper wondered if he needed some more motivation. She was getting ready to state the reasons with more specificity, but she didn't have to, Sam walked over to his parlor office. He turned some pages in a book. After he found the number he was looking for, he picked up the phone and dialed Anderson's Funeral Home. Sam waited for the connection. "Hello, this is Sam Murphy, is Erik available? Yes, I'll hold." Jake looked to Cooper; he motioned for her to walk to the patio. She obliged Jake's gesticulation. Jake faced Cooper, and spoke softly to her... "Erik Anderson is another customer of ours. Several years ago, he was faced with very few options in continuing his family business. After his parents died, they were probating a devastating tax burden. These folks knew how to bury people, not attain or manage wealth. The long and short of it came down to Erik needing a new place of business. The old property was sold to settle outstanding bills." Cooper was following Jake's 411. "He had some resource, but not much. If he could get the hole dug, he could manage the finance for a prefab structure. Sam and I had heard of his circumstance, I forget who approached who. None-the-less, we got to dig his hole, we even contracted the form guys to make it work. We were doing well, and figured, at the very least, and by the very worst, we could be silent partners. Erik agreed to sign off on a blanket form of debt. We tried to structure it as if we purchased a bond. So, if what you say is right, Erik is the man to pull it off." Cooper remained silent, but affirmed what Jake had said with a nod.

Sam was finishing up with Erik. "Okay Erik, and Thanks again... Okay, _____ bye now." Sam returned the phone to the cradle. As Jake and Cooper watched Sam return the phone, the sound of another car arriving at Sam's house offered the three another focus. The two detectives appeared at the door and knocked, without really having to. Jake waved them in and offered a greeting. "Good morning Detectives, just in time for coffee." They both declined the offer, they seemed anxious. Hendrick spoke first.

"Sam, Jake, and Agent Cooper sorry we are late. Agent Cooper, here is your requested copy of the crime scene report." Hendrick extended his hand holding the paperwork; she reached to receive it. "Thank you Detective Hendrick," Cooper took possession. Hendrick spoke some more... "Detective Jameson will be the lead on this case. I'll be assisting Jameson as I can... 1 month ago I had submitted my retirement paperwork. Forgive me in being... well not capable of seeing this investigation through." Agent Cooper was flipping through the report. She seemed to be looking for something, or trying to put something right in her mind. She looked at the photos comparing them to the actual areas of incident. She began moving around the house doing the same. Sam was fidgety he moved from the kitchen towards the patio door. While Sam removed himself from the three others, Jake sparked up conversation.

"So Detective Hendrick, What's gonna occupy your time, when you give up the donuts?" Jameson wanted to laugh, but he covered effectively. He might have lost it if Sam's face could be seen. Jake stared Hendrick down with a patient and awaiting grin. "Well, Jake, that is pretty good, never heard it said that way. But I think I'll just enjoy my family some." Jake's grin had released slowly; he couldn't resist one last shot at Hendrick. In Jake's mind, the guy came up short by dropping the lead off to Jameson. The rest of the world went on even through retirements. "Well Detective Hendrick, that sounds like a fine life; that is, of course, if your family doesn't like donuts as much as you…." Jameson couldn't cover his response. He actually got upset with Jake's humor. It was too funny. Jameson really didn't want to laugh at his partner, but Jake's dryness killed him. Hendrick smiled at Jake, he had a sense of humor, even at his own expense. Hendrick looked at Jameson's loss of control, and nodded. "Jake, you sure are the comedian, and it is fine. I guess I deserve worse." "Be that as it may, Detective Jameson here, well, he will be an extraordinary detective. You and Sam are in quite capable hands." Hendricks hand moved as to display Jameson. "Jameson here has already started a task unit for this investigation, he reports directly to the lieutenant of the division."

Agent Cooper came back to the group. She seemed to have a curious nature. "Detective Hendrick, a question?" Hendrick focused to Agent Cooper, "Yes Agent Cooper?" "There was no weapon recovered?" "Correct, No weapon was recovered." Hendrick waited for more than one question. Jameson wasn't sure, but it sounded as the rug was about to be pulled from under Hendrick, he wasn't laughing anymore. Jameson interrupted. "Agent Cooper, excuse me, wouldn't you rather ask me?" "No Detective Jameson, I think I've got the right man." Jake smelled blood in the water; he sat down and lit his cigar. He sipped his coffee and watched the show.

Detective Hendrick didn't see the train coming nor did he hear it coming. "Maybe you should have offered the lead to young Jameson before you wrote the report…" Hendrick didn't know what just happened, but he felt warmth rising in his neck, he knew where this would end up. He was going to get a sharp ass chewing. He sucked it up and spoke. "Agent Cooper, I'm not sure of what you're referring too, maybe you could be more specific in any criticism?"

Cooper was in disbelief, but Hendrick made a request. She allowed him some courtesy.

"Very well, Detective, __ I find it odd that the kitchen area hadn't been dusted. No weapon found, and no weapon considered…" Hendrick had heard what she said and realized the implications. *Kitchen Utensils??* Hendrick had to sit. He couldn't believe he missed such a no-brainer. He obviously took it harder than Jake thought he would have, but Jake knew how bad a pecker spanking could be. Jake could only imagine, *What if this would be, the last work you did before retirement?* The silence was broken by Cooper's directive to Jameson. "Okay Jameson! Get those CSI guy's back over here right now." Jameson headed for the phone and made the request. Sam walked back into the room. He pulled up a chair next to Hendrick. The rest of the room was silent. Sam placed his hand on Hendrick's leg. "Detective Hendrick, don't be too hard on yourself. My experience of this whole nightmare has been chaotic. Chaos is never really handled, it is only managed. When an operator of our machines has a split second lapse, very costly resolutions need consideration. You might use this experience to not feel shame, but to protect Jameson from himself. I am speaking of your experience. I'm sure he will need some solid help right about now. Maybe you can use this err, so as to, cover his back. This might be a more fruitful path in finding redemption, as well as, value recognized in this redemption." Jake whistled loudly. "Shit Sam, you should be writing Chinese Fortunes for those cookies... That was so moving, I think I'll have a cry. Boohoo Whooo. Hahahahah!"

"Detective Hendrick pulled from a crash and burn, Oh Man you're one lucky man detective!" Jake got up and went to the bathroom, as he did he loosed a comment to Jameson. "Hey Young Jameson, you'd better be the better for what your partner just went through. I don't think Cooper will be so kind with a kid like you!!!!" Jake disappeared.

Sam looked at Hendrick, "Forget all he said, he was just a kid who liked the taste of soap!" Hendrick laughed, he looked at Sam, "Thanks for being so understanding Sam." Sam patted Hendrick's leg. "Detective Hendrick, I've always known success lies beyond mistakes. Mistakes are a given in life, they are the means by which we refine ourselves. For me, and anyone around me, we always exploited them, rather than wallowed in them. We were very successful." Jake came back into the room, he had heard all that Sam had said, and yielded to it. Jake was just the witness providing humor to what he saw. "Hey Sam, you can take your head out of your ass any time. We still are successful, just limited. After you get your beautiful face cleaned up, you can live by that which you have offered in advice. Use your sorrow as a compass leading you to the guilty. Damn you just need to find a bearing." He winked at everyone. Cooper asked Jameson, "ETA on the investigators?" Jameson came alive. "I was told within the hour, they had to notify an off duty officer." She continued, "What about the uniforms that were here?" Jameson qualified, "Do you want them to respond here?" "Nah, it won't be necessary right now, but they are available?" "Yes." Cooper seemed satisfied for the moment.

Hendrick stood up. He was still smarting from his err. He walked to Agent Cooper. "Agent Cooper I want to apologize again to you. My attention to detail was less than diligent." Cooper took a moment. "Detective, Take only what you can gain from, leave the rest behind and revisit it when you need to be humble. There is no foul here, so no harm. Sam seemed to cover it well, don't you think?" Hendrick nodded, "Kinda blew me away, if I say so, myself. Hard to believe a man in such pain has those kinds of insights, I'm not sure I'll ever forget his kindness." Cooper nodded, "Now we must proceed in this investigation. We must do it as though our lives depended upon it." Cooper shook Hendrick's hand, and went back to examining the photos. Hendrick moved to Jameson and had a few words, they both agreed to what their decision had been. Hendrick left the house. Jake watched Hendrick leave. When he was safely out of earshot, Jake looked towards Jameson. "So boss, is he gonna get a demerit?" Sam looked at Jake. He shook his head. Sam had given up on convincing Jake to hold his tongue. So, when Jake was pressing a point, Sam let him hang himself. Jake read the mood of the room; he didn't see the reaction from the others he had intended. "Damn, we all were having such a laugh." Jake pouted and plopped down onto a chair. There was a silence between the men, Cooper was shuffling photos around, looking for any other bombs, and none seemed to be evident. She folded up the file and took a seat near Jake. When she saw Jake pouting, she thought of something from her youth. Her mouth opened and said an old rhyme she recalled. "Jake Blaques, You take that frown and turn it upside down!" Jake looked surprised and Sam took notice. Cooper was wondering if her foot needed extraction from her mouth, and if she did? What kind of assistance she would need? "Did I say something wrong??" Jake raised his eyebrows indicating he didn't know.

Sam spoke coldly. "No Bina, you didn't say anything wrong, it's just... Monica cajoled the children with the same words you had mentioned." Cooper inhaled realizing she was safe; her timing and word selection was just inconvenient.

She decided to go for broke. She realized what she was about to utter, could be construed as manipulative. "Oh, so if Monica were to suggest what I just said, you'd be doing it?" The men were speechless. They were so startled they had to force themselves to think on it. Jake was surprising. He kept his mouth shut. He might have bent the rules, but he knew the limitations. Sam offered a guess. "Monica would have Jake smiling while she expected him to walk on a bed of red-hot coals... and he would have done it. Anyone would have done what she asked." Sam was sliding a bit. Cooper changed up. She hoped Sam would welcome the distraction. "Well, Mr. Blaques? What about that sorry puss and frown?" Jake played along and smiled. Cooper nodded, "Don't let me catch you losing that smile either." Jake was contemplating Bina's skill as a helpful person. "Yes Ma'am!" He saluted her. As he did, he thought of the similarities, Bina shared with Monica. Jake always accepted natural tendencies. He thought it was a loosing battle to defy them. Part of his humor was a direct assault on people's inability to deal with what couldn't be changed or helped. He thought of it as a cosmic equalizer. He saw Bina, and he thought of Monica. As far as Jake was concerned, Monica was taken and Bina was delivered. There was no arguing it. It just was. Of course Monica would be missed, sorely. The kids would be missed sorely, and he was doing all he could, to keep his best friend out of a place with no escape.

Jake took a look around the room; he knew he was supposed to be doing something; he just wasn't in tune with the natural flow. Most of the time when he felt like now, he cracked jokes or made someone aware of their own stupidity. No one was available for his usual joking behavior. Jake had reached an interesting point in his life.

He was out of his usual loop, so it was time to find another thing or person, for his own amusement. The more he thought of his options, the less he had. He couldn't go to work for his friend needed him. Oh, how he wished to be left to his work. Jake was working himself into a fit. He needed to make a change. He decided to kidnap Jameson. "Jameson, feel like a stroll?" Jameson was content to wait on the crime seen guys. Bina added in. "It is okay boys. When the crime seen investigators get here, I'll tell them what they need to do. You go out and play, and listen for the dinner bell." The guys looked at Bina; Jake was going to have a word with that woman. "Okay then, we'll all see ya later then." Jake was looking back at Sam. Sam's hand waved without looking back. "Yeah, here we go Jameson, it is a good thing you're a cop! At least the law will be there, when I'll need them."

Jameson really didn't know how to take what Jake had said. He was hoping Jake was kidding, he wasn't sure. One thing he did know, Jake must have been feeling like a long tailed cat in a rocking chair room. He seemed somewhat anxious. Just as they were leaving, Sam spoke up. "Jameson, he's all bark, don't let him get ya worked up too much. Besides, we need ya back here to weave the local flavor into this fabric." Jameson didn't know what to make of the last part of Sam's cryptic message, the first part made him feel better, but the second part, well it didn't sound right. He looked at Jake. Jake shrugged and rolled his eyes. They both left.

Cooper looked at Sam to see how he was managing. She was trying hard to keep notice of Sam, while figuring if the file was complete. The photos had become a preoccupation. "What the heck, was it?" She started focusing on her confusion, and forgot all about Sam. She needed to relax a bit. She felt her pulse beginning to work on her temporal region. She broke away from her increasingly uncomfortable study. When she looked up Sam had moved. He was no longer in her field of vision. She took a couple of steps toward the kitchen she looked out onto the patio, and saw Sam. She was relieved. It might not have been too good, if Sam made his way to the bedroom. Her concern for Sam was contributing to her discomfort. She knew he was PTSD. She wondered where in the grieving process he was. He remained aloof, and somewhat skeptical.

She recalled the grieving process from psychology. Sam must have been somewhere in that process. When she expected anger, he displayed compassion and understanding. She started to realize her involvement, was the reason for the stress. Concern for Sam was a distraction. Empathy for Sam was shaking her confidence in being an investigator. She had not welcomed this past year and a half's change; she made her way through it, by what worked for her. What seemed to be logical, as a plan developed, offered new and unfamiliar complexities. She made more mental notes. She decided to put the file down, and develop more of a bond with Sam. Cooper placed the file on the table supporting the phone and walked towards where she thought Sam to be. She hoped he was approachable. When she finally came upon Sam, she noticed he was starring at a garden. "Ah Sam? Do you have a moment?" Sam didn't turn to face Cooper; he stood there and gathered some composure. "Sure Bina, I was just thinking about how Monica had to nag me to put this garden in. Tim and I made a big joke of it... Monica fought hard to enlist Tim in her design." The two of them had conspired and here is the result. It had remained a subject of welcome controversy. Cooper waited on Sam to finish his daydream there really wasn't much she could say. "So Bina, ever been married? Any kids?" Sam finished up. "No Sam, neither for me." Sam turned to face Cooper. "The hard thing is only having memories." "Realizing that is the hardest thing. I can't imagine what that is like Sam." Cooper thought she could be honest, fortunately so did Sam. Sam was not expecting to hear what Bina had said. He looked to her and nodded. "Even if you had a family, it would be hard to imagine, I suppose, but thanks for being candid." Cooper was intrigued by Sam's comportment. She almost lost the train of thought, which brought her to interrupt Sam. "You had asked for a minute Bina?" "Yes Sam! I'm sorry for spacing out Sam. I wanted to take some time and have a meeting of the minds as to how this would be playing out. If, that is alright with you?" "Yes Bina that will be fine." Sam appreciated her notion of progress. Sam always wanted transparency in his dealings.

"Well then", Bina gathered her thoughts. "I'm sure you're still wondering what it is that I see as worthy of being here and investigating the crime against you and yours. So, here it is. The program I designed was specific to crimes like this. This program lacked input because all of the victims except you and me are dead. In my surviving of this attack, the result was obvious, the guy screwed up. Not completely though, he is still free, and they have breathing room as I am no longer on any real investigation." Before she could continue, Sam interrupted. "Bina your tools of the trade, lead you here. You don't need to qualify how you ended up here. Being redundant is either a specific function, or it is a problematic circumstance. You seem to be effective in your vocation, so there is no need to explain your methodology. I am concerned by one thing you have said. That would be 'they,' Just who are they? Is this a conspiracy, or your opinion, that it is a conspiracy?" Sam offered a pause. Cooper underestimated Sam's ability to articulate the obvious. She hadn't expected having to rationalize her position. "It is my opinion." Sam acknowledged her statement. "Very well Bina. What do you think it is we need to accomplish, so that we may validate your theory?" Cooper was shocked! She was so predisposed to having to fight for her opinions, with Sam there seemed to be no obstacle. He listened to what was tabled and worked through it. Cooper thought the only man she knew like this, had left this world, when her father died. "I think we need to pull Jameson into the 'gray side' of the law. He will be ready to report all our doings to either his lieutenant or to Hendrick. I'm not suggesting these guys are bad, just extra baggage. Policy always screws things up Sam." Cooper winced. "Correction, not policy, __ but agendas, yes agendas." Sam rubbed his chin, he was thinking of a connecting thought. "I think you are right about agendas and I'm glad you qualified it. The choice of diction means you consider it all the time. I am similar in my business. I'll assume your choice of the color gray was specifically chosen, and I'll also assume this grayness isn't illegal." Cooper nodded. Sam's character was developing right in front of her eyes. "Well then Sam, you're assuming, I will not make an ass of either you or me, especially not Jameson."

"Bina, I'm not suggesting a need comes along, which forces choices. These choices leave one in difficult position as to chose right or wrong. That is not what I meant. What I meant was this: If we would want Jameson to step beyond the bounds of his oath, we should make him aware of the peril of his actions…. That's all. If he makes his decisions, they are his. And, when they are his, he will be as effective as he can be." Cooper considered what Sam had said. She was floored. Before she could respond, Sam added some more food to her plate. "I saw the way you pinched Hendrick this morning. He had it coming. I was glad to see him suck up his ineptitude. However, that man has been at this game for sometime. He deserves some leeway at the end of his career.

He was helpful on the terrible night of my families' murders, and that goes along way with me. It buys favor with me. I think he will do his very best regarding Jameson. He'd be a fool otherwise, and he doesn't strike me as a fool." Cooper was still getting her footing from what Sam had said previously, this was over the top. "Agreed Sam" they stood in silence. Cooper was still trying to figure out what was happening. Sam had realized Bina's confusion. He allowed her some time while he turned his focus to the garden once again. She was realizing the richness of Sam's experience. She was realizing Sam, as being an asset to the job. She was going through her listed mental notes about the beginning of this investigation, she found herself, behind a need. Her need was to realize trusting Sam became a priority. Her predisposed assumptions, of figuring Sam's personality, were no longer needed. Sam punctuated her thought speaking of Jameson. "While you're refocusing Bina, don't waste any time wondering about Jameson. Did you know Jake could talk to dogs?" Bina looked at Sam incredulously. "No, no, I swear he can. Ask anyone who knows Jake. Can't you see the puppy-like characteristics of Jameson? Old Jake, ___ hell, Jameson will come to eat from his hand. By the way, Jake is with me..." Sam flashed a smile, Cooper might have thought impossible for Sam to wear. She responded in kind. She liked the odds, four victims and four investigators. Sam focused back on Monica's garden. She excused herself to make some notes in the file she left inside.

Chapter 10

Jake had suggested that a stroll might include policing the reported escape route. Jameson agreed to the suggestion. While they retraced the escape route, a question developed in Jameson's mind. "Jake, I'd like to ask you something, if it is alright?" Jake stopped his forward progress, and offered Jameson his ear cueing Jameson to proceed with the question. Jameson stopped as Jake had, he assumed a comfortable position, and fired it to Jake. "Is it usual for Sam to do that calm kind of thinking and speaking?" He winced in anticipation of Jake's response, wishing he'd not asked it. Jameson was rightly intimidated by Jake, he was confident in having this insight. The cigar in Jakes mouth was a huge distraction. The only way Jameson thought to attain a modicum of Jake's respect was to get beyond that distraction. Jake's proclivity to make one aware of their folly was the quicksand he wanted to avoid.

"Young Jameson what you witnessed is all Sam. What you didn't witness is what it takes for Sam to loose his cool. Your virgin eyes need to see that happen. They will never be the same again. I guess it is easier for Sam to be nice. When he gets stressed…. the man is as slick as slick gets. He remains cool, and if you are reporting to him, you'll do well to keep that in mind! He does have a fearful side. You might have thought I was the one to reckon with, and you'd be wrong. It isn't that I wouldn't deal out attitude adjustment because I regularly do… but, with Sam, he gives solid advice and strong consideration to all he does, unlike me." Jake rolled that cigar over on his tongue, as he prepared to continue. "I saw Sam go after a vandal we caught some years ago. This unfortunate former employee was letting some of our equipment have it. Nothing too serious, but enough to get Sam all worked up. Damn, some of the graffiti was down right good. This couple of months made Sam crazy. He couldn't get over the fact that someone could show such disrespect. He kept asking if the dipshit had a problem, why couldn't he talk about it as a man? That is all Sam kept asking. We had grown tired of it. I grew tired of Sam's agony. I couldn't stand to listen to it anymore." Jake found a light for his cigar, after he spit what he was chewing. Jameson was content to wait.

"We had the idea to ambush this fool. So, we planned a strategy over a couple of days. Once Sam had a resolution, he got to his usual self, kinda like you asked about. I guess he was patient even satisfied

that our troubles would soon be over. I was just glad for the relief...
so, we end up shutting down for the day and left. We made it appear
as though we were offering up another few 'canvases' by moving the
machine to favor the graces of more masterful art work. The move also
played reasonably. The machines needed to be moved to complete the
next phase of the job...remember, as slick as slick gets! I come by and
pick up Sam on my bike. We had optics, and we had a perfect perch.
We brought some beer and holed up. Sam didn't say much, but he
didn't need to, his appearance said it all. Payback was his. Forget about
our payback, I was like a sideshow. I was getting tired of the whole
thing even as it was my idea. I had different wishes for the evening, fine
young lass, with a tight... Well, you get the drift?" Jameson enjoyed
Jake's recollection, and how he could tell a story. He nodded and winked
at Jake's last thought. Jake drew on his cigar. He spoke through his
exhalation. "I was just getting ready to depart on my lustful tendency.
Wouldn't ya know it? The little bastard we stalked walked right in on
the seen." Jake grabbed his arm as an example Jameson could feel. "Sam
grabbed my arm! I couldn't break his grip. The harder I worked, the
tighter his grip got. It was Sam's way of telling me, he wasn't going to
allow me to spook him. So we waited, Sam was right. The guy waited
some time to commit, so we waited until he made his move. As soon as
Sam saw the opportunity, we moved and I mean *moved!* The sound of
the guy's spray can must have dampened our approach; to this day I'll

never think we'd have caught him. To me, we sounded like a stampede. He didn't even notice that we had his escape of convenience cut off. When he finished up and turned, he suddenly knew his trouble. Sam was standing full of recoil, ready to spring on the guy. Get this! Sam says, 'Show yourself!' The guy was hooded up, when he said it I about jumped back. The guy tried to retreat, and at the first move, Sam lunged at the guy. The poor bastard was like a cornered mouse, and the cat was tired of playing with it. Sam reaches to the guy's hood and revealed the identity of our frustration. It was Bruce Dodson! He used to work for us. For a second, Sam looked like he had lost his breath. Sam was exchanging deep breaths as he threw this guy off the machine he just painted. I guess Sam thought the guy's head and body would be a good start at cleaning up the fresh paint." Jake shook his head as he recalled Sam's action. Jameson was engrossed with the tale. Jake pulled again on his cigar.

"Young Jameson, I don't know how Bruce survived the attack. Hell I wasn't sure I was gonna get through the battle I had with Sam in trying to remove him from delivering such a beating. I had to consider dropping Sam with a piece of wood for a second there. It was a viscous beating. I know I'd hate to have been carrying a can of spray paint anywhere close to those machines, watching what poor Bruce was enduring."

Jameson thought his jaw had dropped, he overcompensated a bite to close his mouth and bit his tongue. Pain riddled his face, Jake watched Jameson accept his own medicine. As Jameson's face changed, Jake started to laugh a bit. His hand rose up, and patted Jameson's shoulder. "Yeah that's kinda how old Bruce looked at the second swing!" Jake's previous snicker had developed into a healthy belly laugh. The kind of laugh, you have realizing, an infrequent recollection, outdone only at another participants similar folly, by context of incidental physical pain. Jake broke a piece off a non-smoked cigar, he had. "Chew on this Young Jameson, and fear not the questions you pose; fear the potential of not having posed them. I know old Bruce wishes he had another bite at that apple. Yep, he had that wish for quite some time." Jake laughed some more. "Poor bastard ate through a straw for 9 months. He still walks with a pretty good limp. Guess Sam saw fit to give him plenty of time, to think about all those pictures he painted…. he'll think on it 'till his very last step."

Jake was back to chewing his cigar. Something clicked for Jameson. The distraction of Jake's cigar was nothing more than Jakes managing pauses in his tales. It was an effective tell. Jake used his cigar for an ingenious management of timing. Jake could pace an audience. Flicking his cigar in his mouth, Jake shifted needed focus from a visual to auditory and back without anyone losing interest. Jameson realized it as a sort of, *hypnotism*. Jameson loosened right up with knowledge of Jake's 'tell.' He felt much better, and busied himself for whatever may have been overlooked. The men were silent for a bit. "Here's a question for you Young Jameson, what's your take on Cooper?" Jake kept his policing activity while he asked. Jameson felt as though Jake was entitled....

"Well pops!" Jake owned a pause and grinned at Jameson. "Pops?" Too bad Jake's cigar wasn't the decoy right then. Jameson wished again for the ability to retract what he said. "Okay, Pops Jake!" Jameson snickered. "She's a Lady that seems mighty sharp... if ya could listen to her, ya might learn some valuable things." "Ya might be right about that Jameson, ya just might be right." Jake shook his head while he considered it. "Hey Pops, I wouldn't mind working with her. She sure seems to have a handle on doing her job." Jake couldn't help adding in. "I hear Hendrick feels similarly. He now sees that, as one of her strengths too." Jake chuckled a bit. Jameson looked at Jake. For an old man he was quick with the tongue. "I'm sure of it Pops. He really stepped on his pecker then, huh?"

Jake grinned and nodded profusely. "Ya know there scup? She could even teach a man, about being a man, long before he'd come to realize it...." "What the hell is a scup? What happened to Young Jameson?" Jameson rebuffed.

Jake grinned his white teeth were whiter than Jameson would consider a smoker of a cigar to have. "Well a scup is......... a little fish!" Jake laughed a bit. "Hey kid, you called me pops and you should be more kind of my senior moments!" Next time Jameson would leave less opportunity for Jake to reverse one of his own jibes, maybe the cigar wasn't the distraction he thought of it to be?

The men continued their policing. Jameson moved ahead of Jake, something had caught his eye. Jake continued in his area as he took notice of Jameson moving. Jake wasn't sure of what he was looking for. His original idea was to evade Cooper's suggestions regarding his mannerisms. Jake lost himself in a moment of recollection. Monica was one who would let Jake have it. But she could. The world they had all designed had been built on coming to each other. On the journey, they had come to know themselves as siblings. Jake thought about his choice of identification and retracted it. Siblings sometimes hated one another. While Jake was contemplating descriptors, he noticed an oddity to the proximities environs.

"Jameson? How is your tongue?" Jameson was nursing his tongue with the piece of cigar Jake had just given him. He paused, considering how his mouth felt. He opened his jaw moving his tongue. He evaluated his senses and peered at Jake. "My tongue, ___ it's not as swollen as I thought it might be." Jake was grinning again. "Okay, what's the difference now?" Jake's grin held steady; his eyes had the alpha quality to stare down an answer. Jameson reached to his mouth, stopping below and slightly away from his chin. His hand caught the tobacco. Jameson lifted it towards Jake. The gesture showed the answer as to the difference. Jake's head nodded his stare had been broken. Jameson smiled and put the proof back in his mouth. Jake broke out in an amused fashion making sounds Jameson didn't know what to call. Jameson realized then, Jake was hypnotizing regardless of the cigar. He was a guy who was rough on the edges, and like it had been said about Cooper, if one could get past, or around appearances, there might be a great value in what one may come to know.

Jake ceased his flow of thinking by asking another question. "Jameson?" Jake waited for Jameson's attention. Jameson looked towards Jake, meeting his stare again. Jake took a step towards Jameson while he retrieved the cigar he had broken earlier. "Jameson life comes down to how you observe things. While some folks deplore these cigars for their offensive nature, they become trapped in only thinking of the offense they observe. And in doing so, they fail to capitalize on what is gained in toleration. While they dismiss the cigar as having any benefit to themselves, their sense of observation is limited to the substance and its benefits. They attained a comfortable proximity." Jake presented the cigar for comment. Jake watched Jameson make sense of his insight. Once Jameson seemed to grasp what he had said, he continued. "When you observe things more completely, your perceptions come from a more suitable foundation. The reason your tongue has less discomfort is directly related to the tobaccos toxic quality. The spit your mouth produces, when it accepts tobacco, prevents inflammation. The bacteria living in your mouth have not the ability to attack the fresh wound, the bacteria, has been under effective attack. Your bodies' defense mechanisms are less taxed. If you could come to see that this cigar is not just a cigar, you'd be more likely, to be happy. People walk away from all kinds of solutions without ever seeing them as solutions; a cigar to them is, undeservedly dismissed." Jameson had heard what Jake had said. He wasn't sure if he captured all of it. He made the connection of how the tobacco, although toxic, could be an effectively used, resulting in benefit for it's use, but he wasn't sure what Jake had meant in being happy about it. Jake had realized Jameson hadn't understood his previous points. He revised his thoughts and attempted another effort. "Let's say, you and me are 2 guys who live with excellence in observing things." Jameson nodded in acknowledgment. "Our foundations are solid, our perceptions are readily flexible. While we know what we want and like, we live happily. Our perception changes as we accept different potentials of what we observe. We always seek happiness, because we can. Those unwilling or unable to live in this wisdom, settle for lack of choice. Their foundation of perception is controlled, because what they perceive comes from limited observation."

Jake lit his cigar again, he watched Jameson, and waited. "Jake, I guess that is another way of illustrating how folks manage options. I'm still not sure of what I should conclude." Jake furiously broke out in laughter, startling Jameson a bit. "Young Jameson," Jake spoke through his laughter. "Your conclusions come at the end of a charge you are fulfilling or have fulfilled. They are not perceptions, they are regrets, they are victories, and they're the continual building blocks of the observable foundation expanding, as our perceptions expand. Do you recall what this stroll is all about?" Jake waited on another response. Jameson was struggling. "I guess the 'why,' serves a few purposes…. you weren't too comfortable about enduring the focus you were receiving. We have come to know more of each other. I'm sure there is more, but I can't articulate it." Jake flashed a rewarding smile his hand patted Jameson's shoulder. "That is good thinking young Jameson! What you're having difficulty articulating is your perceptional disconnect from observable fact. We are taking this stroll, for all that you have thought and just mentioned. Here is the kicker! Your observation was taken on another's ability to have effectively policed this area." Jameson nodded as following. "If you had repeated the same steps taken, would the report still result as the same with a different observational perception? If you observe statements of fact to be fact, how can you be sure of factual validity? Might those reporting a lack of evidence, have a lesser foundation of observation, than you or I?"

Jameson was like a kid figuring out for the first time, he discovered the art of shoe tying. "Damn Jake, we are looking for that which is yet to be observed! Too bad it is a cold seen!" Jake turned Jameson by his shoulder. When Jake had finished exposing a view to Jameson, his hand directed attention to an observable area, which they covered and which had yet to be surveyed. "Do you think Ginny Holman saw the perps here, or back there?" Jake pointed to an area they had walked by. Jameson gave it a second. "Back there!" The two men walked back to the entry. "Do you think her proximity was considered, when Ginny had stated an observable perception?" Jameson's pace quickened. "That is a good question Jake, let's take a look." When the men had reached an area where Ginny could have seen them, they discovered her statement was not actually factual. It couldn't have been. Her field of vision ended before she could have seen the suspects enter the path. "Damn Jake, how is knowing error supposed to make you happy?" Jake's laughter was approaching a level of contempt for Jameson. Jake realized that Jameson's frustration was rising. He cooled the laughing some, but the grin was permanent. "Jameson, it seems to me, realizing err, provides alternative perceptions... and, the flexibility of options expands. What wasn't there before is now available, or another bite at the apple?" Jameson looked like he had figured the secret out of a double knot in tying the shoe. His confusion and frustration evaporated. He saw the light. "Hey pops that sure is some piece of thinking! Whad'ya say, we go check out Cooper's report and refine our observation?" Jake was swimming in the light for the moment. He had already started for the others. He was laughing the whole way. "Feeling happier about it now Jameson?" "Well Jake, I don't know about happy, or that I would call it happy, but I sure got some more detecting to do, and busy beats bored any day of the week."

Jake had felt as though he mentored Jameson enough for the moment. "I'm pretty sure you'll find what wasn't found before, nobody disappears just like that!" Jake was satisfied to leave Jameson as the messenger of good and bad news… he didn't know if Jameson saw the reaching implications of what still needed to be discovered. Hendrick had dropped the ball once again. The difficulty was realizing how a set of bad observations left you a path of perceiving another possibility. And seeing how difficult a passage from that place of perception would be.

Chapter 11

Just after Jake and Jameson had gotten back to the house, the crime scene investigators had arrived. While Jameson rifled the report Cooper used to possess, she directed the investigators to dust for prints around the area in the kitchen where the knives were stowed. Jameson was almost frenetic in finding the statement Ginny Holman had given. When he found what he wanted, he looked at Jake. "Jake it appears no reference was given. It doesn't say where she had seen them…"

Jake placed the file down, and invited two investigators to follow him. Sam looked at Jake. Jake smiled and laughed. "Apparently, no one considered where Ginny Holman had seen the suspects flee. What was her position, or vantage?" Sam's head reeled when he understood the implication. Cooper had also heard what Jake had said. Her reaction was more animated. "Where did these police learn investigation protocol? Did they get their training from a Bazooka Joe comic collection?" The investigator started to laugh, he wasn't aware of how cutting Agent Cooper could be. "What are you laughing at? This is your second time here, isn't it? Just what the hell is your excuse?" The investigator wasn't laughing anymore, he was getting busy, the new blush in his face seemed to regulate his focus, it had been slow to come, but it had defiantly arrived. Jake realized the second bite of the apple wouldn't ease the frustration, which was developing; too many were looking for the second bite. He sensed this whole investigation was shady from the start. Any credibility associated to any work or effort was waning, with regards, to what was apparent. He looked out the window. Jameson was pointing out that what had been searched before might not have been the stated escape route. Jake could tell by Jameson's hand motion, he was directing the investigators to survey the general direction of the original witness statement. When a plan had been delegated, Jameson was off to Ginny Holman's house to get more specificity to her statement. Jake lit his cigar, and grabbed another coffee. He sat down and observed the work of the fella dusting. He also waited.

Cooper was showing her teeth a bit. She was entitled. Sam was considering her pointed criticism. He decided he liked it. It was fair, and it was beyond dispute. Sam never minded that a more capable individual would point out weak actions or thinking by others considered to be peers. The obvious result being... those who some call peers are not peers at all. And transparent thinking combined with deliberate action was an individual difference of misnamed peers. Once again, Sam loosed a comment to the investigator. "Excuse me." Sam interrupted the dusting process. "Apparently, we are aware of a need to revisit this crime scene. Correct me if I am wrong, but this isn't the first time you have revisited a crime scene, is it?"

The investigator thought about the question Sam posed. "No sir, as a matter of fact, it isn't. We have questions posed to us all the time that would be a different thinking, and there by, need a different analysis." The investigator seemed to have claimed redemption, and got back to work. Sam looked at Cooper and winked.

"While you are completing this differently understood analysis, might you also consider what else might have been overlooked?"

Cooper was skeptical of Sam's line of thought, and the skepticism came from doing things her own way. Usually to root out err, of others. She had been blown away by the investigators response. "I could do that!" The investigator's focus no longer seemed to be motivated in anxiety. Sam was contemplating one more offering… "Yes, I think that would be a huge help to getting this crime solved, wouldn't you agree Agent Cooper?" "I am certain of it!"

Cooper had once again seen Sam deal with a bad circumstance, and exploit it. She thought again, of what hadn't made sense to her, regarding the photo's she studied. She decided to have another look.

She reasoned if the known information wasn't seen clearly, what were the details that had been missed? She became satisfied in a potential new discovery of yet unrealized evidence. She calmed down, and picked up the file Jameson seemed to find new direction from. Once Sam saw Cooper had a new directive, he turned to wink at Jake. Jake already had his thumb up. Jake looked out the window again and saw Jameson leaving Holman's house. He was on his radio. Jake thought he might be calling the uniforms back to the scene. Jake watched as Jameson made it back to the house. His facial expression wasn't pained, and it wasn't happy. It was deliberate. Jameson came back in through the door. "We were right about Ms. Holman' vantage, when she claimed to have seen the suspects flee down the path. Her field of vision left a much larger area to be policed than was originally thought. More police are on their way." Jake had snickered a bit. "Good work, Young Jameson. Do you think you can hold the fort down while we three take a ride?" Jameson nodded affirmatively. "Yeah, we can manage now."

"Good!" Jake had turned his attention to Cooper and Sam. "Let us 3, take a ride!" Before anyone could offer objections, Jake spoke again. "I'm pretty hungry." Sam and Cooper thought about their own hunger and decided it was a good idea. Without comment, they nodded and collected themselves to depart. Jake asked if Jameson was hungry, and if he wanted anything on the way back. Jameson indicated he was fine. They headed for Cooper's car. On the walk to the car, Jake suggested a place in the form of a question. "Sam, why don't we pay a visit on Mike and Brenda's eatery?" Sam peered at Jake. "You are bad. You're a bad man Jake Blaques!"

Jake giggled and snickered. Cooper saw surprise within the invitation to eat. She ignored Jake's antics. Getting to know Jake meant realizing in some strange way, that she would be a participant, willingly or not, to Jake's sense of fun. She wondered if his sense of fun would fall victim to her sense of priority. "Which way boys?" Jake told her the directions plainly.

Only a few minutes down the road was where they headed. Cooper watched Jake in the rear view mirror. She knew he was designing something. Jake was teeming with anticipation of their arrival. Besides being hungry, there was a little issue of payback going out. Jake held his tongue, and remained silent. Cooper could no longer resist. "Jake, I'd swear you're growing an ant farm in your pants! What has got you so wound up?" "What? Can't a guy get excited about breakfast?" He refused to give it up. "Well Jake, I guess if you get this worked up about breakfast, I'm glad not to have met you suffering from Blue Balls!"

Jake ceased feeling anticipatory. Sam busted out in a laugh, which left him crying. Cooper no longer wondered if Jake's sense of fun or humor had been well matched. Jake was pouting again, leaving Sam obliterated. The two of them picked it up in unison, "Now Jake, take that frown, and turn it upside down!" Jake relinquished a smile. Jake had thought to himself, *he'd been got.* "Hey there Bina, you are okay, that wasn't bad at all." Just as the two have recited together, they burst into laughter, after hearing Jake's come back. Sam held up his hand, trying to control his outburst. "Jake! HaHa _____ Haaaaaaaaaaa! You never got ripped like that before! And, that was one, for the ages my friend!" Sam continued to laugh. Cooper stole a glance in the rear view mirror, just as Jake held his hands up for surrender, "Guilty as charged, Guilty as charged!"

Between glances, Cooper saw a smile Jake produced, after he put his hands back down... Cooper considered that Jake wasn't done. She parked the car. They took egress from the squad. Whatever Jake's design it was right through those doors. Sam seemed to be content. Cooper abided the spirit of things. *This was like the trips to the canteen, from the Quantico days. It was 'Chow-Time.'* They entered the diner and took the same booth Sam and Jake sat at just after the murders. Brenda wasn't anywhere to be seen; Jake rolled his cigar in his mouth.

He was trying to avoid revealing his disappointment in not seeing Brenda. A second later Brenda appeared through a door leading to the back area. She was fixing her hair as she entered. Jake's titillation, betrayed his earlier concerns of concealment, Cooper was reading the play. She nudged Sam's foot with her own. She didn't know why. It might have been apprehension. Maybe Jake was playing too close to her liking. She was just trying to minimize the shock effect in letting Sam know, she knew, _____ that it was beginning. Sam acknowledged her silently nodding. Jake was very likable. He grew on you. Trusting him? Well, Sam was an easier case. With Jake, you never knew what or how, you only knew. Brenda was bringing coffees. She seemed to have primped herself; she definitely looked to be nervous. Cooper pondered the circumstance.

When Brenda delivered the coffees, it became apparent to Cooper that Brenda had a crush on Sam. Cooper understood Jake's motivation now. She sat back and observed the interaction. She wondered just how Jake was going to manipulate this. She decided as soon as she knew what Brenda's gig was, and, she didn't like Brenda. She welcomed the opportunity of Jake's intention.

Brenda managed being a waitress. She wasn't particularly proud of what she did. It was a job until Brenda could find an unwilling host for her parasitic lifestyle. "Good morning Sam!" Brenda presented herself as though Sam might have been a King, picking a wife. She looked at Jake with a smiling contempt. "Hi Jake." "Morning Brenda." Let me introduce you to a friend... "Brenda, meet Sabina Cooper." Cooper cleared her throat. "Nice to meet you Brenda." Brenda looked quizzically at Cooper. "Sabina? That's a strange name, Hi." Cooper grimaced a little; she flashed a look towards Jake. She hoped Jake realized how pitiful this was. Jake just held on to that stupid grin he had on. Sam had extended some politeness. "Good morning Brenda.

How are you?"

Brenda had developed a slow motion gaping, in her mouth. When she realized a response was needed, she became a little flush. Brenda spoke as she thought of what to say. "My, my Sam, aren't you just the angel? With all your troubles, you still have time to be a gentleman?" Sam smiled, "That is so kind of you to say Brenda." Her face flushed so she could feel it. She displayed a cute smile. A smile worn by a woman caught in a nasty little secret… one ready to share, with a man like Sam.

"What will ya have folks?" Brenda was ready for Sam's order. "I'll have my usual." Jake got his first. Brenda scribbled Jakes order. Cooper assumed Jake's style. "Brenda, I'll have a steak, medium and 2 eggs, scrambled, some rye toast, and some orange juice." Scribbling Sabina's order just wasn't happening. The needed penmanship for a successful meal, hung in the balance of trusting Brenda to get the order right… Cooper wondered if she would be in need of some antacid after this meal… "And, what will the angel Sam be having today?" "I think I'll have a bowl of Grape nuts, with a blueberry yogurt." Brenda wrote the order, but couldn't recall taking this before for Sam. "Wow Sam, I can't ever remember you having that for breakfast." Sam looked at Brenda. "You are right about that Brenda. Guess I figure a change would be helpful in coping." Once Brenda heard the word *change,* she seemed to lose her focus, just slightly. Maybe she was frightened about her fantasy actually having potential. Whatever it was, the table's conversation had been crippled. Jake bit his cigar end off. He seemed to be upset. He spit the chewed end out in the ashtray. He proceeded to light his cigar, and take a hurried but deliberate sip of coffee. Cooper was astounded. Just like that. Sam trumped Jake's folly. The real kicker... nobody had seen it coming. Not even Brenda.

Sam pulled a cigarette out and lit it. He looked at Jake. "Hey partner, your ant farm must be hibernating, what's up, you okay?" Jake grumbled, as he rolled his cigar over his tongue. "Sam, you get real! Don't play that innocent look with me!" Sam raised his eyebrows. He feigned surprise! Cooper couldn't help but smile. Jake just sneered. "You know what I'm talking about." Sam looked at Jake, then at Cooper. "Some people get mighty short tempered when they're hungry." Cooper pushed toward Sam. "Would you excuse me? I need to use the bathroom." Sam was caught off guard. "Sure Bina!" Sam exited and permitted passage. Bina made a beeline for the restroom. Sam watched her disappear into the back. Cooper couldn't remove herself fast enough. She entered this small restroom and locked the door. She closed the seat to the toilet and sat herself down. This feeling she was having was one she feared. She only came to know it, when Sam had mentioned how short tempered people could be. *Sam was too polite. Sam was in complete control!* Some tears well up around her eyes. She rolled off some toilet paper and tended her face. She thought to herself, *Sam is a vigilante!!!* All the signs were there. Sam was too cool. And, Sam was saving this newly found hate, just as she was saving her 18-month, hate. There was a God. Cooper had been considering pay back for quite some time. She too saw a real potential of her fantasies' deliverance. She was aroused, not frightened like Brenda. What she pitied earlier she had become. And, that wasn't a reality Cooper dared consider. She stood up and rinsed her face. She gave herself the twice over in the mirror. Cooper had little use for serving needs, which delivered misery. She had been with likeable men. But, there was never the feeling she just had, this frightened her. She finished up and returned to the table.

The men looked up as she came back to the table. Jake had gotten up before Sam could. She squeezed in by Jake's side to a place setting that wasn't there before she had left. Brenda had been busy. Sam noticed a difference about Cooper. "Is everything alright Bina?" Cooper noticed Brenda was looking to engage Sam's eyes. She decided some womanly wiles were appropriate. She extended her hand to touch Sam's forearm, she glanced up at Sam once her hand was targeted. "Sam everything is just fine, Thanks so much for asking. Just a moment of sadness, I'm sorry." She left her hand on his forearm for a second or two then retracted her hand. Jake had found his grin again; his designs might yet be salvageable. Cooper was glad to allow Jake this hope, he after all was Sam's partner. Like Sam said before, "Jake is with me." Brenda brought the food to the table. She was definitely aggravated with Sabina. That was clear by how she placed the steak and eggs down. It was more of a slam. Jake was ecstatic. Sam thanked Brenda and she looked over the table. She ended up emptying the ashtray, not because she would have done it for her job, but because of Sam's convenience and for his kindness. She left them to eat. The only noise between them was the sounds made of people eating. They all seemed to focus in their own little worlds, which were expanding every second. After the meal, Sam paid the bill and thanked Brenda again. Both Jake and Cooper had a feeling. If Brenda were to die one minute after they left, she'd have died happier than before they all came in. They were fed and on they're way back to Sam's house. The ride was silent. Sam broke the silence, minutes from the house. "I think I'm going to sell this house." Cooper didn't say a word. Neither did Jake. She parked the car, and they slowly got out. Jake looked to Sam. "Really, sell this place?" Sam nodded. "Sure I am gonna sell it. That might have been my home once, not anymore! I'd end up shooting myself staying here." Jake grunted, "I'd guess you know."

Sam was viewing his house once more. "Back, in another day, this house protected me and mine. I never needed protection, not for myself. This house would serve another family better than me. Better to sell it." Jake and Cooper considered what Sam had said. It was, unexpected. Not so much that Sam might consider selling the house, but the suddenness of his conclusion. Jake had been more inclined to accept Sam's decision. He'd been doing that for most of the relationship, they shared. Cooper on the other hand, was witnessing a process. Much time had been dedicated to understanding actions, as a developing unforeseen problem. Cooper considered the past 3 days. Sam's comportment through this tragedy was not what would be considered normal. In fact, the wrong Agent might have read Sam's disconnect, as a consideration, in qualifying him as a suspect. Cooper realized the gravity of the situation; she needed some help. She also realized, that help was right next to her. "So, Jake, I need to pick your brain." Jake raised one of his eyebrows, his grin came to life. His look alone said it all. "Be careful there now big fella, I just might have to use handcuffs on you!" Cooper nailed the only weakness Jake had. The grin she expected to come was delayed but delivered. And it was priceless! Jake added a long soft whistle. Cooper was not lacking for a workable vocabulary of the non-spoken conversation. She after all was the law. Not the local law, or even state authorities, she was the law of the land. She took a quarter-step to face Jake, she took a stance, which clarified what the law of the land was; punctuated with warning seduction.

The look on Jake's face startled submission. The pair seemed to be speaking just fine. Jake had a bit of advice for Cooper. "Agent Cooper there are some that say the way to a man's heart is through his belly. How do you propose to find the path to my mind?" His grin developed a chuckle. "Mr. Blaques are your affairs in order?" A rhetorical pause ceased further chuckling. Cooper parried. "We could look at this merger 2 ways, the expedient way, or the considered and deliberate way. The expedient way assures your every wish and fantasy come true. You'd be lucky to survive. The considered and deliberate way, well, I fear you stand a lesser chance of survival in the context I'm thinking about." She snuggled up to Jake, offering the forbidden fruit. She wanted to trust Jake, she need not. She could manipulate any need she had. She hoped Jake understood. "Jake, I really do need to talk to you. There are concerns, developing concerns I have regarding Sam." Jake's appearance responded silently. The gravity of what Cooper had said was like a mental-erectile dysfunction for Jake. "Yeah, that's the way it always goes…a great fantasy you only have once."

Jake hung his head, like a dog would when people would retract an invitation to the canine's presence. Cooper couldn't help but to laugh at Jake, he was such a ham. She hugged him in a thankful gesture and smacked his cheek with a kiss. Jake accepted the rejection, "Yeah, go on, go ahead rub it in." Jake passed on the forbidden fruit, they separated, and he looked at Cooper and continued some non-spoken language Jake meant, your loss. He looked at the house. "Do ya think a second go at it, reveals any pearls of wisdom?" Cooper giggled. She giggled again. "Jake? Did you say pearls? You know? I'm a girl who is fond of a pearl necklace." She reached over and gave Jake a slap on the ass. Jake hadn't expected it he turned to look at Cooper. "Hey Bina, you know, I'm a guy known to give pearl necklaces. But the pearls I meant wouldn't be on your neck... they'd be in there." Jake pointed in the direction of the second Crime Scene Investigation. Cooper nodded and took his arm. "Shall we precede, Sir Jake?" "Yes Agent Cooper we shall undertake this dreadful process. I'm available to you, at your convenience Agent Cooper. May I offer a relaxed and suitable alternative of discretion, so as to offer you my brain?" Bina looked ahead to watch Sam enter the house, and turned to Jake's ear. "Might, you have meant your lovely, **Buried Treasure**?" Jake acted as though he was impressed. The reality was he expected her to follow his lead. She had effectively demonstrated her capacity of exploiting foresight previously. Having two choices for Jake wasn't good to begin with. The outcomes Cooper predicted were worse. That was bad. And, if Jake didn't survive, well that was 'really bad.' Jake wasn't the type of guy to face his end without an option. Jake believed fate existed. He also believed it existed so that the human spirit could overcome predestination. "Agent Cooper, you did say something about victim insight? Isn't it ironic? Your treasure revealed, onboard The **Buried Treasure**?" Cooper smiled at Jake's conclusion. "Indeed Jake, ironic indeed. Better even yet an excellent alternative!" They had reached the threshold of the house. Inside, a 2nd bite was being taken. They were hoping a 3rd bite would not be needed.

Chapter 12

Sam's parlor was a hopeful place, for the moment. About seven people were waiting on print results the technician was trying to lift. He explained to Jameson, there were some prints that hadn't been wiped. The technician was of the opinion, that the surface had been wiped, but not completely. He was just finishing up with the samples he'd taken. Jameson instructed the technician to leave the scene, and process those prints. The technician acknowledged Jameson's directive and left other tech's to finish up. Jameson turned to face Sam. "I'm sure sorry for not managing this investigation more diligently Sam..." Jameson had noticed Agent Cooper and Jake just coming in. "And, thank you, Agent Cooper. I really am looking forward to any of your guidance and help." Sam raised a hand to pat Jameson on the shoulder. "It appears, the right man, has the right job." They shared a look into the others eyes. Both saw everything had settled out, it was justly even.

The interaction ended. Cooper saw Sam's interaction. She was relieved. She was distracted, when an officer came into the house. "Detective, you might want to come with me. Something needs your attention." Jameson looked towards the windows, "Okay let's go and see." The only remaining people in the room were the technicians dusting, as their boss had told them to do. The four of them, plus the officers made haste. As they crossed the road, a car had to brake unexpectedly. No one even noticed the car; it was a minor nuisance, seemingly just a moving obstacle. Respect for the high rate of speed of a heavy object never crossed their minds.

Jake was cautious, as they got to the area of inquiry. "Sam, why don't we let the cops do their job?" Sam came to a halt after Jake asked. Jake held a cigarette out for Sam. Sam took it and waited on a light. "Yeah, Jake, that might be a good idea."

Jake struck a match and lit Sam's Smoke for him. Bina and Jameson went in through a door opening. It was in an alley, which was perpendicular to the original search area. "You know what this reminds me of Jake?" "No Sam, I'm sure I don't." Jake looked to Sam as he exhaled the smoke. Sam smiled, "Frigid' Hide and Seek. Almost like the second or third time you get ready to hide. You already know the better hiding spots." Jake rolled his cigar in his mouth. "Like I said, I'm sure I wouldn't know Sam."

Jake had thought, sometimes Sam was flaky. He took another

look and shook his head. Jake considered saying something. Before he could, Jameson and Cooper had emerged from the door. Cooper reported. "Sam I think your comment about the right man for the job was very appropriate. The boy's are bagging coveralls they have to be analyzed. DNA breakdown will be a couple of day's minimum but it may prove to be valuable as the investigation goes forward."

Sam seemed to be agreeable to all that Cooper had said. He was confused as to her somewhat cryptic meaning of value and the investigations evolution. It could wait, Cooper was thinking through some unmentioned items. Sam extended patience. "Jameson... Here is what to do." Jameson perked up. He was hungry for some of Cooper's wisdom. "You oversee the isolation and identification on the print from your end. I'll get this back to FBI crime labs, it will be the most expedient means to get a marker." Jameson nodded as he heard her directives. When she finished, he paused a moment to collect his presence. "Guy's this is good work." Jameson believed in giving credit when it was due. "But, it is not 'new work' or 'first time work.' We need to make our first error right!" "This," Jameson held up the evidence bag, "is a great and worthy effort! So now we really need to make sure we get it right. The witness had the place wrong, but she said two men. This," he raised the evidence bag again, "is from one individual. Re-check your areas already surveyed, look to expand the area, there might be more! Keep up the good work and Thanks." Jameson took his presence along with the officer and evidence back to the station. He winked to the others as he left.

The three of them turned back to the house. Jake was happy. Sam and Cooper were skeptical, but redemption was well received. They did have more than before. As they walked back to the house, a car approached. It pulled up as close as it could and parked. The driver's door opened. Jake was the first to make the man out. "Stephan!" "Sure is." Sam chimed in. The three of them converged at Stephan's surprise. Stephan was very surprised when Jake was around. He was afraid of Jake. "Oh, Sam, ____ Hello. Ah, Hi Jake." Sam reached for the disc Stephan had brought and was holding. Stephan loosed it without even realizing it. He was too occupied by what Jake was doing. Maybe even hoping, delivery of the disc would somehow be like a crucifix in the face of a vampire so, as to protect him. "Thanks Stephan," Sam handed the disc to Cooper. "Allow me to introduce Agent Cooper from the FBI." Stephan couldn't help to keep an eye on Jake while he said hello. "Hello Agent Cooper." "Hello Counselor." Shaking hands Cooper said, "Thanks for making my job easier." "Yes Agent Cooper, you're quite welcome. Ah, if there is nothing else, I am late for appointments! By the way, Sam, I already contacted everyone else. You know the Life Insurance Company and well you know." "Before you go Stephan, I'll have need of a realtor. I want to sell the house." Stephan repeated the question with surprise, "You want to sell the house?" Jake spoke up, "Hey Stephan, would you rather he'd sell your house?" "No Jake... Ah Sam, I'll have someone get a hold of you today. Will that be satisfactory?" Sam beat Jake to the punch, Stephan was visibly nervous. "Yes Stephan, that will be fine, thanks again." Stephan replied, "Okay call if you need anything else, I really have to go!" "Stephan it was nice to have met you." Cooper was watching Stephan clumsily step back to his car. She wondered if he'd trip or something before he got back into his car. Jake had him rattled. Stephan finally did make it back without injuring himself on the way. He started the car; Cooper had noticed Jake holding a scowl over Stephan. She reached over towards Jake and slapped his shoulder. He turned quickly to address Cooper's slap. When he saw her eyes, he relaxed. "You be nice Jake Blaques! Be NICE!" Jake ignored what Cooper had said; he glanced back at Stephan just as the car pulled away. Jake had caught Stephan's eyes briefly and squinted for the second. He turned back to Cooper. He smiled, as though nothing had ever taken place. Once Cooper had read Jake, she squinted at him. "I got your number Mr. Blaques. Pretense might serve you now, but I've got your number."

Sam watched the two carry on. It reminded him to be sad. And, Sam's mind was not interested in sadness. He knew he wanted answers to this confusion. From there, he could focus on managing, making it right. Sam imagined himself being sad over this for the rest of his days. He experienced a brief sadness. He allowed it. Then he placed it in storage. There was work to do. He didn't yet know how Jake would be receiving his other intention. He wasn't overly concerned. Jake could have a positive outlook towards selling the business to Stan and George. It was in fact their plan to have the company buy their shares out. The paperwork had already been written up. There was only a difference in time passed. It came earlier to Sam than he expected. Sam was sure it would be unexpected for Jake as well.

Jake interrupted Sam's daydream. "Sam, Cooper here wants to load this disc in her computer." Sam nodded, "I'm going into the house to pack some clothes, and I'll catch up in a bit." He turned and walked into the house. Jake and Cooper headed for her squad. She popped the trunk with a remote key chain. When the trunk opened, Jake whistled. "That is your computer?" "Yes Jake, it is." Jake was in for another surprise. She pressed another button on the remote and the computer came alive. Jake stopped his approach. He might have even backed away by surprise. He looked at Cooper with wide eyes. "Did it just arm itself?"

Cooper laughed. "No it hasn't yet..." She ceased laughing as she put the disc into the machine, the CD ROM started. "Geez Cooper, your some kind of secret agent, are you not?" She turned to look at Jake. She raised an eyebrow recalling Jake's proclivity to make faces. Jake felt like melting. "So Bina, ask me something." "How's this Jake?" "I say something, and then I'll ask something, Fair enough?"

Jake nodded Cooper proceeded. "I'm wondering about Sam. I have noticed a behaviorism in Sam that worries me." She looked at Jake and asked, "Does he seem Postal to you?" Jake was waiting for the other shoe to drop, but he didn't have to wait any longer. "What else do you want to know?" Cooper frowned over the detached and redirected response. "I thought I asked the question clearly enough." She waited for a response. "You asked your question clearly enough, I can't answer it. What else did you want to know?" Cooper accepted the frustration, which developed from an unexpected response. She considered what else she wanted to know. She drew a blank. "Nothing for the moment." rolled off her tongue as the blank moved on. She watched the screen as the disc loaded. When the machine prompted its readiness she entered commands. The machine obeyed. A power booster engaged. Jake smiled. "Auxiliary Power!" Cooper reached up and shut the trunk lid. "That's it?" Jake shrugged. "For now, that's it." Jake asked, "No more questions? Wasn't this a time for consideration... a question of survival?" Cooper looked at Jake. "Yes, now even more so." "Whad'ya mean, More so?" Jake was chewing on his cigar. Cooper was regulating her behavior, even her responses. She had Jake's curiosity. "Do you know something Jake? I think men are okay in general. But then there are times, I swear! Let's take you for example. The response you offered! What is that all about? My question was qualified and then asked. I know you can think with the little head, but how is it that your larger thinking apparatus, can instantly take a vacation? Is it a Macho thing? You would know the answer if it was in your ass!"

Jake busted out laughing. His gut collapsed a bit and his hands rested upon his knees. "Oh, ho, hooo, Agent Cooper! I think I'd rather be in your line of sight, than the subject of your diatribe! Ha Ha Ha ha... I don't think I ever caught it like that, too bad Sam wasn't here." Cooper just stood there shaking her head. She walked to the house, or tried to. Jake's hand reached her shoulder. Jake was aware of her injury and was delicately holding her back. "Do you know Agent Cooper? I was sympathetic for your explanation, even a little aroused, especially, when you had mentioned my ass Ha Ha." Cooper squinted, and tried to move away. "Really Cooper; wait a second for an old man, won't you?" Cooper no longer intended leaving, as long as she could provide a little more ass chewing.

"That's another thing I told you about old men and me, yet you still test my ire! Jake! Either you're an old man, or you're a man! Take your pick!" Jake came to his senses, his facial gestures changed, he looked more serious. "Okay, here it is, I'll be a man." Jake watched Cooper regain some of her composure. "The notion that Sam may be Postal is a valid question, however, as the friend of a man enduring the grieving of his entire family, I can only tell you he suffers. Sam does not consider morality as you have chosen to reference morality asked in your question's context." Jake paused. He tossed his chewed cigar away. He reached for the one he had previously broken and lit it up for a smoke. Cooper waited for further clarity. "Sam is moral. His sense of right and wrong was evident, by the happiness he had. Now that they are gone, I expect most of his happiness will too be gone. If you want to know what Sam's condition is, you'll have to ask him. If you want to know what his potential is, I think Sam would also be the only source of the same information. I have never known Sam to endure such loss, and therefore couldn't mention on the new possible potential." Jake smoked some more of his cigar. Cooper was quick to see his point. When she realized Jake's explanation was rooted in logic, she apologized. "Your explanation justifies your position, forgive me for over reacting." Jake acknowledged, "There is no need to forgive a process, which leads us forward. In fact, your recovery is in realizing your error and admitting it. Now then, when I was admiring your computer I had a thought."

Cooper gave Jake a quizzical look. "Wouldn't you be glad to know my thought has evolved and, we may be able to investigate your original question? Is that right?" Cooper seemed impressed. "Oh yes, it is true! We men have our own wiles, don't you know?"

"Yes Jake, I know, but I feel as though there is a handy lesson in this evolution you speak of."

"Bina, you know all the words I love to hear, ass and handy."

"Jake, answer me this?"

"Did a girl ever do you, just to shut you up?"

Jake smiled; it was wonderful having a girl around who could hang with the guys'.

"Well Bina, I'm sure if you thought it, others must have too, and I wouldn't presume to know. If it were true, as you have proposed, they would most definitely been pleasantly surprised otherwise." Cooper smiled and laughed. "So, you must be every girl's dream?" Jake rolled his cigar. "Isn't that another unanswerable question?" "Maybe it is Jake!"

Cooper thought of the potential of transparency that Jake brought to a conversation. She was considering potential disadvantages she might foresee. She was wondering why she drew blanks for this investigative process.

"Try this on for size Bina. Maybe you are used to deductive questioning techniques. The process of deduction left with Jameson. You might consider a more constructive format in asking questions." Cooper thought about what Jake had said. "I think you explained it before... something about victim profiling, or was it victim insight... the polarity in that example is congruous to my last suggestion. Does that help a bit?" A light broke over Cooper's face. She did now see the context Jake was speaking to. "Yes, Jake, very helpful." Jake smiled for her realization. "Good, then we are ready to answer your original question. We'll need to get Sam, and then, __ off to **The Buried Treasure**." "**The Buried Treasure?**" "Why yes Bina, Sam is very approachable on board." "That will be fine Jake, let's go find Sam."

Chapter 13

Jake and Cooper had entered the house. The crime scene personnel were just packing, their investigation and fingerprinting was complete. Agent Cooper addressed the officer in charge. "Did you manage to get any other lifts?" "Yes we did Agent Cooper, nothing very clean, but some good partials." "Very good, your efforts should be helpful, Thanks!" The officer nodded and turned again to his work.

Sam was not within sight. Jake had made his way to the bedroom, he found Sam packing a bag with clothes. "Sam, do you need a hand with anything?" "No Jake I'm all set. Remind me to get a storage bin." "Sure Sam, why don't you let me take care of it?" Sam stopped packing then he looked at Jake "If you're okay with it, go ahead. By the way, I needed to speak to you about something." Jake grinned, "Well wouldn't you know about that?" Sam focused on what he was doing. "Imagine that." Sam figured spending less time in the room could be accomplished by getting done with the task at hand; listening to Jake get to a point didn't require his complete attention. "Bina asked me a question. She requested from me, an opinion relating to you. I couldn't give her an answer; I suggested we get to **The Buried Treasure**."

Sam moved to his tallboy. He rummaged through the top drawer selecting some personal items for packing. "That was part of what I wanted to speak to you about. If it is okay with you, I'd like to camp on her." Jake nodded affirmatively. "I appreciate you asking, but it was not needed, you know that!" "Shit, Jake, all that I knew here is gone. But yeah, I did know that, thanks." Cooper came up behind Jake, he turned to look at her and flashed a thumb's up. She winked back. She left the men alone.

Cooper walked back to the patio area. She panned the back yard. When she had finished, she reversed her visual sweep. The second sweep gave her mind time to absorb nuances of the property. These were the descriptors or reference point the photographer, hadn't included in his shoot. Cooper was still concerned over the fact that something did not look right in the report's photographic evidence. She'd bring the file to the boat with her. As she gazed upon the small yard, she smiled. She made a mental note not to use the term 'boat' when she was on board **The Buried Treasure.** She really grinned when she thought of the possibility of ribbing Jake. Maybe she would adopt an attitude removed from honoring, *Mariner Lexicon*. She sensed Jake could be drawn into one of his rants. There was something very enjoyable in the prospects of pulling Jake's leg. Her musing ended as she heard the men moving. She turned to the inside and walked towards the file, they met in the parlor, Cooper asked, "Are we ready?" The men's heads nodded. They were passing through the door. Jack offered a suggestion. "We all ought to take our own vehicles." She added, "Okay I'll follow you."

As they made for their own vehicles, Cooper's cell phone rang. She answered her phone. "This is Agent Cooper." She held her hand up suggesting that they hold up a second. "That is great news Jameson. Now we are heading over to... Jake's boat," she figured Jake could stew on it for the ride. "Yes, bring it over. __ Yes, right now! Okay, we'll meet ya there." She disconnected. "Okay, Jameson got a hit! He's bringing the file to the boat." Sam dropped his head and shook it. "Well is that all?" Jake asked obviously upset about the 'boat' reference. "Agent Cooper you might want to keep up, otherwise, you'll end up at a boat, I'm heading to **The Buried Treasure**." Cooper smiled, Jakes retort proved to be a certainty, she knew Jake would fume the ride over. When she looked at Sam, he had a smile while he shook his head. They got into their vehicles and drove to the marina. Cooper followed Jake. Over the tailgate of his pickup, Cooper could see Jake having an aggravating conversation with himself. She was amused. She giggled to herself while she checked Sam in the rear view mirror. As she followed Jake, she noticed he had thrown a cigar from his window as he drove.

She hoped by the time they got to **The Buried Treasure,** something would present itself, so that Jake wouldn't be so course in defending the correct word usage regarding his vessel. She wondered if Sam was going to be as ambiguous as Jake had been. She thought it wouldn't take much to get Sam to reveal how he was feeling. She figured timing would have a larger play than expected. Actually, the 'boat' comment was subterfuge.

Jake enjoyed going on about insulting his prize, she was hoping that might prove enough to reach the needed level of distraction, if that was unsuccessful? Jameson would be bringing the reinforcement of distraction. The new I. D. from the print would trump any of Jake's need to go on too long about Cooper's intentional faux-paux. Her motivation was to give Sam a distraction, by laughing with, or at Jake. She knew what she needed to ask him could backfire and, badly. She also hoped Sam would be as kind to her, as he was to Hendrick. She figured it didn't matter much anyway. What would be would be. She couldn't do anymore in preparation before the circumstance unfolded. She went over her checklist, and she covered it all. Development of trust, work practices resulting in appreciated credibility, and sincerity. She was confident in her ability to do her job. She followed Jake watching the rear view mirror occasionally. Sam was a fair distance away. He left plenty of distance between them for the ride.

They passed through the marina entry and made their way to a proximate parking place where **The Buried Treasure** was secured. In Cooper's mind, the boat was more than a boat. It really was a splendid vessel. Jake did have a solid reason to be proud. She would pay proper homage to the boat's identity when she thought Jake had heard enough. They exited their respected vehicles. Cooper went to the trunk and opened it by remote. She had gotten busy manipulating the computer in the squad. The program had sorted the information on the disc Stephan had dropped off earlier. The information needed to load to the computer was unavailable as of yet. When Jameson pulled into the parking area, she had been waiting to load his newly discovered identity. Jake and Sam had already made their way to the slip area where **The Buried Treasure** awaited them. The loading of the information into the computer didn't take long. It was simply loading what the NCIC had already provided. This was the identity of a potential suspect. Once she entered the info, she had grabbed the wireless unit for portability and handed it to Jameson. She retrieved a pullover for cooler climate on open water. She was familiar to water recreation. She closed the trunk, and relieved Jameson from the assistance he provided to her. They too approached, **The Buried Treasure.** Jameson could hardly contain himself; he didn't have water recreation experience, which Cooper had. He was like a big kid facing a new wonder. When they arrived at the end of the dock Jake had looked at both of them. "This is what I get? Are you part of the crew, or are you just passengers?" Cooper couldn't resist. "This boat looks as though it needs passengers, maybe even a crew too." Jake was getting worked up again. His body language appeared very aggravated. "Cooper it is customary to ask permission to board a vessel! Mention 'boat' again and you'll be keelhauled." Cooper looked at the sky, and the water. She noticed the fine weather they were ready to sail in. She looked at the men and wondered what Jameson might think about keelhauling her. She handed her computer once again to Jameson. "Would you be so kind as to get permission from the captain as to board the vessel and take those with you?" Jameson nodded affirmatively. "Captain Jake, request permission to come aboard?" "Come aboard young Jameson!" Jameson proceeded with landlubber steps. Jake laughed, while taking notice. "Did you bring Dramamine Young Jameson?" Jameson drew a blank; he didn't know what Dramamine was for. "It is for seasickness." When Jameson had realized the potential of getting sick, the look on his face provided an opportunity for Jake and Sam to laugh heartily. "Don't worry Jameson… before we get underway, the mate will see to your needs." By the time the men finished busting on Jameson their attention went back to Cooper. She had taken off her top shirt revealing her womanly curves. She was very attractive and easy on the eye.

"Permission to board Capt' Jake?" Jake had forgotten about the keel hauling when he had seen her. "Granted Bina!" She didn't have the difficulty Jameson had, she proved to be nimble on her feet. She wasted no time getting below to stow her gear, which Jameson had brought on board for her. She couldn't help but notice the cabin's utilitarian elegance. There was no sign of a woman being here. She could see how Jake had an eye for décor. Jake was a man of taste, and utility. **The Buried Treasure** was well outfitted. She employed her observational powers instinctively. Cooper always noticed things where others failed. Her mind might have been considered as being a photographic memory. She attributed it to insight, rather than profile. She smiled during a last look around. When she appeared topside she remained silent. Sam noticed her return and waited...

"So Bina? Are the accommodations acceptable?" Jake stood proudly on the cabin cover; he managed the mainsheet with a confident smile. "Well Captain Jake, It'll do." Jake frowned; it was a disguise for anger. Everyone saw it clearly. Cooper realized how timing here was crucial. "It'll DO!!!!!!!!!" Jake's hands started trembling. His neck was beginning to visibly pulse. Sam managed a smile and dropped his head. "What the hell do ya mean?? ' It'll DO...' " Cooper appeared to have thought about the question Jake had just asked. She was timing him. "Captain Jake, for the flirt you claim to be... I would think your boat might be a little more romantic??? You know, softer for the passion..." Sam silently started to shutter. His body convulsed without expelling the appropriate noise. He wasn't sobbing this time, his head rolled back as he straightened his back up. At the stop of the motion, Sam exploded with laughter, Jameson wasn't far behind him, and Cooper had jumped onto the opposite side of the cabin cover, getting right into Jake's face. Jake stomped off towards the bow attempting to release building frustrations, mumbling as he moved forward. The men had another outburst of laughter. Cooper was relentless; she went after Jake to grab him gently by the elbow. In her best flirtatious way, she warmed up to Jake. "Ahh Jake, I'm just pulling your leg! **The Buried Treasure**, she's a fine and proud sloop." She clung to Jake with some tenderness. Jake calmed himself a bit. He didn't release his frustration completely. "You know the water do you?" Cooper nodded agreeably giving Jake more pause…

He dropped his head and shook it from shoulder to shoulder. When he could, he offered another statement. "God Damn it Bina, it is not an honorable seaman, which belittles a mans ship." Sam and Jameson could not contain their laughter. They broke up so hard, even Cooper had to smile. Cooper had remained focused on Jake, she saw a glint of wanting to participate, but Jake would never admit it. She had felt good about the sail, and context of what needed to be discussed. Humor was truly an effective cue. Soon, all would be right and Jake could grumble at any long pauses the discussions might have. The distraction would be helpful. She smiled at Jake. Jake noticed her facial gesture. He dealt his own diversion, barking surprisingly, "No one sails idly on **The Buried Treasure**. Get busy with your seaman skills! Sam, get

Jameson busy." They all laughed some more but a directive had been called, the crew responded to the captain. Jameson and Sam cast off the slip tethers. Jake started the *Auxiliary Power*. Cooper manned the main sheet. They were motoring out. Cooper was waiting for the opportunity to raise the main. She didn't have long to wait. Jake had caught the off shore breeze, she noticed and raised the main sheet. Jake slipped the power to neutral without mention. They all watched Jake catch the wind's power gracefully. He managed as an effective sailor. After he shut the power off, he turned to Cooper. "Very nice read Bina, but I usually give the orders to hoist the main." Cooper had smiled with a look, which drove men crazy. She coyly saluted Jake with her hand. "Yes Sir Captain Jake." Then she giggled in a show stopping way. After another pause, Jake interjected a response. "Let this be a lesson for you swabs." "This is the deception of secret agents, with womanly wiles, masquerading as a seaman." Jake scowled at all present, with a crazed but informative look. Everyone lost the ability to contain his or her laughter. Sam and Jameson had tears in their eyes, they were experiencing difficult breathing. Cooper had to cross her legs to avoid having an accident. Jake sailed on. As soon as Cooper was able, she excused herself to the head. Jake had found a tack and held her lightly. Sam went below to retrieve beverages. He asked Jameson what he would have. His indication was water. Sam passed him a bottle of *Poland Springs* drinking water. He also asked Bina through the head hatch what she would have. She mentioned coffee. Sam went to work. While he got the brewing started, Bina had exited the head. Sam was starting to pour Jake's drink, his own after Jake's. Cooper ascended to the cockpit. "You men! Didn't you know girls shouldn't laugh so hard? Men are much better prepared for these moments than I was just then. Besides, we have business here." She looked around hoping she was convincing. She didn't want to have to abide another trip below. The men missed another good laugh. She had been thankful for that. The gravity of the sail was like an observable front of weather. Everyone knew its proximity. What they did here would minimize exposure to the oncoming elements. Those elements were coming. Of this, there was no doubt. A poorly chosen course leads to doom. A well planned choice lead around doom's address. Now, Cooper was sailing a vessel made by the four, as captain. Her crew was ready for orders. And, no one really likes orders. She decided to replace the orders with a more contributing effort, but she was in leadership, and they knew it. Cooper pulled out her laptop. She turned it on and waited for the signal from the squad computer. "You are witnessing a wireless connection to the squad's computer. All the information offered by Jameson's ID of the of the perps, with your company's records have been cross-referenced. We will see any connection of the two, if any exists." Jake was behind a bit… "There's a connection?" "Not yet… but that may change. This is a search program. It accesses taxable records to the suspect's work and pay record. Any company employing him that you have had dealings with will be revealed." Sam waited because it was the thing to do. He didn't believe for one minute there would be any connection. In thinking over it, Sam-Jak's business was fair, and if it wasn't fair... Sam-Jak had nothing to do with it other than being present when the injustice was being realized. Jake wasn't quite as confident as Sam. He after all was the operations guy. In his experience, there were some unruly guys out there who probably would have liked to take a shot out of anger and or resentment. Jake could think of a few. The computer produced its results and just as Sam had thought; there was no connection. "Very well, this avenue of investigation has been exhausted." Jameson was truly amazed. Cooper's results would have meant hours of office work for him or any other detective at the station. He had a taste of professional law enforcement. He was ruined for the job he had. "Okay Agent Cooper, what next?" Jameson awaited her response. He really wished he could participate in her thinking. Cooper folded her machine up. She wasn't going to explain how her computer had been damaged by a sudden splash of water while she was on a boat. "Well Jameson, now we proceed in Brainstorming... and there is one thing, we all must agree on." She waited for appropriate responses. "Justice will be served." There she said it. She knew she was an equal part of serving justice; Jameson had taken a similar oath. She didn't see anything in Sam or Jake's response indicating any hostility for the proposition she tabled. She breathed easier. She finished her coffee. Jake broke the silence first.

"Bina, I am not sure about any kind of justice, which could be applied making this right."

Sam ignored the conversation. Jameson was appearing to avoid interaction until he had to be a part of the conversation. "I think you are right Jake. Sometimes the wrongs perpetrated are calamitous. And, only scar remains. At that point, many vacate hope along with any possibility of reckoning. This is no way to live. And, precisely why, I called for agreement to see it through." Each tended to their drinks as **The Buried Treasure** abided the waters motion. The wind was steady without much variance, no gusting. On every few sets of swells, the bow would force the water it displaced into mist. It had a cooling effect on the sun's radiance.

As Cooper relaxed, she continued. "Sam, I don't think this was a random attack. I think you were targeted...." Jameson had to break in. "Cooper, Come again?" Cooper looked at Jameson after he asked. "I think Sam and his family were targeted."

"I heard what you said Agent Cooper, I was looking for a qualifier..."

"Jameson, there is no qualifier..."

The group was quiet. Sam and Jake had consumed their drinks. Sam was grabbing Jake's glass as he went to refill. "Jameson you all set?" Sam asked above the soft breeze. Cooper indicated she was ready, Jameson needed another as well. He asked for his same as they were drinking. Sam got below seeing to Cooper's coffee and drinks. He was anxious to hear Bina continue. He wanted to hear her strategy before he decided for himself. He didn't waste time. He passed the drinks through the hatch. Jameson extended a reach and assisted Sam. Cooper was the last to receive her beverage. They all sat down once again. "There is something else... this suspect, _____ he will be found dead some place." She sipped her coffee. The men wondered of her thinking, nobody said much. "Why would he be dead?" Jake had asked. "The likelihood of not accomplishing a hit isn't a profitable equation. Imagine having to say, you screwed the pooch to someone paying for death?" Jameson didn't appear to like what Cooper had said. He grimaced a little then shifted his seating. Jake heard what Cooper said. "Well, if those who hired him killed him? He is better off." He looked to the water's horizon and called to come about. Sam managed the jib sheet Cooper handled the main sheet. The maneuver went smoothly and Jake was smiling. Cooper had noticed how Jake beamed. Jake said, "Not bad for the likes of this crew." He smoked some of his cigar and sipped on his drink. After the new course had been attained, they settled back in.

"Another issue we need to discuss will take some patience to understand.... Sam you and me are the only survivors of the crimes I am investigating…" She took a sip of coffee.   Sam put his drink in the holder next to him; he reached for and lit a cigarette. "And this means?" He waited for her to continue.   Cooper had expected another response from Sam. Her hesitation was realized but not with lessened credibility. "I do not believe this is the work of a lone serial killer." She saw the looks the men had after she said what she said. "I am of the belief that these crimes are being arranged in a conspiracy. The Bureau believes… she frowned and looked to the sky…. God I don't understand what they believe." She shook her head with what appeared to be despair. Jameson knew exactly what she meant, and was the likely sympathetic ear. He too was in a bureaucracy. Sam saw what was happening. He had to forget and sacrifice his sorrow to keep things going here. It wasn't a choice for Sam it was just the way he was. Sam shined during difficult times. "Seeing as it is only us four, I doubt that the bureau has anything to say. I would imagine we are to proceed with a real awareness of the protocols of both of the law enforcement communities present." Sam sipped his drink. Both Jameson and Cooper were speechless. Jake chimed in as Jake always completes a thought. "Yes I agree. What they don't know won't hurt anyone, unless of course we draw attention to ourselves in a violation of policy… otherwise known as stepping on our peckers!" The crew smiled at Jake. He always had an ability to leverage some kind of humor out of serious circumstances. "Seeing as you have no pecker Bina, maybe Jameson would serve double duty and offer you his when the stepping needs to happen." This last comment sent the crew into laughter. Sam had a good laugh but it was short lived. He was still anxious of Cooper's line of thinking. "Bina, one might infer that I am still in danger... is that accurate?" Sam tossed it in more or less for a cue. After Cooper had collected her composure, she answered Sam. "Sam, I think you are still in danger. We need to address that circumstance." Jake laughed out-loud. "Sam, show them! And don't be slow about it, we still need to navigate!" Sam stood up indicating to the two to follow him below. He made his way to the bow berthing area and to the bunk, where he and Monica had made love. He opened a panel under the bedding. An arsenal was revealed. The looks from both of them showed disbelief and a cautioned curiosity.

Cooper had organized the arsenal in her own mind, Jameson was extremely nervous. When they had their fill of observation, Sam closed up the bunk. Cooper was contemplating this unexpected awareness. Her mind blazed through scenarios. She couldn't fathom that these two were so well armed. They made their way back to the cockpit. As they ascended, Jake was instructing another coming about. The course change had been satisfied, and Jake had a grin to beat all grins. The maneuver went as well as the last, which made sense for his facial gesturing. But, there was so much more to this grin. "God Damn it Jake, What are you expectin' World War III?" Bina shook her head, after she vented. "Well Bina, really I was only expecting pirates... then the Towers fell, and well everything changed, didn't it?"

Quiet embraced *The Buried Treasure.* It was quite a revelation for the law agents to consider. Cooper's worst fear had just come true. These men were willing to listen to reason, but their intention had none. None that law enforcement could abide. The game was different. Jameson and Cooper realized this new potential. Jake and Sam had noticed the change. Sam looked to Jake wondering without speaking if showing them was the right thing to do…Jake anticipated it and spoke once again… "Geez what happened here? You all look like you just found out you had two weeks to live…" Jake smoked his cigar, Jameson and Cooper looked at Jake with serious faces. Jake continued his rebuke. "What in the hell did you both think?" Jake paused before he fired off another question. "We would wait on you and others to make this right? Please…" Jake rolled that cigar twice over his tongue, gathering his thoughts. "Ya know you said it yourself Bina, Sam is still in danger! And, in a case of realizing danger or the possibility of danger, a man would be a fool to not take protective measures." Jake humph'd as he refocused the water.

They both realized by bureaucratic flaw, he was right. They settled a bit. It was still difficult for them to grasp, but the groping through victim empathy had begun. It was also apparent to Jameson and Cooper that these men were as cool as cucumbers. They realized how much they had underestimated both Sam and Jake. It was humbling.

Jameson had little experience in this, far less than Cooper had. He was truly lost at the prospects of working with 1 victim, and a friend having an arsenal greater than the department he worked for. Thoughts of these two held up, and avoiding capture, were truly unsettling. They were motivated, and they had resources. Jameson was glad to know they were law-abiding citizens. He pictured a scenario where many police would try to apprehend both of them. It would be the last day of their careers, judging by what Jameson had just seen.

Cooper would waste no time trying to convince them that they had gone overboard with 2nd amendment rights. She quickly realized the need to get them carry on permits. "Jameson, would you be able to get them carry permits?" Jameson frowned hearing this question. He thought so all could see his contemplation. "I suppose I could expedite the need to the chief. But, I'm not sure; he has got a protocol which is highly scrutinized." He sipped some water. "Young Jameson." Jake said, "If you asked me as chief of police, like you just did... you'd be walking away empty handed. Shit, you got to tell him that these permits are what you need!"

Cooper nodded in agreement. "Yes Jameson, you are running the show. Your request can't be a request. See to it!" Jameson nodded affirmatively. He would need to work up his confidence before the request took place. Jameson asked, "And you will vouch for this Cooper?" "If you think it will help? Yes I will; however, if you do this thing right, I doubt any vouching will be needed. Yes that is right young Jameson. We are the four musketeers! One for all, and all for one!" Jake giggled to himself. Sam remained uninterested.

Cooper thought of the next play… she was working out of her pocket now. She needed to exercise great care. She could afford a little breathing room, the kind Jameson was stuck with. She knew The Coast Guard is only a phone call away. If the men became unbalanced **The Buried Treasure** would become **The Sunken Treasure.** She did after all have the pipeline to Homeland Security. She wouldn't hesitate to have this vessel declared a terrorism target. 2 F-16's would pay a fateful visit. 'End of problem.' She tried to ease Jameson's worry. He would just have to accept it as it was, until she could get him to the side for explanation. Her evaluation left her knowing this was a crucial time. She could extend the trust already developed, or kill it. She opted for the former. The armament issue would have to wait. She closed it with a progressive suggestion. It was time to move on. "There is a general attitude at the Bureau. Today the priority is terrorism. Although this is a form of terrorism, it isn't the priority you might think. Islamic Muslim Terrorists are the priority. As our condition meets the minimum criteria to dedicate resources for investigative purposes, it also removes us from the chokehold of direct supervision. This means I am flexible. Apparently, this option for flexibility is a fortunate thing."

Cooper stood up after finishing her coffee. She moved towards the cabin hatch. Before she lowered herself she mentioned to Jake she was anticipating the complete revealing of the armaments. Jake developed, a *not me look on his face.* "Oh yes Jake, the full accounting. I mean it!" Jake dropped his gaze. She clearly established Alpha dominance. The interaction confused Jameson. He had no idea of the stern berthing; the thought never entered his mind. "You mean there is more?" Jameson choked on his water. Sam looked towards Jameson with a kind of '*keep up Jameson'* look. "Yes Jameson, there is more." Cooper requested Jameson's presence, he responded. Cooper spoke to both of the men. "Would you excuse me along with Jameson, for a minute?" "Surely Bina, you may complete the tour as well." Jake smiled at Sam. Sam was unaware of some of the newer items Jake had purchased since the deaths. Sam nodded towards Jake. When Jameson had taken some privacy with Cooper, he asked "What's Up?" "Are you okay Jameson?" Cooper looked into his eyes for truth. "No, this is crazy!" He whispered a roar. "Yes it is… but you'll have to trust me." Jameson nodded back confirming he understood. "We should see what the other armaments are like." She moved towards the aft, Jameson followed her.

Sam watched Jake as he was moving for a come about. Sam manned the jib sheet while Jake managed the wheel and mainsheet. The two nodded as to go and **The Buried Treasure** rolled over. Jameson and Cooper were both a little surprised. Cooper grumbled, "God Damn it Jake!" Jake waited for her dissent and then busted out laughing.

Cooper moved to the berth and felt for a panel. She found it and opened it up. Both stood in tremendous disbelief. She dropped the panel back down. They both heard Jake cackling after the sound of the panel dropping. Cooper wanted so badly to lose control on Jake. She was livid! It was all she could do to remain composed. Jameson was extremely worried. Cooper saw Jameson's reaction. She expected the worst. Jameson had to say something he just couldn't get the words out. Jake continued laughing. "This is more than I expected." She whispered. "But yes, I still need your trust! You mustn't lose it here Jameson." Jameson nodded working to compose himself. "Don't you recall what Jake said about 9/11 changing everything?" Jameson nodded in a positive manner. "Good don't forget that! It'll be alright, we want them to trust us, don't we?" Again, Jameson nodded. "Alright then, let us move *this* back atop." Cooper moved so Jameson would have to move Cooper had indicated she would be doing the talking. She ascended first, then Jameson. Jake didn't have a smile; he was perusing the waters horizon. Sam looked at Cooper. She just raised her eyebrows with a frown. Sam looked at Jake. He got the same look Cooper did. They both sat in the cockpit. "Sam… if it's not too much trouble, I think a drink is in order, what do you say Jameson?" Cooper looked for an answer from Jameson. He nodded, saying little if nothing, Sam took it as a yes.

"So Jake, were you planning on shooting down seagulls?" Cooper was laid back. Her voice carried a less friendly intonation.   "Well Agent Cooper anything attacking **The Buried Treasure** from the sky is a target. And, let us not forget the man below pouring both your drinks. I believe he is still a target." Sam passed a drink to Jameson, he handed it off to Cooper. Sam followed with a beer for Jameson. He went back to the galley to get Jake's drink with his own. As he got above he handed Jake his and sipped his own. "You are right about the targeting of Sam, Jake. I was just surprised at what you have stowed." Sam looked at Bina quizzically. It became evident to Cooper that Sam might not have known about some of the stores. "When did you think to let us in on the Battle Station Order?"   Cooper took a swig and waited. Her intonation had lightened up considerably. "Well Bina, I was kind of thinking **The Buried Treasure** would be the last place of retreat. I kinda thought the battle would be already engaged by the time we all got back here." Sam just waited. Cooper was a little unnerved. Jameson had just about finished his beer. "Jameson, help yourself to whatever you can find." Jake rolled his cigar from one corner of the mouth to the other.   Jameson raised his hand to acknowledge Jake and passed for the moment. Cooper thought to herself just how prepared these two were. She had been presumptuous and it wasn't fun to realize.

"Okay Jake, I was horrified, scared and confused. Jameson is as well." She folded.

"Well Bina, you seemed to handle it just fine to me." Jake took a belt off his drink. It was decided as he raised the glass that he would empty the single malt whiskey. As he swallowed the drink he grimaced and stared at Cooper. "Time is close to coming about! Let's watch the boom!" Jake cackled a bit. Everyone had listened to the order, Cooper thought it was a convenient distraction, and she respected it. Jake did things almost planned. It occurred to her that she would have a difficult time tracking down these two. They all did what they needed to do as the vessel came about. They had settled back into a new course to contemplate the rest of Cooper's thinking. She had finished her drink and sighed. "I guess if we can get the perpetrator Jameson came to identify, we will have more information to get this behind us, because the perpetrator is only the arm. We need to locate the brains. The subterfuge has been well constructed. Looking to the obvious answers won't do." She sat back and let the sun shine on her face. Sam finally brought his part to the discussion. "I have something to add. And, I think you all need to hear it." Jake looked towards Sam. When Sam made announcements like this, it was usually worth listening to. Everyone did listen.

"My life, my being and purpose have been ripped away in such a cruel fashion. I have always been a law-abiding person and I think I will be the same. After this work is done, yes, once we get this behind us, I will have very little left to live for." He lit a cigarette. "Jake I want to sell the business, it is time to let George and Stan take control of it. My friend this work will not allow distraction provided by the demands of earning a living. The living I worked for no longer exists." Sam smoked as he thought what to say next. Jake had anticipated the fact he wanted out of the business, it was the likely step to follow, after wanting to sell the house.

"I believe whoever is responsible for this has eyes that see my actions... It is time to utilize this advantage of stealth. What we need is to root out this evil! I also think orchestrated efforts by you Jameson could prove very useful in aiding this work by distraction. Press releases suggesting the police could use help from anyone having knowledge might set a decent level of comfort for those avoiding the light of justice." Sam thought and redirected to Bina. "I have a question for you Bina... have you moved in this investigation silently?" Sam pulled on his cigarette and waited. "Sam I don't think there would be a way to have my efforts compromised. The Bureau doesn't like shooters of agents any more than they like terrorism, however I can double back to seal up any potential revelations. We are pretty good at concealing this types of information." Sam frowned a bit, and smoked some more. Cooper immediately understood the frown was presented because they hadn't prevented Sam's family from being executed. She couldn't do anything about the past, but she could manipulate how things would be from here on out. Sam finished his smoke, and flicked it overboard.

"Well please do make sure there aren't any possible leaks. We want to keep them in the dark."

Cooper was now in the co-pilot seat. Sam had taken over. She wondered how this happened. While she tried to figure it out, Sam finished his drink. Jameson was ready for another beer. He got up and took the place of getting beverages. "Thanks Jameson."

"Jameson, Bina... I have no desire to draw attention in doing these things that need doing. I do not wish to produce a blood bath like that which was inflicted upon me. So, as far as policy of both of your departments, I don't think we will be giving your superiors any reason to worry, and I am content to allow Justice to assist us in the tracking down of those whom are responsible." Sam took a breath and thought for a second. "If what you say is true Bina, the killer we seek is the map to those responsible, No?" Jameson had a drink ready for Sam. He took it from the arm reaching through the hatch. Cooper grabbed hers and Jake's from Jameson. He then joined them in the cockpit. "I think your understanding of the situation is accurate Sam, and I'm relieved to hear that your thinking is considerate of our positions. But, there is more, isn't there?" "Yes, there is Bina. This person or people will be made an example. This insanity must stop and not only stop, but give others of the same contemplation a reason for pause. That is what I am working towards while I abide by the law. You can take the killer and do as you wish, but nothing else. If you can't agree with this I suggest you place me under arrest now. Those responsible have no idea of what they have started."

Jake frowned. He had heard Sam when he was deliberate before. He had seen how Sam would persist until his desired result was accomplished. Jake knew this would be very nasty because it was a side of Sam he had never seen. He was worried. "Sam I think we all want what you want, and you know you can count on me." "There is one concern I have, and that is your focus on this deed coming. It may be that your drive or need, sabotages the very stealth you seek to operate in. You know how you get." Sam looked at Jake; he understood his position and respected his counsel. Jake had often proved to be a stabilizer for Sam when he was on a tear. Jake wondered if he could protect Sam from himself. "Sam let us just remember what you have said, you know how you get when you have an obsession." Cooper and Jameson listened to the interaction. They weren't happy at what Sam had just plainly said. They could empathize. Without saying a word, they both understood all that Sam had said. He would not put them into a difficult position regarding the oaths they took for their jobs. It was a moment of easy breathing. "Well Jake, you couldn't be more right about the way I used to be… The fact of the matter is I believe I can avoid this obsession, as an obsession. My remedy is to remember what I built my life on, and that they are gone. Vengeance will be mine and it will be constantly tempered in the grieving process yet to come." If Jake had any doubts before, they were removed now. Jake saw a look in Sam's eyes he was familiar with. The difference now, was the lack of warmth in his friend's eyes. Jake could remember Sam always paying attention to detail. He would to give an even application to the task at hand, and he always proceeded with consideration of the unseen problems. He had an ability to be flexible within the fairness of principal business dealings. Everyone who knew Sam knew this to be true about him. Jake noticed the lack of warmth in his friend's eyes. He lit his cigar and made course for the marina. "Who wants to bet there is new information ready for us?" No one offered a take. Jake shrugged, "Okay, I'll bet Erik has got something for us." The details were where the devil was. Sam thought about Erik and his work and shut down. He finished his drink and excused himself. He wanted to rest; the thought of his family laid out on Erik's tables was too much. He went below without saying a word. His motion through the cabin, lead him to the bunk he knew. Sam wondered how he would manage this pain he couldn't fathom. It was greater than all he had accomplished in his life, because it removed his need to be what he had been. Sam knew what emptiness was; he just had a difficult time accepting the newness of this horrible feeling. He could cry no more. He placed this rage into a safe place. Sam's essence had changed. He could only accept what had been delivered to him. Just as those, would have to accept the intention of his delivery of justice. This is how he would manage this loss, in anticipation of the day when he could mourn. He dreamed of that day as he fell off to sleep. It beat wallowing in his loss. Sam was through resolutin'.

Jake had brought the boat around on several tacks to get back to the entry of the marina. There was very little conversation during the trip back. When Jake had come to need to start the Auxiliary Power, Jameson had taken the wheel. He listened to the simple instructions Jake had given to him. Cooper and Jake manned the sails and secured them while Jameson motored closer to the slip. When the two were finished securing the sails Jake came back to the wheel to relieve Jameson.

"Very well done, young Jameson, very well done." Jameson relinquished the wheel to Jake and he steered the boat to the slip perfectly. Cooper had jumped to the dock and secured the tethers that Sam had released earlier. The sun was falling off to sunset as they secured the rest of the rigging. They continued in silent activity. When everything seemed to be in order, Jameson requested leave to go back to his squad. "Once this vessel has found it's berthing Jameson, you no longer need permission, do what you need to do." Jameson looked at Jake and nodded. He departed from **The Buried Treasure** and made for his squad.

Jake looked at Cooper. "What do you think now Bina?" "Quite honestly Jake I'm upset about this. I didn't need such a surprise." Cooper looked beaten down. "It really doesn't matter any more though, it is done. As far as Jameson goes, well I'm pretty sure he is worse than Sam… I wish you had used more diplomacy in revealing your cargo, but again, it is done. I think Jameson will come around, but geez it is his first real doing as a detective…" "Yes, I'm sorry about how this worked out." Jake's apology seemed sincere. "But sorrow can't be an obstacle for what needs to be done. As shocked as you both are, it is the last of any surprises you can expect from us." Cooper looked at Jake. "He doesn't even know about those missiles, does he?" Jake shook his head negatively. "He does not know, and it wouldn't matter any way. I don't need to explain things to Sam. All he needs to know is what he knows, I'm in this for a penny, and if you're in for a penny you're in for a pound. It has never been that way between us. We have no judgments of each-other. He knows I have his back… it has always been that way." Cooper looked at Jameson getting to his squad. "You know how all of this would have played if Jameson were Hendrick don't you?" Cooper retorted. "Yes Bina I do." Jake looked at her coldly. "Hendrick would have been found washed up somewhere." Cooper squinted as she heard Jake's comment. She looked to him and glared. "I'll pretend I didn't hear that Jake!" Jake looked at Cooper with a cold stare she had not expected to see. It was so cold she developed goose -bumps. "Here it is Agent Cooper." Jake seemed to be staring right through her. "Anybody becoming a hindrance in this process will be dealt with harshly, and by any means available. Am I making myself clear?" Cooper had lost the upper hand. She was down on herself for allowing this to happen. There was really nothing, she could say. "Crystal Clear Jake, I'm going to check with Jameson to see if your bet pays out. These past hours… have only given my position more responsibility to yoke, So Thanks!"

Cooper hopped off the boat to the dock. She was upset; it showed in the manner she hastily departed. Jake shrugged. He finished the battening of the sails. He collected the glasses and bottles and went below. There wasn't much for Jake to do besides rinse the glasses and tote the newly produced garbage from the sail. He checked on his friend, Sam was in the throws of his torment, or as Jake thought, the torment he was planning for those responsible. Jake reckoned Hard Justice was coming. There was no possible way to stop it either. Not without *putting his friend down* and that would never happen as long as Jake had a say in it. Jake gave thought to what Cooper had said, she was right. But right had no business here. The harm done to Sam went beyond rational thinking. A man left in this condition was easily beyond realizing what is wrong and what is right. Jake wondered just what level of wrong Sam was willing to exact. He wasn't happy about the prospects. His friend wanted out. Out of everything! He was worse than a wounded animal. He was a removed man. In Jake's estimation, there was nothing as dangerous as a man like Sam being put in a place of being removed. Jake poured himself another drink in the glass he just rinsed. It was gone, in a gulp. Jake's body accepted the drink without shuddering like before. There was no pain they could endure which would be comparatively worse than what they were realizing now. Jake knew it was coming and it would be very bad... *Hard Justice Indeed.*

PART 2

Chapter 1

Agent Cooper caught up with Jameson. He was in his squad staring at **The Buried Treasure.** He said nothing, yet his facial expression could have inspired a short story. Cooper realized this detective had gotten a crash course in victim tenacity. She figured it was better now with no bullets firing than later. She approached Jameson deliberately. She was attempting to demonstrate an air of being in control. After all, being in control was what saved lives in their business. Jameson was sitting in the driver seat of his squad. He was at a loss. He was aware of her approach towards him but his earlier motivation seemed to have vanished. Cooper found a comfortable proximity and stopped advancing. She contemplated what needed to be said. She observed him and determined he may not be where she needed him. He did have three beers rather quickly, thanks to Jake. She attempted a verbal connection with him. "Sorting it all out?" He looked at her finally.

"I never thought a day of sailing could be so… enlightening." Cooper was content enough with what she heard. She knew he was thinking through this enlightenment, and that he was still trying to articulate his feelings. She was somewhat relieved that he hadn't become a basket case. Jamesons' face was different now… He was the kind of guy who didn't speak as he thought. This was probably one of the reasons he got detective rank so early. Cooper was considering all of his strengths.

It was always helpful in bringing those qualities up when dealing with a load of doubt. "Agent Cooper, Jake had said some things about observation and perception earlier when we came up with the inconsistencies of the Holman reports." Cooper was intrigued. Here was a rookie, faced with a huge contradiction, going through the back to basics investigating skills. She felt better in listening. "Did he now?" "Yes he had, and we scored with the coveralls by his insight." He added, "I'm sure glad those two aren't the bad guys." "Yes Jameson, these two are resourceful. Are you ready to do our brainstorming, or should we wait?"

Jameson looked back at **The Buried Treasure**. Cooper felt a need to surmise the obvious. "I guess we have come up short, apparently we have been out thought." Jameson heard her assessment. "Yes Cooper, that is a good thought and the sooner the better, I think." "Very well Jameson, here is one bit of good news… they have shown their full hand, Jake says no more surprises." Jameson looked at Cooper with hesitancy. He frowned, "Yeah and the checks in the mail." Jameson wasn't about to get hammered by unknown details anymore. He was feeling just a bit betrayed and used. Cooper felt the same way, but the feelings they were experiencing were due to lack of knowing and could always be changed. "Jameson don't be so hard on yourself. Investigation is nothing more than discovery of new details." "Yeah, well this discovery is one, or many, big and lethal details." "Agreed Jameson, agreed. So we were short on the uptake, it could have been worse." Cooper was thinking about what Jake had said regarding Hendrick. She figured that would send Jameson to the place she really didn't want to know about. "Okay what was it about Jake that intrigues you?" Jameson took a breath and again formulated his thoughts... "Why aren't these two guys working for us?" Jameson blurted it out without realizing the genius in the asked question. "Well Jameson they sort of are doing that. Remember these guys are self employed, and apparently very good at running their own show too, so in a way they are working with us. Their needs are parallel to ours, and I'm glad they aren't the competition." Cooper looked at the night sky. "Well I need to get registered in a hotel, it is late."

Jameson seemed to have been surprised by her comment. "Agent Cooper, if you don't mind bachelor pad accommodations you can bunk with me. I have a house with plenty of space, I'm sure you would be comfortable there." "That would facilitate 'the sooner' Jameson. Sure it sounds like a plan to me." Jameson got out of his car and faced

The Buried Treasure. He watched Jake going over the securing of his fortress. "I'll be right back Cooper. I'm going to straighten some things out with Jake." Cooper was surprised and pleasantly so. Jameson was back.

"Okay Jameson I'll be at my squad playing with the computer." Jameson was off as she gave her intentions. His frame wasn't large, but as she watched him, his figure did move with deliberate intention. She saw the development of an excellent Law Enforcement Agent in the making. Her hand rose to her shoulder as she walked back to her squad. She felt tightness in the healing wound. Her previous doubt had been displaced by Jameson's interaction. She walked to the squad and released the trunk with her remote. She was thankful Jameson was who he was. To Cooper's surprise an old friend had emailed her. He was one of the guys, which graduated from Quantico a year ahead of her. While she was enduring the rigors of the curriculum and gender disparity of the bureaucracy Nathan had become a big brother to her. There was a supportive relationship between them that she couldn't have done without. Nathan had gotten his Special Agent status for a very brief time. The CIA pirated him not long after 9/11. Cooper had opened the email and read a short note. She had thought her day was chock full of surprises... Here she found another smack of reality. Apparently, Tenant was resigning, which made everything chaotic within the CIA to say the least. Cooper looked back at Jameson and Jake speaking to each, and remembered what Jameson had asked earlier. *Why weren't these guys working for us?*

Her mind swirled with info… she waited for Jameson. She wondered if there was an upside to this email she received… She watched Jameson break off from Jake. He was making his way back to his unit. *Why weren't these guys working for us?*

Jameson seemed to be beaming as he returned. Cooper had since secured her squad and waited to follow Jameson to his house. Before he got into his squad he motioned to Cooper to follow him. She acknowledged with a wave. They were leaving. While she followed Jameson her mind took inventory of where she was. Her career at the FBI was on vacation. There was still a gender difference at DOJ. She wasn't sure she would be as effective as she wanted in her current position. She considered the Oath she took as an FBI Special Agent… this case was definitely leaving her out on a limb. She already had a black mark against her with this shooting incident and wondered when the hammer would be coming down. The thing about the DOJ was everyone was in CYA mode even at the expense of one of your own. If her superiors had known just what was developing here, she might find herself in Leavenworth. This was a reality weighing heavily within her rationalization. Retirement was making more sense as time marched on. She wondered if the chaos within the CIA could be beneficial to their circumstance. She thought about Nathan and his recruitment efforts. She decided maybe a career change was appropriate.

Jameson was pulling into his driveway. She pulled in behind him it was a narrow driveway. She parked the squad and got out. Her trunk was open and she retrieved her portable laptop. Jameson had been waiting for her to come up. "Welcome to my humble home Agent Cooper." Cooper hadn't really thought his description was accurate. It was not extravagant but it was not humble. She responded to Jameson. "Thanks Jameson. I think this is going to be very helpful." "Well, let's get inside. I could use a shower and another couple of drinks." Cooper nodded and followed Jameson into the house. Once through the doorway Cooper had taken an overview of Jameson's dwelling. She noticed once again Jameson was humble in self-description because this was no bachelor pad. As a matter of fact, Jameson had some very fine taste. "Jameson I like the diggs. I don't know that you are a traditional bachelor, so tell me, why is it that there is no Mrs. Jameson?"

Jameson didn't respond to her directly. He didn't offer her the grand tour either. He headed straight for the bar. "I usually have a couple of beers at night. Tonight beer won't be enough. Would you like a drink?" Cooper nodded as she continued looking around. "Scotch if you have it, neat, please." Jameson busied himself making the drinks. Cooper walked near the couch, which was better than her own. Jameson asked her to have a seat as he brought over the drinks. Cooper noticed a stack of coasters on the table, she reached for two and placed one on the table for her drink and handed one to Jameson exchanging it for her drink. "Thanks Jameson."

Jameson took his coaster and sat on the chair off to the side. He placed his coaster down on the lamp table next to the chair. He sipped his own drink and placed it down. Cooper had a sip of her own and did the same. "I noticed you seem to have been a little more up after you spoke to Jake." Jameson nodded. "Yes, I did feel better about it afterwards."

"That is good Jameson. I'd like to ask you some things if you don't mind?"

"Sure Cooper, ask away." He grabbed his drink again and sipped as she started.

"I noticed that you seemed to come alive in this investigation... It seems to me that you have realized a greater potential than being a detective in the Lyme Police Department. Is that accurate?" Jameson smiled a bit before he answered. "The fact of the matter is yes. This job is, or was, just yesterday something I thought I would be content to have until retirement. I saw myself making a mark greater than that of Hendrick." He had another sip of his drink. "But the toys you have, well that excites me. The cases you work on... that excites me too. It kind of opens my eyes." Cooper was holding her drink allowing Jameson to loosen up. Jameson sighed as he thought how to answer Cooper's question of a Mrs. Jameson. "After 9/11 everything changed.

The Mrs. Jameson to be died in the WTC attacks."

Cooper went blank. This revelation was sobering even while having a drink. A world of understanding had been revealed to Cooper as she listened. "Jameson I am so sorry."

He finished what was left of his drink and got up. "I think I'll take that shower now. Make yourself at home, I won't be long." Cooper nodded and watched him leave the room. She rubbed her shoulder again thinking of how Jameson now played into this investigation. He, too, had very little to share, as it had been removed from him so suddenly. She knew about loss from the 9/11 attacks. Several people she knew had died as well. And she decided to give Nathan a call. She thought while Jameson was having his shower it would offer some privacy, something you wanted when you were having a conversation like the one she would be having with Nathan.

She made her way to the phone and dialed his number. He answered the phone but said nothing. "Nathan? It is Bina…" "Hello, how are you Bina?" "Did you get the email?" Cooper spoke into the phone. "Yes I did Nathan, how goes the battle?"

Jameson didn't really want to reveal his loss to Cooper. He was sick of the sympathy, which came along with stating the loss. He disrobed and turned on the shower. He waited for the water to heat up. After it did he entered the shower and let the water soothe him. Jameson was the kind of guy who would carry his loss. He wasn't one to share it.

He held the soap and washed his body. He had all the psychology he needed. Therapists had tried to get him to unload his burden, but he couldn't bring himself to do so. It was a private thing. He did what he had to do with his future in-laws. There was no body recovery. There was no trace of his love. It was almost as if she never existed. When he finished with the soap he reached for the shampoo and washed his hair. He showered methodically just as he lived in this house. Detail was what he and his fiancée were all about. This was the only way he could keep her close to him. After he rinsed the soap out of his hair he turned to shut the water off. In the corner of the shower was a squeegee, he grabbed it and pulled it across the shower surface. He had not been raised this way. This was a learned behavior from his love. He didn't know why he did it. Maybe it was his daily commemoration to her. He found comfort in the ritual.

Jameson exited the shower after he dried off. He stepped in front of the sink vanity mirror. He reached for a comb and pulled it through his hair. He brushed his teeth quickly and rinsed down the sink. He made his way to the adjacent bedroom door and dressed into his comfortable clothing. A sweatshirt and some elastic waist flannel pants. He donned a pair of slippers as well. He gave a once over in the bathroom and satisfied, he proceeded in rejoining Cooper.

When he entered the room where the drinks had been drunk, he noticed Cooper was on the phone. He didn't know if she required privacy as he retrieved his glass. He went back over to the bar and poured another. Cooper looked as if she could use one, he held the bottle of Scotch in an asking way, and she nodded positively. He took the bottle and poured her glass full and returned the bottle to its home. He sat where he was earlier and relaxed sipping his cocktail.

Cooper was finishing up a conversation; seemingly there was a meeting-taking place. With whom and where were not apparent to Jameson. He sat and worked on his drink. He decided that he was hungry and he would wait to see if Cooper was brave enough to have a bite with him. He was actually a pretty solid cook. He missed cooking for two, as he hadn't in quite some time. He laughed to himself, making sandwiches wasn't cooking. Cooper had hung up the phone and Jameson surmised it was a friend of hers by the one side of conversation he heard. "Thanks for the refill Jameson." She sipped on it and settled back down. "You're welcome Cooper; are you hungry at all?" "I think I am, do you have anything in mind?" Jameson put his drink down. He seemed to think of what he might be able to scrape together. "I think I have some frozen Pasta Sauce and some spaghetti. I did go shopping just a couple of days ago." "Well that sounds good to me Jameson. Will you need any help?" "No. You can shower up if you'd like while I get busy." "Hhmm. A shower would suit me just fine. I just need to get my luggage." Jameson offered to get what she might need but Cooper wouldn't have it. "Okay I'm off to put the food together. The bathroom is down the hall, and towels are in the closet."

"Thanks Jameson." He disappeared into the kitchen. She got up and went out to her squad. She unlocked the vehicle by remote and retrieved her suitcase. She moved back into the house and proceeded to the bathroom. Just before she shut the door, Jameson had made his way towards her to show her what room she'd be bunking in. "Cooper this is the guest room." He showed her the room and apologized for not doing so earlier. Cooper thanked him again as he went back to the kitchen.

She noticed that there was a woman's touch slight as it may be. The house was clean... cleaner than if just an average man was living here. She unpacked what she needed for a shower and undressed. She grabbed her robe and put it on and headed off across the hall to the bathroom. After she started the water she felt for the temperature, it had warmed right up. She doffed her robe and entered the flowing water. She made a mental note to thank Jameson for some good advice. She let the water flow on her shoulder; it never ceased to amaze her how healing water was. She lathered up and rinsed off. Then she shampooed and conditioned her hair. When the soaps had been rinsed away she let the water flow against her shoulder a tad bit longer and shut the water off. As she opened the curtain she noticed herself in the mirror. Her scar didn't offer her the same pain as in the morning; she had much to discuss with Jameson. The call to Nathan had been a fountain of unrelated, but cogent information to the case. She dried off and put on similar attire to what Jameson had dressed in. She hung the towel up as his had been hung up and moved back to her room. She reorganized some things in her suitcase and left for what at least smelled to be a splendid dinner. When she got to the kitchen she noticed Jameson was a much better cook than she could ever dream of being. She whistled at what she saw. Here was Jameson fast at work. He had been making a salad, warming some bread and heating water. The kitchen was a working kitchen, not just wasted space for processed food storage.

"Jameson I am amazed! I never knew you had it in you." Jameson had lost a motion in his preparation. "Well Cooper some of us can and some of us don't. I can. This is enjoyment to me.... cooking. My mother always used to say, 'A man who can cook doesn't need a wife.' I never understood what she meant by that, but there was no way she would send me into the world without the knowledge of cooking." He finally stopped to have a sip of his drink. It was a pause between tossing the salad and putting it into the fridge.

Cooper asked, "You don't know what she meant by that Jameson?" He shook his head. "Do you want to know?" Jameson gave her a quizzical look trying to figure out how Cooper knew what his mother meant, "Sure Cooper." "Men who can cook have a defense against the wiles of bad women." Jameson stood there expecting to hear more but Cooper sipped her drink. When she put it down she smiled at him. His look made her laugh. "What?" Cooper asked. "Is that it?"

"Yes that is it." Jameson busied himself again tending to the food; the water was heating up nicely so he added some olive oil to it. He put a pinch of salt in the water as well. "You really don't get it do you Jameson?" He looked at her without a clue. "Well Jameson don't worry about it, you're too smart for the wiles of a bad woman." Jameson shrugged and got the now defrosted sauce out of the microwave. He opened the container it was in, and poured it into a Dutch Oven Pan. Cooper watched with interest; she had never seen this done before. Jameson had a wooden spoon in the sauce as it heated up. He placed the spoon into a spoon holder on the range top. Cooper watched with hypnotic eyes. She was fascinated at Jameson doing his thing. He was so busy he hadn't taken notice of his audience. When nothing more could be done; he reached up for the tableware so as to set dinner places for them. Cooper insisted on helping him out. He decided to let her help although he'd rather she didn't. After Cooper had set the table she returned to the cooking area. She continued to watch Jameson in *his* kitchen. Jameson had already put the pasta into the water and turned back the boil. He was busy turning the warming loaf of bread. His sauce had been starting to steam up more quickly than she had thought it would have. She also noticed that each utensil Jameson used was put to the dishwasher as he had finished.

There was very little cleanup by the time the dinner was finished.

Jameson had timed the meal to be ready simultaneously. Cooper thought about how she could never manage everything to be ready at once. Before she knew it, the meal was being delivered to the table all together. They both took seats and began to eat.

Cooper was in heaven. The sauce was fabulous, the spaghetti just right and not sticking together. The bread was warm while the crust remained crisp but not nand. The salad was about the best she could remember having. She was glad Jameson asked about eating.

"Oh that reminds me Jameson." "Thanks for inviting me to take a shower, I needed that." Jameson waited to swallow the food in his mouth. "You're welcome Cooper." "And this dinner is delicious, you really are handy in a kitchen." Jameson held off on eating so he could thank her again. "Thank you, although this is really nothing to write home about."

The rest of the meal was enjoyed without comment. Jameson asked if she wanted anything else; she said everything was delicious and she couldn't take one more bite. Jameson stood up and cleared the table. Cooper didn't offer to help, she thought she might get in the way. Besides, Jameson had it cleared in two trips. The only thing suggesting that an excellent dinner had been eaten was the aroma of the earlier cooking. "Jameson that was a delight, tell me are you as good with your weapon as you are with kitchen utensils?" He responded to her question with a smile and a nod of positive indication. "There are some things we need to speak on Jameson." "Yes, I know. Would you care to talk outside looking at the sound, or inside?" Cooper responded by asking, "If you view the sound I'd prefer that."

He stood up and motioned his hand in the direction of the deck. Cooper followed.

They did have a splendid view and they settled into chairs placed closely enough together so as to converse. Jameson waited for her to sit and then did so himself.

"I'll tell ya Jameson I feel much better than I did leaving **The Buried Treasure**." Jameson seemed to be in agreement. He offered a thought, "Dinner and a shower along with a couple of wash downs is helpful." "It sure seems so Jameson, and Thanks again."

Jameson nodded substituting a bow. "Tell me Cooper what is on your mind?" "Well Jameson I'm wondering what your take on the survivor and his partner is?"

"Well, Cooper, I think they are motivated and somehow crazy. Not dangerous, but a little daft." Cooper could help but to giggle. "That is an interesting take Jameson." She asked another question. "Can you go with it as you know it now?" Jameson responded. "Honestly, I don't know. I have half a mind to arrest them, but by what they have got on that boat makes that unlikely, considering our departments' resources." "I seem to be in a pickle." "I understand Jameson, that which we saw was unbelievable." "Do you still trust me?" Jameson took a long sip from his drink. "I guess I have to Cooper, this is way beyond my experience." Cooper nodded she understood what he said. "I'd like to talk to you about that phone call I had when you were showering." "If you think it is necessary, Cooper, please feel free." "I do think it is necessary. So I will. The person I was talking to was a fellow I went to Quantico with, his name is Nathan. He had told me some very interesting things which are going on at the CIA. Do you know who George Tennant is Jameson?" "Certainly I do Cooper he is the appointee from Clinton to lead the CIA." "That is right Jameson, he is resigning very soon and the company is in chaos. Nathan is looking to recruit me from the FBI, and I am of the mind to jump ship." This got Jameson's attention. His eyes squinted a bit and he excused himself to get another drink. "Would you like another Cooper?" Cooper nodded positively. She looked across the back yard her eyes gazed upon the shimmering water of the sound. She realized Jameson had a lovely house. She made a mental note on Jameson. He seemed to talk things down; never being an exaggerator. While she was filing that bit of information, looking to the water, Jameson reappeared with the drinks. He handed Cooper hers and reclaimed his seat.

"So, you are thinking of a new career?" Cooper nodded again positively. "Is it likely to be problematic?"

"I don't think any significant problems come along with this package." She looked to Jameson.

"But do you remember what you asked earlier?" Jameson drew a searching look on his face… "Oh, the 'why don't we have these guys working for us' one?"

"Yes, that one." He nodded to her. "Do you think that you would consider being employed in the CIA Jameson?"

He almost spit his drink up as he choked hearing the question. Once he squared himself away, he thought on a reply. "It never would have occurred to me to consider such a thing. I don't really know."

"Well you should. My friend Nathan listened to our predicament. Can you guess what he suggested?"

Jameson's head dropped, his hands lifted him off his seat; he needed to stretch.

"Let me guess? He said we could come on board and the CIA would take the case off the DA in CT."

Cooper smiled, "No, that is not what he suggested, not as you said it."

Jameson looked at his glass. He went to it and downed all, which remained. He went back into the house and returned with the bottles and a bowl of ice. When he sat down he said, "Cooper why don't you explain just what this Nathan suggested?" "Jameson you are a pretty bright guy. You are closer than you think."

"Okay, I'll explain as he did to me. There are so many things going on at DOJ and the CIA along with Homeland Security. And now that the 9/11 commission reports are out, everyone is scrambling to get some forward thinking implemented." Jameson nodded as to show he was with her. "Foreign Policy is as it is, but domestic strategies are where the need has to be fulfilled. Once I explained how my *victim insight* got me here, he practically begged me to come aboard. He said I could bring a team." Jameson was visibly excited by this news.

Cooper had a long pull on her drink. "This Nathan must have some juice." Cooper nodded to confirm what Jameson had observed. "Not only are they looking for translators, they are looking for operatives with construction experience. He also seems to think that my hunch about the killings as a hit is dead on. They think cells in the country are sabotaging businesses so as to give them opportunity for legitimate business concerns; to this time, no one has been able to prove this, but chatter supports the strategy. I am meeting with him tomorrow, in New York."

"Are you telling me that all of us could be employed as CIA operatives?"

Cooper nodded again. "Certainly you and me, Jake and Sam would need to be approached and vetted, but other than that we'd all be paid by a company funded by the United States. Oh yes, you can forget about that business of getting those nut jobs permits." Cooper laughed at herself. "Ah, yes, the perks of that type of employment.' "Honestly Cooper, I thought after some time in the Lyme Police Department I would have the ability to maybe get an interview with the FBI, but this is a dream come true. And I'll tell ya why. I am much like Sam; we both have loss. Granted mine can't compare to Sam's but never the less, I want to kill some of those who robbed me." Cooper interjected, "Nathan thought that might be a helpful motivator." Jameson drank his last drink smiling. He got up and said he was going to retire, he had enough and certainly needed rest for tomorrow. He thought to strategize with her, but a solid buzz was the result of his drinking. He decided to wait until the morning.

Cooper said she would be finishing her drink up but wanted to enjoy the view for a bit. Jameson smiled and wished her a good night. He left her there gazing at the sound.

Chapter 2

Sam woke up to the still of morning. The time when quiet is minutes away from the busyness of life awaking. Sam felt as though this would be the way he woke for the foreseeable future. The anticipation of warm morning greetings from his family was extinct. He was lonely and this time of predawn still was a future he'd rather avoid. Sam thought he'd rather be with them, wherever they were, than here alone. So much for what Sam wanted. He lost an ability to be grateful for the days to come. Sam followed his drive for the business of exacting revenge. In his pain he did keep a small amount of humanity, by knowing he would do all he could to prevent this from happening to anyone else, even his former enemies.

Sam raised his body off of his berth. He ran his hands over his face and head. He felt his hair being pulled through his fingers. He also felt the growth of his beard. Sam's sorrow was eclipsed by his need to be effective in his new direction. He hated the fact that he had become less than keeping in his appearance. It was an outward sign that maybe the loss of his family had ruined him. It did ruin him but the appearance of not being ruined was what he wanted to display. Sam stood up and went to the head. He relieved himself as most men do and grumbled about his appearance, which he saw in the tiny head mirror of **The Buried Treasure**. He forced himself to consider allocating time for himself, as he had done religiously when his family was with him. He made a choice this morning to hold onto his humanity. He no longer could abide feeling sorry for himself. The pain would never be far from him, he was sure of that. He reckoned when time was available he could mourn and grieve by thinking of happier times. He did want to avoid that as much as possible.

While he was in the head, Jake stirred and woke unlike Sam. Jake's only consideration was how his friend was doing. Obviously, Sam's movement was an alarm clock for Jake. Once Jake realized his friend was awake he jumped out of his own slumber. He went to the galley and prepared coffee. Better to formulate plans of the day over a cup of joe. He wondered if Erik would be ready with the family... Sam emerged from the head and offered a morning greeting. "Hey Captain." "Morning Sam, did ya rest well?" Sam yawned and shook it off. "Yeah I guess." After Jake finished with preparing the coffee for brewing he repeated Sam's action in the head. Only he did so with a welcoming Sam couldn't seem to find. Jake loved everything about bodily function. His favorite time was relieving himself and so he celebrated every time he did so. He really didn't care what others thought of his animated response to bodily functions. As a matter of fact, Jake would engage others if they chose to shun his celebration. Jake had a default position along these regards. He would say to anyone offering a criticism; "Imagine if you couldn't and had to go through the rest of your life with the discomfort of needing to do so." Generally most people got his point. Those who didn't get the point suffered even more by Jake's witticism. He would suggest that they were miserable because they'd rather be full of shit, piss or gas than enjoy a good bit of relief. Once that had been delivered most hearing Jake's reasoning had a good laugh. He wasn't going to give Sam the benefits of this celebratory ritual; Sam had already heard them, and he was after all indisposed by the loss of his family.

After Jake had emerged from the head Sam offered a default statement of his own. "Feel better Jake?" Jake just nodded positively. He was being careful to feel out how Sam was doing before he would launch into his philosophy of life. "Good because today has got a hill to be climbed before it is over." Jake nodded again in the same manner. "Sam how do you think the law is going to respond to the discovery of our package?"

"Well Jake, there seems to have been a dramatic reaction to our package, more than I would have expected."

"Ah, I think you're right Sam, want to see what it was all about?" Sam nodded as he did. "Check the panel in the aft berth."

Sam did so. While Jake heard the noise of lifting the panel and shutting it, he waited for a verbal component. None came. Sam came back out to the galley area and said, "Damn, Jake, I guess the notion of world war III was appropriate." Jake was focused on trying to figure out Sam's take on the newly acquired addition to the arsenal. He offered none. He tossed a line out for a nibble. "Think I overdid it?" Sam knew better than to engage this discussion with Jake before having a coffee.

Sam simply made a statement. "I wonder about Erik's progress." Jake was disappointed. He expected something from Sam; to either support his doings or to condemn them. Getting neither he rolled off a comment about Erik. "Erik is doing all he can and I'm sure when he is ready for us we will become aware of it."

Jake grabbed a cigar from the box in the navigation desk of **The Buried Treasure**. Sam ascended to the cockpit to watch the coming sunrise. He brought his cigarettes with him. Jake waited on the coffee and handed Sam his cup when it was ready. Both men sat back and watched the world come alive… The stillness, which Sam had awoken by, yielded to life's business. Birds were flying about seeking breakfast. Water and wind began a ballet as thermal temperatures increased. Other neighbors of the marina had also begun life's business. Sam was haunted by life's business, as his past life's business was just a ghost. He tried to filter out the noise he once embraced but succumbed as he had to, being alive.

"The extra cargo is going to force them to do something." Jake paid attention to Sam's verbalization. "You would think so." He also realized enough time had passed so that Sam was now ready to bandy any ideas about it. "How do you think they will react?" Sam pulled on his smoke and coffee. "I don't think they will react." Sam stood up and once again began resolutin'. Jake worshiped this resolutin' Sam did. It was his favorite characteristic of Sam. He actually was in awe of this ability Sam had. "I think Cooper is smarter than that. I think she is gonna settle Jameson down and come off with a feasible way to manage it."

Jake considered what Sam had said. He did feel as though Cooper had it in her to overcome that which Hendrick would have fucked up 'til Sunday. Jake remained silent.... He figured Sam wasn't done. "Cooper has an idea that the guy who shot her is the same who did this to me. I think she can make this case, the framework she has laid out is reasonable. So why would she drop the hammer on us over this cargo if she knows we are a necessary element of her own vindication as a law enforcement official? She does have her own stake riding on this." Sam concluded his resolutin'. "Nah I think she is about to drop a bomb on us without becoming authoritatively prohibitionistic. And, she doesn't need much to convince Jameson, he is ready for the big time like no one else I have ever seen."

Jake nodded, "He is a hungry one. But you think she sticks with our play?"

"No Jake, I think she is going to show a necessity to redirect it."

"She knows more about us than we probably do and has formulated opinions as to where she thinks she can lead us. She has our files." Sam looked at Jake as he does when he is resolutin'. Maybe he wants to see if Jake thinks it carries any water. Jake rolled his cigar in his mouth. He had more coffee, and thought about Sam's resolutin'. "Let me get this straight…. You think she plays a mean game of chess?"

Sam looked at Jake. Sometimes when Sam was resolutin' he got ahead of those counting on him, but Jake seemed to be right by his side for this session. "That, Jake, is a fair assessment." Jake got up and descended to the galley. He brought the pot of coffee back up to the cockpit and poured Sam and himself warm-ups. He took his seat again. The sun was now breaking westward in its full glory. It looked to be a day, which would reveal answers to some of the questions being raised just now. The men sat finished their smokes and coffee and waiting.

Chapter 3

Cooper woke to the smell of coffee and some heavenly aroma of morning baking. She hadn't gotten the best sleep, but it would have to do. Her head was a little foggy from the previous nights digestion of a splendid meal and relaxing effects of imbibing more than she usually had. She raised herself from a more than comfortable mattress, and went to the bathroom to fulfill the morning's needs. After she was done she went to the origin of the wonderful aroma Jameson was responsible for. He was just taking homemade corn muffins out of the oven. "Good morning Agent Cooper, did you sleep well?"

"Good morning Jameson, not as well as I have, but whatever you have prepared makes the difference up, it smells wonderful."

"I have a little nourishment on the deck out back, why don't you have a seat and I'll bring the muffins out to you." Cooper followed the directions asked of her. When she reached the deck she was very surprised. Jameson had created a honeymoon breakfast. On the table were freshly picked flowers with glasses of orange juice, cups of coffee and some fruit. She took the seat she had from the night before and gazed over a different sound than she had seen last evening. Jameson appeared with the muffins and placed them next to the preset table. "Jameson I never thought you were such a home body!" Jameson smiled, "Well Cooper, I'm glad you have taken notice." Cooper didn't need an invite to begin helping herself to what had been prepared. It was obvious to her that consuming the result rather than talking about it would show her appreciation for Jameson's efforts more. Besides…this was just what her body seemed to have needed. She began and enjoyed. She had briefly wondered what it would be like to have a manservant like this, but she got lost in the dream by what would be expected from the kindness. Jameson had none of those expectations. She realized he truly enjoyed being a homebody. And, that he took pride in it.

After she had paid enough of a compliment to Jameson's efforts she gave mention to the remainder of the day. "Shall we discuss just what our plans should be Jameson?" "Yes, that would be helpful as long as we can be brief about it. I do have a boss to report to." "Fair enough Jameson. I think you should go about the regular business of the day." Jameson nodded with agreement. "I don't think you should mention anything about the phone call with Nathan, or even the discovery of the arsenal to anyone…. keep it as though it never happened." Jameson looked at her quizzically. "Is that even possible Cooper?" "It is not only possible but essential. Here is why I think so. These two have now shown their hand. They are expecting something from us, and expecting will have to be their focus until my meeting with Nathan. What they don't understand is that they think they have placed us in check, like in a chess game." Jameson frowned a bit, knowing the reality of the position they had, fully armed. Cooper read this in Jameson and continued with her explanation. "These two have one direction... that is to exact vengeance. What they don't know is the game they have just entered, and neither do you. You have had a glimpse of it and are hungry for it; that is the game of information and exacting justice." Jameson reflected on all that Cooper was saying. "The CIA is the board which chess gets played on. They are also the pieces used to win. Rules even I am unaware of and even frustrated by, are the new way of doing things, and there are very few variations of the game they set up. It is a game where life and death are the boundaries."

Jameson tried hard to understand the metaphor of the CIA being the chess game. He seemed to trust all, which Cooper was saying to be true, but just couldn't believe it. "I have heard what you have said Cooper and I want to believe it will work out, I'm just short on faith thinking about the arsenal they have." Cooper finished her coffee. She looked at Jameson and verbalized a link for thought. "Jameson having faith is the last thing to worry about although very practical. These two have prepared for what they think they will need in an upcoming action. They present no real and immediate danger, they are just covering their bases. Actually, they are very good at placing themselves in a position of being victorious. Have faith in the fact that they are as determined as they are now, in exacting justice they understand only now. After this meeting with Nathan, they will be able to see something they never would have considered as being justice."

Jameson seemed to have been okay with all that Cooper said to him. He couldn't think of anything to say which would result in making him feel any better about what was coming. "So your advice is just to do my thing?" Cooper nodded positively. "One other thing Jameson, don't mention anything of this meeting to anyone in your department. The CIA will take care of all of it, okay?" Jameson nodded and excused himself to go to work. "I'll clean up this wonderful breakfast you have made." Jameson nodded and thanked Cooper. "Oh Jameson, I'll be finding you okay?" Again Jameson nodded and left. Cooper sat for a little bit before she showered.

Chapter 4

Jameson was in his squad heading for the office. He was experiencing something he was familiar with. Exhilaration! He was surprised at the overwhelming sensation he had. He was feeling totally in control. He had no idea what had become of the investigation or even if his speech to the others had given them the motivation he wished to convey. He didn't care... He was 'wired' with principal and virtue; holding the biggest trump card any investigator could have. And, when he did become aware of any changes he was going to be delegating action like he was veteran. He no longer needed to have a concern with policy as authoritative, only that he maintained it so as to not tip his hand. When he got to his office he reported to his boss. Surprisingly, it was a very quick meeting. There was nothing to do except give the normal report. He went to his desk; Hendrick was where he normally would be. "Morning Hendrick."

"Good morning Detective Jameson how is it with Sam and Jake?" Jameson suspected something by the way Hendrick had greeted him. Somehow Hendrick knew… "It seems to be going well Hendrick, we had a second bite at the apple and it turned up some more evidence."

"That's what I heard… good work Jameson."

"Thanks Hendrick. Actually, I'm waiting to hear on some of the results of those findings…"

Hendrick smiled, "Yeah, Johnson had dropped some paperwork off. I have it right here." Jameson still feeling charged and less suspicious took notice of Hendrick beaming. "Is that right?" Hendrick nodded much like an instructor holding a final exam of a mediocre student plagued by the unknowing of pass or fail. "Jesus, Hendrick, is there anything there which helps us go forward?" Hendrick lost his superiority complex and even seemed a bit rebuffed. Jameson gave a stare to Hendrick as to suggest getting on with it. Hendrick wasn't about to succumb to offering his perception, that, he would leave to his new partner… "Have a look for yourself." He got up off of his chair offering Jameson to sit and review it while he went for coffee.

Jameson went to the desk and sat down. The blood test on the pair of coveralls were tested and matched to several blood types. Two of the types were possibilities of the victims… the third wasn't. Jameson figured one of the perps had sustained an injury. Another report suggested that no other clothing was found and there was a descript area pointing out what had been searched. The last bit of work was reviewed. The last known address of this id from the thumbprint needed to be checked. Obviously the guys were busy following up on the second bite. Hendrick returned with two coffees. He placed one down on the desk in front of Jameson. "Thanks Hendrick" "Don't mention it, by the way on your desk is the rap sheet on the thumb print; his place of residence is empty and it is clean. I already have the uniforms checking last known employment; however, I don't think much will come from that. Agent Cooper postured this as being a hit isn't that right?" Jameson nodded while he swallowed a sip of coffee. "Why don't we take a ride Jameson? Bring your coffee." Jameson stood up and closed the file; he grabbed his coffee and followed Hendrick out. They got to the squad and Hendrick got into the passenger side. Jameson assumed the driving position. "Where we headed? Let's take a drive by the fella's construction sight"

Jameson backed the car up and made way for Sam-Jak Inc. work site. "Hendrick that was good follow up on the last known address." "Yeah, well, we have been busy, new information needs to be examined. That Agent Cooper is pretty sharp. I haven't had all that much experience with the FBI, but I have heard how sometimes they only come and go, leaving everyone feeling as though they were left with a S.N.A.F.U." Jameson seemed to be listening to what Hendrick had to offer, but was less attached than previously. "Is everything alright Jameson?"

Jameson was perplexed by the question. "Yeah why do you ask?"

"I don't know it seems as though you are preoccupied..." Hendrick sipped his coffee.

"I don't think so Hendrick. Maybe being lead detective just makes it that way." Jameson ventured a sip of his coffee. "You might be right Jameson." Jameson wanted to let Hendrick know about some things, but couldn't. He knew his hunger had changed. Hendrick did drop the ball. Maybe he realized that the better years of service Hendrick could offer to him were over. Realizing the old veteran is nothing more than the old veteran, could be seen as being 'preoccupied.' Maybe Hendrick was looking to apologize in an off subject kind of way? Jameson had found new exhilaration in working with Cooper. It paled Hendricks' ability to offer any mentoring... so Jameson thought.

"Jameson, I got a call from a friend and he had some interesting news." Jameson was waiting to hear what Hendrick had to say considering the suspicion he felt from his greeting earlier. "You had an interesting call?"

"Yes, I sure did. I thought I'd wait for your point of view until I went anywhere with it."

Jameson tried to exhibit a matter- of- fact nature to his question. "Okay, give it up and I'll let ya know." He sipped his coffee as they were getting close to the work site. "Why don't you park for a stake out position at the job?" Jameson did as Hendrick suggested. When the car was parked and the men could see the operation Hendrick spoke up. "Apparently Mr. Blaques has been making some substantial purchases of firearms." Jameson decided to play it the same way as his pretense from before. "Yeah he showed them to me and Cooper on **The Buried Treasure**." Hendrick thought he would get more play from this tidbit of information. But amazingly, Jameson was already aware of the arsenal. Hendrick sipped on his coffee, as did Jameson. He tried another way. "So, Jameson, you wouldn't by any chance, be trying to cut me out of a last hoorah would ya?" Jameson read him wrong. He torpedoed Hendrick with a quip, which stung. "Hendrick, Cooper is FBI. If she thought there was any glory in nailing these two for illegal weapons don't you think she would? More than likely we wouldn't even know of this if she weren't here." Hendrick got out of the car and shut the door with a little extra push. He slammed it. Jameson was tired of the dancing around with his partner. He opened the door and got out slowly remembering not to show his hand. "What bug got into your ass this morning Hendrick?" Hendrick turned and said, "S.N.A.F.U. is the bug which got up in my ass." "Well then you had better shit it out Hendrick." Jameson was a rock.

Unfortunately for Hendrick his mistakes in the first investigation had created a monster. "Look Jameson I just want to know how it is developing. I don't have any intention of breaking any murder investigation over a weapons charge... I'm not the enemy!" Jameson realized Hendrick did not yet know about the really lethal cargo. Jake must have used a contact Hendrick couldn't possibly have known about. "Okay fair enough Hendrick let's just relax. Look all I can tell ya is this, Agent Cooper and I were with the guys on the boat last night brainstorming. That is when we found out about the guns, it was around the end of the trip. Nobody was happy about it, least of all me. When we got back to the marina Cooper let me know what she had thought about the guns… it sounded completely rational. I guess she feels as though these two are going to be instrumental in solving this case. She said let it ride, so I have. She also wanted to go to a hotel. It was late so I offered her a guest room and she took me up on it. I finally got a chance to work in the kitchen again and feel as though my skills were appreciated. She had also made a call to the CIA a fella named Nathan; she was returning a call from an email she had gotten. Today she is meeting this guy in New York. Her last instructions were to keep things going on as they could and that she would find me."

Hendrick looked to the guys working. "Tell me Jameson did she appreciate the cooking?" Jameson smiled and nodded positively. "I think her comment was 'I didn't know you were such a home body." Hendrick grinned and asked, "Feel good to cook for two again?" Jameson thought about his bride to be, and how much she enjoyed and appreciated all that he did for her. "It was strange having another woman to cook for. Oh yeah, she told me what my mother always said about a man being able to cook and what that was all about."

"Did she Jameson, and what was her explanation?"

"Cooper says that a man who can cook can avoid wicked women with wiles or something like that…" Hendrick couldn't help but laugh. "Geez I still don't know what that means." Hendrick laughed even harder…

"Well you are still in love Jameson you won't be meeting any wicked women." Jameson heard this from Hendrick and shrugged. "So what were your plans while you were waiting on Cooper to return?"

"To be honest with ya Hendrick, I wasn't really sure. I was hoping for more availability of a match between the perp and the finger print." Hendrick seemed to consider what Jameson had said.

"Hoping isn't detecting Jameson." Jameson looked at Hendrick. "Well, Hendrick, what else can this ride reveal as in detecting?"

"This ride was for nothing else than to get up to speed with your doings concerning Sam, Jake and Agent Cooper. Can you tell me anything more?"

Jameson shot back a simple response. "No I can't, there isn't really much to tell."

Hendrick postured a look, which showed disbelief. Jameson thought to himself, *what the hell would get him to look ahead, rather than to disbelieve what he had already said?*

"Okay here is a development… Sam is selling his house and staying on **The Buried Treasure**." That announcement seemed to interest Hendrick.

"He is selling the house?" Jameson nodded positively. Hendrick thought about that. He seemed to be running it through his skeptical awareness. "Was there a reason as to why and why so suddenly?"

"I think Sam was deeply rooted in his life... his family apparently meant an awful lot to him. I think the house was the nucleus of his being, and not having them would be like serving an unending sentence in the home." Hendrick looked straight into Jameson's eyes.

"So then he is highly motivated to serve his own justice?"

Jameson looked at Hendrick with disbelief. "Yeah, Hendrick, I think he is highly motivated to serve up some justice. I don't think he was considering using the arsenal which became evident to us yesterday either. According to Jake, the guy doesn't need any weapons to handle himself, which leads me to believe that Jake is the guy doing all the buying."

Hendrick nodded in agreement. "Yeah that follows."

Jameson couldn't fathom what Hendrick had on his mind. He was growing weary of not knowing the context of what Hendrick had been thinking. "Listen Hendrick why don't you just come out and say what it is you are thinking?" Hendrick really didn't have a direction, he was more or less fitting pieces like working on a jigsaw puzzle, but Jameson's frustration struck him curiously. "Jameson I really don't have much to say of what I think, I'm just doing what I have done for the past years as a detective. Quite honestly it was only till a few minutes ago that I figured Sam didn't have anything to do with this. I am just going over what we know." Jameson realized his frustration was bringing him close to revealing his secret. He offered a ploy as to why he had a heightened frustration. "Hendrick I'm sorry… I guess the *cooking for two thing*, has got me a little bent out of shape. I thought it was helpful, but now I'm not too sure." He hoped that would be an excuse Hendrick could chew on.

Hendrick finished his coffee. He took another look at the job sight. His gut told him there was more than just not feeling right about the *cooking for two thing*, but he'd let it play out and see what happened.

"Jameson you are gonna have all kinds of reminders of your loss in this life, the trick is very simple. You just have to live with it the best you can. Everyone goes through loss. Some worse than others, but everyone suffers it." Jameson frowned. He knew Hendrick was right, and he did understand all that he said, he was just not solid in telling a falsehood to his partner. But his partner was in fact retiring.

"Hendrick forget how this investigation has developed… if you were to have the information we have now and you had just become involved, what would you do next?" The question seemed to be enjoyed by Hendrick.

"Jameson, now you are thinking with me instead of without me, and quite honestly, I would try to understand the motivation here. Knowing that it isn't the husband… I would have to review possible reasons as to why the Murphy family was killed."

"Could it be that these perps were just killing randomly; there is no evidence to suggest that, so we have to assume much like Agent Cooper has; there is another reason. The big question is this…. Was Sam supposed to be there as well, and if he was, why? The next thing I would look to was the numbers of the business… was the partnership weak? Was there any gain for Jake to kill his partner and family?"

Jameson followed Hendrick and deemed his thinking to be deductive; however, he wasn't up to speed with the two, so he couldn't possibly know he was covering ground, which would ultimately offer no fruition.

"Let's say that Jake isn't the guy…where then?" Again Hendrick looked at Jameson. "Jameson, are there any working over there, who stand to gain from such a crime?" He pointed to the crew working. "And if there are none, who would gain, could any of them be aware of something the other two aren't aware of?" Jameson squinted as he thought through that which he heard. "How do you mean?"

Hendrick asked a question to illustrate what he meant. "Are all of those guys 100% behind the decisions of their bosses? Would any of them be likely to have an axe to grind over a beer after work to a total stranger?"

Jameson hadn't thought about that. "You mean like an unaware stool- pigeon?"

Hendrick smiled... "Yes kind of like that. Here is my thinking.... These two seemed to have lived and worked above the board. Everyone says that they were straight guys, and fair. But fair doesn't necessarily have to be appreciated. Let's think as though somewhere in the history of employing these guys a circumstance came up, which was seen to be fair, a give and take kind of thing...." Jameson nodded signifying he was following. Hendricks continued hypothetically; "Okay, maybe the fairness of the circumstance caused resentment, even if it was deemed to be fair by all parties. A guy expecting a bonus doesn't get one from his own doing, but he has counted on an item that this bonus would deliver... the guy doesn't earn his bonus, but still owes it, maybe to a girlfriend."

Jameson thought a bit. "You mean like a vacation or piece of jewelry?" Hendrick nodded positively but offered another choice, which a bonus would provide... "How about a new car?" Jameson looked at the parking lot where the guys had left their cars to go to work. All but one were late model cars. Jameson looked to Hendrick and realized an extra set of eyes was extremely helpful. "How do you want to do this?' "Well we could go over there and stop production finding out who owns that car, or we could get a feel for it from the two giving out the bonuses."

Jameson headed for the drivers seat. Hendrick followed his lead. They got into the car and drove off to **The Buried treasure**. As Jameson was driving, he hoped Jake and Sam wouldn't be getting the wrong idea. He didn't want to be greeted by a shower of metal rain. Nonetheless this was a good distraction for what was yet to come. He thought about how Cooper was making out with Nathan, and remembered her last words. Pretend as though all is normal.

Chapter 5

Jameson and Hendrick arrived at the marina. They got out of the car and headed for **The Buried Treasure**. Jakes' and Sams' vehicles were parked; leaving them to believe they could ask some questions of the two. As they approached the vessel they noticed both of the men were lounging onboard. Jameson didn't think they had noticed their approach. "Ahoy! Permission to come aboard Captain Jake?"

Jake turned and smiled... "Granted Jameson, come aboard with your sidekick."

Both men did go onboard and took seats opposing Sam and Jake. They greeted each and commented on the fine day. "So aside from the politeness of the greeting and small talk of the weather, what is on your minds?" Jake waited for the reason.

Hendrick broke the ice. "Jameson and I had a brainstorming session this morning. We took a ride past the Sam-Jak job sight and asked ourselves some questions." Sam raised an eyebrow; the part about the drive by the job sight got him curious. "Well detectives what seems to be the answer you need?"

Hendrick continued… "We were simply wondering about your compensation packages to your employees." Jake couldn't let it go. "Why are you thinking of a career change?"

"No, Jake, not at all." "We were specifically wondering if you fellas offered your guys any compensation in the form of a bonus?" Sam spoke up and answered for them. "Why, yes detectives, the guys can make bonuses."

Hendrick moved along, "Do all of them make it as a group or is it for individual performance?"

"We use two forms of bonus pay; one as a group bonus, which is less than the individual bonus program. Why do you ask?"

Jameson took it over from here. "Sam, Hendrick and I had long since deducted that both you and Jake are not suspects… therefore we wanted to know how the perp had gotten his info on you and your family."

"We figured if one guy had not made a bonus for one reason or another, he might unwittingly prove to be the connection." Jake was absolutely aggravated with the questions and reasoning… he couldn't believe any of the guys would do such a thing. "Are you suggesting that one of our guys could have a part in what happened to Sam?"

Jameson hoped this wouldn't happen and Hendrick dowsed the incorrect assumption Jake had put forward.

"No, Jake, that is not what we are suggesting at all. But we still need to figure just how someone knew how and when Sam's family would be home. Generally a simple conversation could be primary information for someone wanting to do harm to another, and if spoken to correctly, without any sense of betrayal, it would appear to be... kind of like a bitch session about a missed bonus at a bar."

The way Hendrick had brought this to a possibility, hit Sam and Jake like it was a well-placed bullet aimed for the middle of the eyes. What Jameson and Hendrick observed was exactly what they thought the missing link was. Sam's essence seemed to be defeated; Jake was even more shaken. The detectives had hit the jackpot. Both men needed a bit before they could respond. They looked at each other as to confirm their worst fear. Sam lit a cigarette furiously. Jake was chewing on his cigar without abandon. After Sam had a deep drag of his smoke, he asked another question. "Let me get this straight! You think because Jackson missed his bonus he would have inadvertently given info to the guy who killed my family?"

Hendrick asked a question to answer his question. "How well do you know this Jackson?"

Jake grumbled loudly, and spoke bitterly, "I guess we know him pretty well, he's been with us for several years!"

Hendrick continued, "Okay, is he a married guy?"

Jake retorted, "Not that it matters, but no, he is or was engaged, and just where the hell is this going guys, remember you two needed a second bite at the apple, are you now ready to play?" Jameson had had enough.

"Hold on Jake… these are essential questions, we are working from the second bite as you have put it front and center, and it would be helpful to remember we both want the same thing." Jake was about to lower his next comment to Jameson, but Sam beat him to it.

"Jameson, let's do this slowly, okay? What leads you to think Jackson is the link?"

Hendrick answered. "His car is what gave us the need to ask. You see everyone else who works for you seems to have earned a good living by what they drive." He paused and took a breath. "What is Jackson's story?"

Jake had calmed down now that the line of thinking had been established. He was still aggravated but the detectives were no longer considered the enemy. "Well, I held up Jackson's bonus, it was by the policy which he knew and understood, and he wasn't too thrilled with it either, but those are the breaks."

Hendrick picked it up again. "What was it that kept him from earning the bonus?"

"He damaged his machine! Operator error is costly enough when something is done wrong like improper grading… but to damage a machine? So if it goes out of service, there is… NO BONUS."

Jameson and Hendrick looked at each other knowing Jackson was their guy. Both Jake and Sam knew, by the way they looked at each other that Jackson had some explaining to do. Jameson spoke again. "So far as it has been established, nobody on your crew knows about this, we came here first. We are asking you, how you would like this to be handled, which by the way is being overly courteous to you."

Sam understood the implication and thanked them for the consideration. Jake would have made them work for it, but he was fit to be tied. Sam thought, in the way this came down Jake would have given his own interrogation of Jackson. And, that wouldn't have been helpful. Quite honestly, it would have been a disaster.

Sam asked another question. "Detectives, do you think Jackson will be criminally implicated in this or is it routine fact finding?" Hendrick addressed the question. "In my experience, it is likely that Jackson had no conspiratorial agency to the killings, but until we ask some questions we won't really know."

Jake spoke up because he didn't think Hendrick understood the question. "Is Jackson going to need a lawyer for Christ's sake? And, just so you don't think we are going to be a hindrance… the lawyer isn't for Jackson, it is so the rest of the guys don't think we hung him out to dry…"

Jameson and Hendrick understood the politics of the guys, and the need to continue to keep trustworthy employees. Hendrick said, "Then, yes, he ought to have legal representation."

Jake looked at Sam. "Jackson can't afford that and Stephan isn't a criminal legal counsel."

"Who do we use?" Sam was thinking... "Well, Jake, I'm sure Stephan knows a qualified lawyer so we might as well ask him."

The two detectives sat back and waited for the plan. Jake chimed in. "Okay, I'm going with these two to the work sight to get a hold of Jackson, you'd be better off with Stephan he is scared shitless of me. I'll make sure Jackson is alright until the other shyster gets to the station." Jake had one more comment before they all left. "We were enjoying a nice friggin' morning sit, Thanks for putting the Kabosh on it guys!!!!"

Chapter 6

Jake was extremely aggravated. He understood how Jameson and Hendrick came up with their thinking, but he didn't want the aggravation that came with interviewing an employee. He hoped that it was benign. Jackson was a wild man. He marched to the beat of a different drum; in fact, he was his own worst enemy.

Both Sam and he thought that Jackson was going to be trouble any way you sliced it. But the guy ran the hell out of a machine. For the most part he made them money more than he cost them. All the guys were aware of the same thing too. Jake just hoped that the guys didn't associate the questioning about Jackson as an association to the murders. Where there is smoke there is fire.

It didn't take long to get to the job sight. And, when they did Jake was out of his truck and waiting on the detectives. He was going to break the news without making everyone completely non-focused on their work. He thought he'd like to slap Jackson for being in the middle of these two and their hunches. Profitability only came from operating machines… not wasting time in a third degree questioning. Jake also hoped it didn't take these two long to qualify their hunches. Jake fumed at the thought of paying for a criminal defense lawyer because Jackson was dopey.

When the detectives parked he leaned towards the window. "Let me handle this okay? Just wait here and then we can decide where we need to go." The detectives agreed. Jake walked onto the sight and had to grab a hold of George. Stan was busy. George saw Jake and obviously was surprised. Jake hadn't been around for the past few days… "What's up Jake?" "George I need to speak to Jackson…"

"Sorry to hear that Jake, Jackson isn't here hasn't been for a couple of days now…"

Jake was speechless…. George looked at Jake and asked, "What is wrong Jake?"

"Jackson said he couldn't start his car one afternoon and told us he was waiting on a chick to come get him. We all thought it was strange that his car was here until we had gotten a phone call… Jackson said he was under the weather and he was taking a couple of days off." George hadn't fully understood what was going on but Jake looked horrible.

"Jake, what is wrong?" Jake finally processed what George had said…

"Nothing is wrong George, I just needed to talk with Jackson. He didn't leave a number to call did he?"

"Nope, we thought he was getting a piece of strange, and off on a drunk. It hasn't represented a problem, he was waiting on work." Jake had a hard time maintaining... "Okay George...Make sure to call me right away if ya see him again."

"Okay Jake... ya sure you're okay?"

"Yeah I'm okay... and keep up the good work."

Jake turned and went back to the detectives' car. George just shook his head and went back to work. Jake got up to the detectives. "He hasn't been to work in two days." Jameson grabbed the radio and got a hold of the dispatcher. Hendrick told Jake to get in and take them to Jacksons' residence. "Jameson we are going to need a warrant, a search premises. Let's get a hold of the D.A." Jameson asked if the dispatcher could do a communication relay to the D.A.? A few minutes later they were starting the wheels of justice. By the time they arrived a cop was on his way with a warrant in hand. They all were looking for signs of life but none were evident. Jake thought that Jackson's woman would be around. Unfortunately the bonus created a rift between the two, and no one was the wiser. Jackson's woman had belittled him to no end and left. Jackson never said a word. Jake wanted to puke. An all points bulletin had been put out on Jackson.

Jameson was wondering if paging Cooper was the thing to do.

"Hendricks stay here and execute the search, I'm getting Jake out of here and getting to Sam, you can catch a ride back with the officer and I'll see ya there, okay?"

Hendricks nodded he wasn't happy about it, but having Blaques around would be worse.

Jameson hollered for Jake. "Let's go find Sam." Jameson was headed for the squad. Jake did so without saying anything else. They were on their way to the office of Stephan. Jameson figured he'd page Cooper there.

Once they arrived, Jameson looked at Jake... "Listen, go in and get Sam." "Don't say anything about this to him until he is here, understand?" Jake looked at Jameson with contempt. "What do you mean, don't say anything until he gets here?" Jameson wished he didn't have to explain. "Look if this guy needed any representation before he needs it now more than ever; if you say anything in front of Stephan now, it could go against us later." Jameson thought, 'poor Jake' the guy was just hammered, he wasn't thinking clearly and in that Jameson knew how Sam did his resolutin'. "Go on Jake just let him know we need Sam now, and that you'll be getting back to Stephan later." Jake did so although you might have thought a mule was more cooperative.

When Jake left Jameson paged Cooper, as he did he thought to add 911 to the number. The page tone delivered the page and he hung up. He wondered about how this would affect things as they were. He knew that the resources of the FBI and hopefully the CIA could only enhance any A.P.B. they had out. He saw Jake and Sam coming out of the door. Sam had surprise on his face. He guessed Jake didn't drop the ball. The phone rang it was Cooper. "Hello Agent Cooper it is Jameson. Yes, we had an important development I thought you should know about." Jameson filled her in and listened to what she wanted them to do. Sam and Jake had already gotten into the Squad. He finished up with her and said, "Okay I'll wait on hearing from you, Uh huh, okay bye."Jameson looked at Sam who was impatiently waiting to hear what the hell was going on...

"Sam, there have been some developments... sorry but I told Jake not to say anything." Jake was finally lighting his cigar; he seemed to be waiting for this explanation. "Sam we just found out Jackson has not been to work for the past couple of days... and Hendrick is executing a search warrant at Jackson's home.... there was no answer at the door, and no sign of life." Jameson had the car moving as he told him. Sam had taken this badly. Not as badly as Jameson had seen before, but it was bad. Jake already had a smoke lit for him. Sam took it without saying a word. "Jake, we are going back to the truck and I'm gonna drop you off. I want you to check with the funeral home guy and get back to **The Buried Treasure**. The ride was short and Jake got out. He looked at Sam. "Ill see ya back at the marina, okay Sam?" Sam nodded he couldn't find it within him to say anything.

Chapter 7

Jameson was driving back to the boat with Sam. He thought about the weapons on **The Buried Treasure**, and considered how the men were taking the bad news. Jameson thought Sam was stunned. He seemed to be internalizing new questions of Jackson. Sam seemed like he was in control but you could never know. He had hoped Jake was okay and not coming undone. Jameson didn't want to be single handed if the guys decided to go postal. Jameson hoped Cooper was on her way back with news that would relieve him of the illegality of an armory. She had developed a way with the guys. She saw how Jake was playing her game. He thought it was pretty cool too. Jameson had not gotten to know any really bad people...

Jameson considered Sam and Jake decent fella's. He thought of their success before all this happened. They had better than average lives. They were the fortunate ones, so to speak. He didn't think these guys were stupid… in fact, they demonstrated it this time, a strategy for working things out, which quite honestly would have left both Cooper and he, himself, stumped. These decent kinds of guys became dangerous only when faced with the worst. Jameson knew the threshold just got closer. Sam had nothing to say for the entire ride. They got to **The Buried Treasure** and Sam spoke in the car after Jameson had turned it off. "Jameson you'll need to calm yourself." Jameson looked at Sam with a need for clarification. "Hell, Jameson, if you aren't thinking of the weapons and our response to hearing about Jackson? Ya got me fooled."

Jameson spoke freely. "Sam the thought had crossed my mind, but only briefly… There is more to you and Jake than just a postal rip. You guys think too much to be guilty of that kind of violence. More to the point, while there is nothing you won't do to exact justice, I doubt you would waste it on the 'doer' instead of the 'thinker'. There really is no immediate danger of you going postal…. there is work yet to be done… Jake is checking on that dreadful business right now."

Sam acknowledged Jameson. "Fair enough Jameson, fair enough." Both men got out of the car and walked to Sams' new diggs. "She is a beauty though isn't she?" Jameson said out loud. Sam could only nod for the moment. Once on board Sam asked if Jameson would like coffee or water… Jameson declined, the men sat.

"In a way Jameson, this boat is what Jake has invested his love in…

He always said a boat was cheaper than a family." "None the less she is something to behold... we've had such good times on board." Jameson thought to verbally agree but Sam seemed to be saying what he thought, he just nodded. After a bit of quiet Jameson asked Sam, "What are some of the vivid ones Sam?" Sam gave his question some thought. "Jameson the most vivid ones aren't for discussion... they are only memories of a privately painful reality. Some of the others are available for discussion, and those could be recounted from an observational point of view, as in an everyday occurrence, probably like anywhere else. We had parties on board when Jake had been an unknowing roast, that delighted most. Only for a brief time, then Jake got to sailing and most understood that Jake was the Captain of **The Buried Treasure**." Jameson had understood Sam wasn't up for telling such tales... he really wanted to try a distracting technique. Apparently it wasn't going to happen. Sam descended to the cabin; he came back up with one of Jakes cigars and performed the ritual of smoking it. After he was enjoying his smoke he asked Jameson a question. "Jameson, how is it that you came by this hunch of Jackson?" The question threw Jameson. "Well Sam, I really had nothing to do with it.... It was all Hendrick." Sam raised his eyebrows exhaling some smoke. "Is that so? Hendricks came up with it?" Jameson nodded and Sam smiled. Jameson was even further confused. He didn't understand Sam's smile. He felt like asking Sam why he smiled. The smile would do nothing for his own inability to

209

have made the connection concerning Jackson.

Sam sat back and smoked some more. The men sat silently for some time.

"Does it surprise you that Hendrick had the insight Sam?" Sam looked at Jameson and grinned. "No Jameson, not really, as a matter of fact, it really follows that he would have picked it off... also says something about experience, wouldn't you agree?" Jameson nodded positively. He didn't say anything besides the nod. He was somewhat disappointed with himself for not being the one to pick it off. Sam sensed this about Jameson. He just enjoyed his cigar. Sam had reflected on the way he had to let things come to folks. He always thought a question got more thinking done, rather than a statement. As far as he knew, he was right. Jameson was filing this circumstance so that it could be processed in the future. Sam felt as though he would use it as strength for the future.

The men continued to sit. Jake's truck pulled up and Jake got out. He had come to **The Buried Treasure** and noticed Sam smoking one of his cigars. He would have normally given Sam some grief about it, but Jake was wrapped a little tightly, both men saw that.

Jameson asked, "How is it with Erik?" Jake jumped on board and went below. It was early but Jake was in no mood for anything other than a drink... it had been a day to forget as far as he was concerned. While Jake was pouring a drink he had mentioned through the cabin...

"He's about finished... says Sam can come by tonight if he wants."
When Jake ascended to the cockpit he had both a drink and a cigar. He
didn't do much besides take a pull off his drink and rush any ritual of
enjoying the lighting of the cigar. He was visibly shaken by the events of
earlier today. He took a seat and growled after his cigar was puffed on.
"Fuckin' Jackson!" Sam looked at Jake. "Jake we both knew Jackson,
and believe me, I don't like how it looks anymore than you do, but lets
not lose sight of the important thing here." Jake took a heavy pull on
his cigar, then on his drink. "I know Sam, I know. But really, let's say
he did give up the info, what then?"

Sam wasn't sure if an answer was needed, Jake could draw his own
conclusions if 'what then' was a reality. Jameson however wasn't going
to wait. "Jake, I'm feeling a little low right about now. I missed that
which Hendrick had seen. To answer your question... this Jackson fella
does have due process afforded to him, the most important part of that
due process is to find out what he knows and see where it leads."

Sam added to what Jameson said, "Remember Jake, we need to do
this without them having a clue as to how we'll be coming at them.....
stealth, right?" Jake thought a moment and agreed. "Yep Sam, stealth
is the key. I'm just a little shell-shocked by this new bit of info." Sam
nodded; Jameson spoke up. "Look here guys, every new bit of info
uncovered in an investigation usually leaves those interested floored by
its own relevance, almost like ya didn't want to believe it."

Sam nodded and Jake frowned. "None-the-less it is another developing piece of the mystery and when seen at the end, it will have made sense." Jameson continued. "Cooper has got the national APB out. This Jackson won't be gone for too long." Sam perked up. "Jameson I know you are new to the detecting business, but did you get, any read from Hendrick as to what he is thinking?" Jameson thought about the question and really didn't have an answer. "No, Sam, I didn't. But I can tell you he thinks this is solvable." Jake wondered about Jamesons' take. "What leads you to think Hendrick thinks he can solve this?" Jameson responded, "Well his track record as a detective supports solvability in most of his cases, so I am considering a little inside experience to suggest it. Shit Jake it is what he does." Sam asked another question, "Do you think he sees it as a conspiracy like Cooper does?" "I'm not sure Sam, I don't think he has such a conclusion, he is the kind of detective that questions things, finds the likely answers and arrives at guilt or innocence. So no, I don't think he has isolated motivation. Apparently, the case is built and motivation becomes evident with Hendrick, as a process of deduction."

Jake and Sam both thought on that. They were a bit surprised. The fingerprint thing didn't seem to back what Jameson was saying, but then again, what Jameson was saying was only what he thought. Jameson read along, and noticed the doubt the men were thinking of. "Hey guys everyone is human and prone to make mistakes, we are just lucky as to have nailed the errors as quickly as we did." Jake raised his glass to silently toast the weakness of human design. Jameson really needed to get back with Hendrick to the office, he was considering as to the state of mind between the two. "Look guys, I need to follow up with Hendrick on this Jackson thing. I'm hoping you will all wait to hear from us before you go around shooting first and asking questions later. Do I need to hope?" Jake laughed out loud.

"Tell me this Jameson… Are you any good at hoping?" Jake elbowed Sam and snickered even more. Sam smiled a bit even though he had tried to set Jameson straight on the issue earlier. "Jameson, both Jake and me rarely get wild as such, besides we are in stealth mode. Believe me, before we get to shooting up anything you'll know about it." Jameson nodded and departed for the office. Somehow Sam's promise was taken a face value, which should be enough so that Jameson could do his thing. He left the men sitting on **The Buried Treasure**.

He headed back to the station hoping Hendrick would have some news that would be helpful.

Chapter 8

Cooper was enjoying her visit with Nathan when her pager went off. She looked at the number and told Nathan she had to return the call. Cooper dialed and waited for the connection. When Jameson answered, she said hello and then listened. She seemed to be committing something to memory and Nathan was curious. After she hung up she said to Nathan, "There is more news." Nathan's eyebrows raised a bit as he showed interest. "Apparently this employee of Sam-Jak Inc., one Henry Jackson has developed a need to not be available for questioning." Nathan asked, "Do you have the particulars?" Cooper nodded and wrote them down for Nathan. He examined them and made a call. Cooper needed to visit the bathroom. The coffee had put her bladder on overtime. She excused herself from the table as Nathan had connected to his office. She sat and relieved herself. She wondered as the panic subsided, how Nathan might have as much pull, as she wanted to believe. When she finished, she rose and secured her pants exited to the sink and rinsed her hands. She left the bathroom and rejoined Nathan.

He smiled as she returned. "Everything come out okay?" Nathan asked. She nodded and took her seat. "So how did it go?" "Well the paperwork for your victims will go through as contractors…. Nothing too difficult… the detective may need the farm and you just need to take an oath." Cooper nodded and smiled, "The Farm, I'm sure he will enjoy it." "Well Cooper with Goss as the new director everything is very fluid. The election plays in our favor too."

"Everyone at the top is in just cover your ass mode. The only good thing about being at war is we are keeping them over there, otherwise it would be crazy trying to chase down these sleepers." "Sleepers…. those are what I think we are up against here." Cooper said. Nathan looked at her very seriously. "Cooper I don't want to say too much here, but these sleepers are taking it upon themselves to come up with creative non obvious ways of keeping us busy. We know it, thanks to the Patriot Act passed. There are so many of them we have to prioritize just who we go after. When the bodies get associated to sleeper cell activity, the standing order is to take them down, otherwise it is to watch."

Cooper thought about what Nathan was saying. She was trying to listen between the lines. Nathan saw this and told her not to over analyze it. He caught the attention of the waitress and indicated he wanted a check. "Listen Cooper, ya need to get to your field office and submit your resignation, we can't have you taking two checks for one job." She laughed. "God knows they wouldn't want to be doing that." Both of them knew that in the bureau and the company the auditors would always get the good guy doing the wrong thing. The standard joke was not to get caught by the auditors. They were murder. After her on the job injury she didn't think too much of the standard joke. She was one of the agents who dotted her I's and crossed her T's. She wasn't too gung-ho and unlikely to take the power of the office lightly. As the waitress came back delivering the check Nathan reached for it and checked it. He said thanks to the girl and got some cash. He tossed a twenty on the table and said keep the change. This surprised Cooper, "Since when did you become such a good tipper?" Nathan said, "I haven't, but getting you on board is this waitresses lucky day." He smiled and stood up. She did as well. "One more thing Cooper… after you tender your resignation get your friends back down here pronto, we need to go through some of the details." She nodded and gave Nathan a hug. They departed. She made her way back to the 'soon not to be her squad' and wondered how things were with Jameson, Jake and Sam. It wouldn't be much longer till she knew, and then of course until they did too. The day was early she had decided on seeing those involved in this case before she resigned. She wondered about going to the office first but maybe more could be gained from having Sam go with her for a return ride… She would soon find out. She listened to the radio. Talk radio news, would give the latest news…

There was a new appointee to the CIA and his name was Porter Goss. She wondered how that would be affecting the transition. Time would tell, besides Nathan had her covered. She listened as she drove trying to get by the talk nonsense for the ¼ hour news reports. Then she'd turn the dial to FM. Maybe she could hook up with some tunes that were to her liking. While she drove something had created a question for her. She wasn't sure what that question may be, but Nathan was the familiar face. She wondered how he might be the source of this unanswered question…

The news started broadcasting… more dead in Iraq, soldiers killed by these IED's. She had a hard time listening; her own wounds had not quite healed… not in her mind. She wondered how these soldiers would be rehabbing. Bush was 4% ahead in the polls, by some polls and there was some brief report of Oil for Food Scandal at the UN. Paul Volker was the new guy heading up the investigation. The commercials had begun and she flipped to the music stations, trying to catch a tune.

Chapter 9

Jake and Sam remained on the **Buried Treasure.** Cigars gave them time to not focus on anything except the ritual. Many cigars would be smoked in ritualistic fashion as these men faced a future neither wanted to comprehend. Their new motivation was still seeping into the voids of their souls. So much had been removed from their life forces. These two were successful at managing full and productive lives. The manifestation of success from one life to another wasn't getting any odds. It was a certainty. They would see to it.

Jake finished off his drink and went for another. He asked Sam if he wanted in. Sam shook his head. "I'm gonna hold off but thanks." Jake descended for a moment and returned. Sam asked Jake, "How did Erik do with them?" Jake sipped his drink and took a puff. "Well Sam he did for them as he would do for his own, you know Erik." Sam just nodded. His fingers caressed the cigar and flicked off an ash head. It projected across the side of the boat. "Ya know Jake…" "We all buried that hamster of Tracy's. Remember that? Tracy was of the mind to hate anything that had to do with death…."

"Yep Sam I recall. She was a different kid after that."

Sam nodded. "I hated that part of it Jake… Tracy's innocence, succumbing to reality. I hated it. Ya know why?"

Jake nodded "Yep, I do Sam. Cause there was nothing you could do about it." Sam nodded. He smoked his cigar. Both men knew loss was a given of life. Both men also knew that within this loss you had limited periods of gain, but that you always lost something as each day passed. Sometimes it was a material loss and not so painful. Sometimes it was painful, very much so. Jake by nature didn't gain so much through his life in a sense of familial bonds. He was quite happy in his friend's familial gain. And, as these two men shared the multitude of gifts offered by Sam's family, they had found a shared experience. For Jake, being Uncle Jake was good enough. And for Sam having an Uncle Jake was just a part of the design. For many years Jake had been the brother to Monica. The burden was Sam's to be sure, but Jake was in it with him brotherly so.

"Hey Jake…. Bina will be getting back here soon, are ya gonna be soused for her return?" Sam waited for one of Jakes comebacks…

"What's it to you?" Jake replied. "Don't ya think she might expect it from me?" Jake smiled a bit as he let Sam consider that.

"Quite honestly Jake… I'm not sure about what she expects…."

"I'm thinking she is going to have some kind of action plan. I just didn't want to have to repeat it to ya if she did?"

"Jesus, Sam, that sounds like a thing Monica would have said." Sam listened and Jake squirmed.

Jake said something that he wasn't sure about with Sam… For Jake even mentioning Monica in that light lent itself to foot from mouth thinking. Sam enjoyed watching Jake fumble in his thinking.

"Yep, you're right about Monica saying that. But look here Jake, she isn't here, so I'll have to pick up the slack."

Jake heard what Sam had said and it put Jake back. "Hey now, Sam, before there was two of ya. I don't know how having both of you in one is gonna be, I don't think it is fair though." Sam laid a gaze on Jake. Jake had seen it few times before. He didn't like it, but then again Jake liked fewer things than most. He replied to Sam's gaze…. "Nothing is fair." Sam stood up and stretched. He was about finished with his cigar and flicked it over the boat's edge. As it hit the water is hissed from extinction. Sam breathed in heavily and exhaled. "Jake. For me they are already buried…. this thing with Erik, well it is a formality. It is a duty which is unfair, one never wanted." Jake finished his drink. He tossed his cigar into his mouth and rolled it over his tongue. He parked it and commented. "Sam… there is, however, a duty and it has got to be honored. What is fair is lost. You had better take something away in this duty." Jake knew that Sam had been rationalizing this insanity the best way he could. Jake further knew that Sam might regret compartmentalizing his loss. He wasn't sure that's where Sam was, but it sounded like it.

Sam just nodded as he looked upon the water finishing up his stretch.

Jake waited and Sam said nothing… he arose and went for another drink. He had seen Sam's family and Sam had not. It was pitiful. And, to find out that Jackson may have had something to do with it left Jake in need of some self-medicating. He wasn't interested in justifying that to anyone. He worried for Sam. He hoped that burying them wouldn't crush Sam. He could only wait. No odds were being given it was a certainty. He could only wait and be there. He pulled off his poured drink and refilled it. This is how he thought best to handle it. To be numb not soused. Jake noticed that the noontime hour had past and after his morning, he felt quite good about his dosage of self-medicating. He returned to the deck of **The Buried Treasure** and to his surprise Cooper was pulling into the parking lot. He had thought she would be arriving later in the day. He perched himself comfortably in the cockpit of **The Buried Treasure** with a feline quality of 'who cares?' He did notice that Sam was more interested in her arrival and he felt good for Sam about that. As far as Jake was concerned, Sam was starving for an elusive plan of action. He would sure get some digestion with Cooper's arrival. He smiled genuinely as she approached. He watched Sam. But the guy was as cold as they come. He didn't move; he just anticipated. Jake liked it like that. He never much worried about anything when Sam got to resolutin.' And anticipation was a big precursor to Sam's resolutin' so things were as they should be.

Both men watched Cooper approach silently. Cooper seemed to be brimming with much to say but remained patient. Jake watched as Sam went through the courteous thing. "Ah Agent Cooper! How was your ride?" Jake was enjoying his numbing state as he usually did watching Sam be Sam. Cooper replied to Sam's inquiry. "Hardly any traffic, thanks Sam." And for Jake it had begun. "How is your friend Nathan, Bina?" She replied again. "He is well and full of direction Sam."

She smiled when she looked at Jake and asked: "Permission to come aboard Captain Jake?" Jake summoned the breath to reply. "Granted." Sam looked over his shoulder at Jake and returned his focus to Bina. Sam waited patiently for Bina to take a seat and settle in. "Would you like a beverage Bina?" She shook her head. "No thanks." Sam found himself a place to recline. Cooper looked at the men trying to figure out what to say. Her instinct about Sam was a little concerning to her. His essence seemed a little controlled. She surmised that Jake, well, he was on the fringes that she might have expected Sam to be in. She didn't question it; she just filed it. Victim Insight required it. Sam was a victim who had exhibited patience and realized that in moments

222

of tolerance there were lifetimes of answers. "Let me see where to begin, okay, here we go. As we sit here and speak, we are part of a transformation. Many things that were recently considered absurd are not so…. Absurd."

Upon hearing this Jake rolled his cigar over his tongue. It provided a pause for them that tested Sam's tolerance from moments into minutes. Cooper noticed this in Sam, she was right not to trust instincts. Sam was maintaining control but he needed direction to be soothed. "Now it is important to realize the simplicity with the statement I just made. First of all, there is no departure from what I am saying here. It has been decided."

Sam seamed to loosen up. "Hendrik just became our lead investigator here." Jake laughed with a sense of curiosity for Jameson.

"He did, and has anyone told him?"

Sam seemingly let the flow remind him of the normalcy of Jake. Cooper pounced on Jake.

"No that is your job Jake!" That got Sam to crack a faint smile.

"And Jake honey?" Cooper waited for Jake to look at her. "That has been decided!"

Jake feigned a look of disbelief. "I have to tell him, why me?"

Cooper looked at Sam and giggled, she enjoyed hanging out Jake. She looked at Sam and mentioned so Jake could hear it without involvement.

"Like he isn't ready to break the news to Hendrick over a drink?"

Sam added. "Yeah letting the guy know his retirement plans just got cancelled?"

They both laughed together. Jake was the expense of this, he thought of the abuse as different but the same. Had Cooper been Monica, Jake would have offered his own retort, which would have split Monica and Sam down the middle, getting her back to his side. He passed on mentioning it. He was just relieved his friend still had his humor left. He knew his love was being placed somewhere. He just hoped Sam remembered where he hid it. "Okay, I'll do it." Jake spoke to this begrudgingly. "But that can't be the great transformation in its entirety? Get on with the rest of it." They settled down as Jake rolled his cigar stub.

Cooper continued. "Yes it seems as though Jameson needs to visit the farm...." Sam considered what Cooper had said. Cooper watched him and that instinct thing changed in her again. What had seemed a little off about Sam had now seemed right, she sensed an ease, which was released in the words she spoke. Jake remained quiet, which indicated to her that both men were considering the implications of this transformation she hinted to. She hoped she wasn't going to sound far-fetched. She felt as though her course of speak was going well, so far.

While the men considered what she had said she stood and started below. "You know, I am parched, some water would be a good thing."

She went below to fill a glass of water then rejoined the men. "So Jameson is going to the farm?" Jake repeated the question. "Yeah I guess someone has to let Hendrick know, hehe."

Sam had developed a question and waited on Cooper to quench some of her thirst. "Jameson is going to be a federal employee. What's that make us, Contractors?" Jake added in his own two cents. "Maybe they call us mercs?" Cooper could say only one thing. "I'm still paid by the same people, just a different department." Both men were intrigued. "So Cooper ya are Company now?" Jake rolled his cigar and waited. "Well, Jake, while you are spilling it to Hendricks, I'll be tendering my DOJ resignation. It is why you saw me earlier than you might have thought. I was looking for a return ride. The car is a department asset and as a government employee I can't afford the cab fare." "Hmmmm, I'm too far numb to drive." Jake excluded himself from the taxi service. Cooper looked at Sam. "The whole trip would take us three hours Sam. What do ya say?" Sam nodded to Cooper. "Sure Bina, I'll go along." Cooper looked at Sam. "Captain Numb are ya gonna make it to the Jameson, or do ya want a drop off?" He declined the ride. He wasn't that numb yet. "Jameson!!!!, I thought I was telling Hendrick. See here Copper, all I got to do is call 911. They'll send all of them out. Jameson thinks we could be Postal." Cooper looked at Jake. "Yep, that is good use of the system..." she smiled, "make the transformation an emergency..." Sam smiled and laughed a bit. "Sure Jake let the guy retiring know of this when he comes with guns blazing…that should work really well for ya." Cooper laughed some more too… "Geezus Jake, ya had better not get the guys drink wrong." Sam and Cooper had started to disembark from **The Buried Treasure.** While they had thought they left Jake in a jive, he caught them unexpectedly. "Well don't forget about seeing Erik tonight." He wished he hadn't said it. But there it was. And there they were, laughing briefly before they thought it unfair.

Chapter 10

Jake was left there on **The Buried Treasure.** He hated the fact that he was left to explain what Cooper had said. He wasn't even sure if Hendrick would oblige the circumstance. He seemed to have been pretty firm in his offering up his papers. Jake thought Hendrick might like going out putting this case to rest, but maybe not. He would have to see. He wondered more about the likelihood of Jameson going to the farm.... He couldn't anticipate what Jameson would say. He hoped Cooper had thought this thing through, not only for Jameson, but it wasn't clear what capacities both he and Sam would have. He didn't really give it too much thought. He poured another drink and called Jameson's line. "Hello is Detective Jameson there please? Okay I can wait." The hell if he was going to drive down there. It would be just his luck... some uniform would bust him for drinking and driving. Jake was just pulling another sip when Jameson picked up the line. It took

Jake by surprise and he swallowed down the wrong pipe. He heard Jameson say hello this is Detective Jameson and then Jake dropped the phone to cough his drink up. He spilled some of it too by the violent shaking of his body. When he realized the disaster this call turned out to be he cursed loudly while he picked up the phone. "Is that you Jameson? This is Jake." Jameson finally spoke to an active listener and asked what Jake needed. "Yeah, Jake, this is Jameson what is wrong?" Jake was still looking at the waste of liquor and grumbling... "Hey, are you and Hendrick available?"

Jameson spoke again. "Available, available for what?" Jake finally got his composure back as he poured again. "Listen, get yourself and Hendrick over to **The Buried Treasure.** Jameson wasn't happy. He wanted to know more. "Listen Jameson, you really need to bring Hendrick and yourself here. I need to speak to ya and I'm not driving anywhere." Jameson breathed heavily so Jake could hear it; it was like a bothered breathing or a sigh. He said to Jake, "Give me a couple of minutes, will ya?"

Jake responded. "I'll be right here." Jake hung up the phone. He plopped himself to his previous perch and waited. He thought about how Jameson might be breaking the news to Hendrick's... he was glad he was self-medicating. He lounged further so he could pillow his head on the cockpit's structure. His eyes had gotten heavy. Numbness lulled Jake to relax his eyes. He was enjoying a brief nod.

After Jameson hung up with Jake, he went to Hendrick. "We need to take a ride to see Jake on **The Buried Treasure**." Hendrick looked at Jameson and ran his fingers through his hair. He rubbed his face and his nose with the palm and fingers of the same hand. "Okay let's go." The two were up and leaving the office. Jameson was first; Hendrick noticed a forced pace. Almost like Jameson knew he had to go but didn't want to. He figured that Jameson might be reluctant to speak up, and let his old retiring partner in on what was going on. Hendrick waited to speak. He walked to the passenger side of the car and got in. When Jameson had started the car Hendrick spoke up. "Hey Jameson, what's the story with talking with Blaques?" Jameson looked at Hendrick and raised his eyebrows offering a shake of the head, like who knows. "I don't know, but I think he had started drinking... he went to talk to the funeral director for Sam." Hendrick wasn't done. "No Jameson that is not what I meant." He paused and thought about being more articulate. "I noticed your pace on the way out of the office. Seemed like you were looking at unwanted duty..."

Jameson thought about Hendricks' elucidation. And as he thought about it, he was going through the motions of operating the car secondarily in nature. "Hendricks... how did you figure that? By watching my pace, is that what you called it? Hendrick nodded. "Well that is just how it feels. Unwanted Duty." Jameson shook his head. He thought to himself, 'How did he know that?' Jameson glanced at

Hendrick pulling out onto the main road.   Hendrick just waited for an answer.

Jameson had lost the focus and this confirmed to Hendrick that there was a preoccupation. Jameson noticed Hendrick waiting. He still wondered how Hendrick nailed his current disposition. "Okay, I guess I wasn't clear enough. I'm sorry but I don't know is all there is." Hendrick shrugged; it wasn't like it would be long before the horse's mouth said it. They drove on. Hendrick let it go for the time while he wondered about how Jameson couldn't respond. This was not critical but it would need some sorting out. He broke it down some more on the ride for future reference. There was always another way to illicit info, even unwillingly offered info. After all, that is what he spent his life doing... figuring circumstances out.

Jameson was still fuming about how Hendricks knew. He thought he was less conspicuous than that. Jameson realized Hendricks was the last of the old guys that he knew. He would miss his mentoring. "Hell, Hendrick, I guess I'm gonna miss that quality of yourself. That way you zero in on someone's thinking. Us younger fella's, well we are envious." Hendrick smiled. "Time is the ultimate teacher, it just comes with time Jameson." The men arrived at the marina. They found a parking space and headed toward **The Buried Treasure**. Jameson said to Hendricks. "She sure is a beauty, isn't she?" Hendricks nodded and said, "Yeah if you like boats." They approached without Jake noticing them. Jameson frowned and Hendrick commented to his frown. "A burning desire to talk eh?" Jake raised an eyebrow a little surprised. "I was just wondering if 911 would have gotten ya here faster than you have. Come aboard detectives, come aboard."

They both boarded. Jake had invited them to sit down. After they did, he spoke to them. "I'd offer ya both a drink, but you might want to hear what I have to say first." Jake waited a bit and laughed. "Hell yeah, ya might be wanting one after this." The detectives were intrigued but growing aggravated with waiting. Jake wasn't too numb to notice. "Okay detectives here it is… The she devil FBI Agent just left here with Sam. Guess what? She left me with a job… and you two as well." Hendrick and Jameson looked at each other…they wondered if this was a joke. Jameson had had enough. "Alright Jake, just what the heck are you talking about?" Jake couldn't help himself. His drink was empty and he needed a break and another cigar. "Heck boys, I'll fill ya in when I get back." He arose from his lounge and descended into **The Buried Treasure…** Jake giggled to himself. Jameson thought he was busy now. That was a joke. Jake wondered how Jameson would be feeling at the end of a month on the Company Farm. He thought more of Hendrick being lead detective on this case. Yeah, that's about right. Here the poor guy thought he was going to retire. Jake finished in the head and poured himself another drink. He mouthed a cigar and headed back up top. After he sat he focused on Jameson.

"What the heck I'm talking about Jameson is this: Agent Cooper is on her way to resign from the FBI. Oh yeah, Sam is giving her a lift back and then he's going to see his family." He had set his drink down and was lighting his cigar. He thought that was enough to chew on for a bit. When he looked at Jameson Jake felt as though he knew what Jameson was thinking, and if he did he was to numb to worry about it. Either way Jameson was less arrogant. Jake shrugged maybe arrogant wasn't the word. Jameson asked abruptly, "Resignation? Jake that just doesn't make any sense." Jake laughed and choked out his igniting puff from the cigar. He looked at Hendrick and asked, "Hey Hendrick… when did you ever know of a woman making sense when it came to work?"

Jake cackled like a fool for a bit. He took another puff and spoke to Jameson directly.

"Look here Jameson, if you think that doesn't make sense, you're about to be floored. Okay, the down and dirty now, hold on." Jake took a sip of his drink then got his cigar a home in his mouth. He held it between his teeth and tongue. As Jameson had nailed it before Jake had used this as a distraction… even if he didn't know it. "Do you have any luggage Jameson?" Jameson thought it was a strange question but obliged Jake. "Yeah, I got some luggage Jake." Jake smiled and said to Jameson, "Good, you're gonna need it. You're in for promotion boy. You got a one way ticket to the Company Farm." Jameson knew what to make of this news. Hendrick did too. He grumbled when he heard Jake say it. Jake laughed a bit. " Hendrick? You were just pulling young Jameson's leg here when ya started with that retirement stuff, weren't ya?"

Hendricks was a tad bit angry… "Hell no, Jake, I wasn't pulling anybodies leg. How the hell am I gonna get this one by the wife?" Jake looked at them and said, "I would've already poured the drinks if I knew you guys could cheat on duty." Both men appeared somewhat confused and neither of them found any pleasantry to it. Jake looked at Jameson and concluded that young Jameson wasn't grasping the idea. Jameson was feigning this confusion as he had let on that he had never heard it. Hendrick, well he knew a tough deal when he heard one…and by the sounds of it, he was still going through what needed to be done by it. Jake giggled some more. Both men were involved beyond noticing his laugh. Jake could see how Hendricks was already thinking about letting the boss at work know what was coming. Hendrick fired a question off. "Okay Jake, when are those two getting back?" Jake played stupid. He really liked doing that too. "I don't really know Hendrick, but the plan was to get back here and see his family, if that's any help." Jake smiled and smoked his cigar, and sipped on his drink. Hendrick got up and said to Jameson, "Hey partner, we still got work to do in chasing down this Jackson fella…. Let's get at it." And then, he left the boat. Jameson had a panicked look in his eye. All he could verbalize was a mumbled question…. "Luggage, for the farm?" Hendrick dropped in before Jake could. "Yeah Jameson, you've been recruited to the CIA. You're gonna be a spy!" Jake couldn't believe what Hendricks had said.

All he could do was ask Hendrick as he stood on the dock. "A Spy?"

Jake couldn't help to feel the numbness giving his eyes some heaviness as the detectives returned to their car. He just kept laughing quietly to himself mimicking Jameson. "A Spy?" Jake finished off his drink and let his cigar cool as he embraced the numbness. It was better than thinking of the nightmare at Erik's.

Chapter 11

As the men returned to the car, Jameson kept his confusion very apparent. He led Hendrick on, as he and Cooper had never had any conversation. He was following directions the best way he could recall them. It wasn't so difficult. He really was surprised at how fast the reality came to him. He hadn't expected it quite this soon. He wondered if he should let Hendricks in on the story, but decided not to. He figured being a spy was or even being a good one came with being able to keep things very close to the vest. He did just as Cooper had said he should.

Hendricks didn't like to dwell on how he felt about surprises. He also didn't like alterations from a chosen course of action. Jake had been accurate in the fact that his retirement was postponed; of course, assuming he would re-take the lead investigators place. As he drove the car he mulled it over in his head. If he did take up the lead, he wondered when this case might be resolved. Even, how it would be resolved. He contemplated that the local investigation was probably near the end, and with federal involvement there might still be a body count left to his department, even if it had been solved. He knew he was going to hold out on accepting this additional responsibility until he was sure that the press would see this thing as a cooperative investigation. That probably wouldn't ruffle anyone's feather in the powers that be. Nonetheless, his point was going to be known before he signed on. Otherwise, one of the other guys could pick it up. And, he knew his boss wouldn't want to hear that. Heck, his boss was gonna be out of his mind at the outset. Here he was loosing two of his detectives over four bodies. Hendrick just grumbled and shook his head.

Jameson remained quiet for the ride to the station. He was happy he would elsewhere. There was such sadness in being here, even with his ascending to the rank of detective. Many things changed for Jameson like many others survivors of 9/11. He thought to himself, how much he had put his work forward in the loss of his fiancée.

He was looking forward to the newness, which would come along as the future unfolded.

The detectives had arrived at the station; they exited the car and stopped short of entering the building. "Hold up Jameson." Hendrick had something to say. "I think we ought to go back in there as we left." Jameson nodded. "Yeah we might as well wait until ... that *she-devil* gets back with Sam. Maybe we can talk before they go to do that dreadful business." Hendrick winked at Jameson, the men re-entered the station as they left.

One of the uniforms Jameson supervised seemed to be doing well. He was waiting for them to return. Jameson was ready to respond to his inquiry. It wasn't an inquiry, and it wasn't for Jameson. "Detective Hendrick, this was faxed to you." Hendricks took the paper from the uniform and looked at it. Jameson waited for a glimpse himself. "Detective Jameson?" The uniform had begun a comment he needed to repeat from the boss. Jameson looked at him with an impatient look. "The Chief wants to see you five minutes ago." He winced as he said it. This had gotten both detectives attention. Hendrick looked up from the fax he was reading and focused on Jameson. "What the hell are ya waiting on Jameson? The Chief is waiting, get going." Jameson frowned, knowing they might have gone in as they left, but someone had noticed the difference. A handful of officers present were watching Jameson with a sense of apprehension. Usually a meeting with the Chief wasn't a good thing. Most going to meet the chief in these kinds of circumstances weren't leaving as police. That was the way of the Chief.

Jameson moved along at Hendricks' urging. Hendrick looked back at the fax. He finished reading it and held it down. He looked at the policeman who gave it to him. "Do you know what this is?" The officer just shook his head and said, "No." Hendrick asked another question of Jamesons' new best buddy. "You and Jameson were doing well with this investigation, weren't you?" This time he just nodded. He waited to follow up on it. He was trying to be respectful of Hendricks. "I guess so detective." "Jameson is a little younger than you and more likely the detective I would be getting to know as you are retiring."

Hendrick turned back to his desk and told the officer to come have a seat. Hendrick laid that fax down on his desk. He looked up at the young cop. "That right there…" Hendrick pointed to the fax. "That is more than likely the car this fellow Jackson used to leave the area. Tell me do you know what DOT is?" The officer stated his answer. "Department of Transportation."

Hendrick nodded, "Yes that is correct."

"When if ever, did you see a fax from the DOT?" The officer sat and thought for a second or two. "I don't think I have ever seen one of them detective." Hendrick looked at him with a faint smile. "Don't worry too much on it, it is one of the few for me too. I can tell you this. That fax is the beginning of something you may never see as a lawman here. That little report will change things here forever. In fact, the experience you all will participate in will be a tremendous resume builder." The officer waited patiently for the old detective to get through his point. "Detective I am not sure as to why the DOT is important as to having transmitted that fax."

"Well, when Jameson comes out of the meeting with the chief you will. He will or will not tell you of the meeting. I suppose that will be up to the chief. But if we are getting reports from the DOT the feds are up to this one and on top of it. I have a strong feeling I won't be retiring as soon as I thought. But I don't think Jameson will ever retire from here."

The officer didn't know what to say. Hendrick didn't give him a chance to think on it. "Have you all looked for the last known friends of this guy Jackson?" The officer nodded. "Yeah we are following up on it, apparently Jackson didn't have many friends except for those he worked with." People who knew him said he was alone most of the time but he kept busy with the ladies, if ya know what I mean." Hendrick just nodded. "Any ladies around who have been with him recently?" " Geez detective... we are having a hard enough time just finding the one's who did know him."

Hendrick looked at this cop. He took a moment to think he'd be handling rookies again. He didn't want to have to explain things to these younger guys. He decided he was only going to do it with one of them. He looked up at the other officers. "Hey guys, why don't you take a cruise for some coffee, I'm buying." One of the guy's came over and grabbed a twenty from Hendrick. He and his partner left, the dispatcher went back to the communications hut. Hendrick looked at the officer. "You like working with Jameson, as we have agreed upon.

You like running that detail because you're the guy dispersing the information from Jameson to everyone else, right?" The officer smiled a bit and nodded, "Yeah, detective, I do like that." Hendrick nodded and smiled more than he could earlier.

"How is it your name is said?" The officer pronounced his name for Hendrik. "Ken-ies-ty-os-ky, Detective, Gunter Keniestyosky." Hendrick looked at the cop. "A guy could strain himself saying that." Hendrick continued. "I asked the others to leave so as to mention to you, that I am going to use you as Jameson did, and that means you'll be up for Sergeant. You have to be sharp as you had been with Jameson. Ya know the go-getter. And by the way, I'm gonna be Jameson." Hendrick looked at Keniestyosky. The young cop took the conversation at face value and beamed.

Hendrick appreciated the fact that the kid knew how to play. He didn't think his choice was bad either. "Now Keniestyosky what do you say about coming up with a plan to find some of those girls Jackson might know." "Those we need to talk to?" Hendrick watched, as the beaming in Keniestyoskys' face became determination. The officer was so focused he almost forgot to acknowledge the request from Hendrick. "Oh yeah detective, I'm working on it now." "Thanks, thanks a lot."

Keniestyosky went back to his work area. Hendrick called after him. "Sergeant Gunn."

Keniestyosky turned to look at him. "I like that name better, don't you?" The kid nodded and restarted his inclination of upward motion in the department.

Hendrick looked at the transmittal again. He figured that a motivation formulated of what Cooper had been thinking might be a workable course of investigation. *If Jackson used the car here, was it likely that a terrorist connection would be facilitated there? And, if it was, what was the next likely step?* Hendrick thought about terrorist distribution. *Terrorists use the most widely used hubs to move about. It is the nature of terrorists. To use and plan in the free flow of any society as the society does. New York to Boston? Boston to Quebec or Montreal? Maybe South?* Whatever the travel pattern of Jackson and his companions were, it sure wasn't here in Lyme as far as they knew? Hendrick thought to himself. *Where there are women around a guy like Jackson, there are many mysterious contacts.* And he was sure one of the women Jackson knew could be connected with somebody else of less moral character. Hendricks had an inside plan. One he didn't need to share with anyone else besides Sergeant Gunn. And Sgt. Gunn was sure to need some tutelage in people of interest and associations. Hendrick knew experience would be helpful to Sgt. Gunn because he was willing to see it as an investigatory asset instead of a part of the job.

Chapter 12

A bit later Jameson had emerged from the Chief's office. Hendrick didn't look directly at Jameson but he did hear him as the door closed. He had a bundle of papers he was focusing on while Jameson moved closer to the desk he occupied. Jameson sat down.

Jameson asked Hendrick where the uniformed officers got. Hendrick replied without changing his focus from the papers... "I sent two of them for coffees and talked to the new Sgt. Gunn." Jameson hardly knew how to respond. "The new Sgt. Gunn?" Hendrick finally broke his focus and smiled as he looked at Jameson. "Yes, Sergeant Keniestyosky, his first name is Gunter so I dubbed him Sgt. Gunn. Don't tell me you have a problem with that." Jameson shook his head. "No. No, no problem at all."

"Good." Hendricks replied.

Hendricks kept his focus on Jameson. To Hendricks it appeared that Jameson was a bit reticent to say much. "So, when are ya leaving?" Jameson responded to Hendrick question with a sense of disbelief. "I am leaving immediately."

"That soon, eh? How did the Chief take it?" Hendrick was curious as to find out how the Chief would be making new arrangements for the loss of a detective. "Well," Jameson started, "Kind of matter of fact-ly." Jameson paused to think of more...

"He was sorry to be losing me, but he seemed to defer to what the CIA was requesting. He told me that if things didn't work out there he would put me back on again... Ya know that kind of thing." Hendricks nodded. "Yep, I can see him being that way. I also think he is probably thinking about how to approach me to maybe stay on a little longer."

Jameson couldn't say one way or the other. "All I know is that The CIA is expecting me tomorrow." Hendrick thought to give some confidence to Jameson. "You know Jameson, that Keniestyosky he is a good patrolman. Your sense of nurturing the uniforms is good, hell it is better than good." Jameson nodded, "Thanks for taking notice Hendrick... I was feeling pretty good about how we were getting it on."

"Yes, well, not to worry Jameson, Sgt. Gunn is in good hands." Jameson smiled and said, "I'm sure he is. I also guess you are going to be seeing this thing through." Hendrick nodded. "Yeah, at least while the Lyme Police has jurisdiction. I got the guys working on Jackson's last known female companions. That shouldn't be too difficult."

Just as the men reached a silence in their conversation, the two uniforms who went for coffee returned. They were getting the coffees out for the ranks. Hendrick made a head gesticulation indicating how Sgt. Gunn was heading in. Jameson watched as his former prodigy engaged the uniforms. Keniestyosky went to the group and proclaimed that they had new marching orders. "Okay fellas, here is the new play…. We are hunting the former play pals of Jackson; the female persuasion ˮ Both of the cops frowned as they were thinking of taking their coffees with them. Keniestyosky had said additionally, "It is a good thing you got them coffees to go. Get the new investigation started right now, Detective Hendrick still thinks this is a valid direction." At that verbalization, the officers had picked up their own coffees and left for their unit. Before they had left, Keniestyosky had barked one more instruction off… "Let's try to get some good 411 on these as yet unknown individuals… ya got ¾'s of a shift left. We want some names and addresses." The officers acknowledged Keniestyosky and were off. Hendrick marveled at the way Sgt. Gunn was taking heat off his shoulders. The details… The details. While Sgt. Gunn was feeling good about himself, Hendrick stuck him with another duty. "Sgt. Gunn?" Keniestyosky turned to heed what he was about to be told by Hendricks. "Sgt. Gunn… you are now going to transport the former detective and new CIA Agent to his house, he has an appointment tomorrow at The Pentagon. I don't imagine that means a whole lot of packing, but there are logistics he needs to work out. So, you will see to it. And while you're at it, do a drive by on the guys… make sure they aren't pumping the dog instead of asking for names, Okay?"

Sgt. Gunn nodded. He waited for Jameson as he packed some personal things from his desk. After Jameson had packed his stuff, Keniestyosky grabbed the package and said, "Detective or Agent Jameson… I'll be in the squad when you are ready." Jameson nodded, "I won't be long." The new Sgt. Gunn was off and Jameson and Hendrick stood to face each other. They shook hands and Hendrick said to Jameson, "Cover your ass." Jameson faced Hendrick with little to say. All he could manage was a simple, "Thanks."

Jameson left the station.

Once Jameson had vacated, Hendrick decided to go see The Chief. He could have waited… he might have if he had not liked The Chief. They weren't particularly friendly, but Hendrick did respect the man, and as far as Hendrick knew, The Chief respected him. He took the DOT facsimile. He wondered how many of those The Chief had seen. The door got a knock as usual, the familiar voice behind the door said enter. Hendrick did.

Chapter 13

Cooper hadn't thought much about the process of resignation from the FBI on the drive. Her mind had wandered to the motivation of how she ended up, here at this moment in time. *The Shooting.* Not Sam's family, but hers. She rationalized that although The FBI had not mistreated her since the shooting, they had also not helped her out. She knew that there was still a fraternity to the DOJ. No one who mattered would ever admit it. She had heard of other Agents (the male agents) being reinstated to duty long before they would give it to her. She pondered it. All she could formulate about the situation was that she would be the only one to help herself out. And, her consistent methodology brought her to a new set of friends. She smiled. Friends... she didn't really have any, not in the DOJ. Her one professional friend was a transfer now recruiting her. She wondered if this investigation, the Murphy investigation would result in maybe making her friend plural. She could imagine Jake as a friend, even Jameson. Maybe Jameson would be a better friend than Jake. She thought about Jake. He was certainly a catch to a single girl not interested in anything serious. Jameson would have been more of an interest to a girl looking for more stability. She giggled. Jameson was *housebroken*.

Cooper had checked her rearview mirror. Sam was dutifully following her. He wasn't tailgating, but he wasn't tolerating any stupidity. She looked back to the final negotiation to the office. Hartford was never as bad with traffic like New York was. She looked again into the mirror, Sam. Would he ever be a *friend?* Could he ever again be a new friend to anyone? She had taken notice of many things when she talked with Sam. Some concerned her. But she understood. Sam would have much rather traded a gunshot wound for his family. Even one worse than the one she had received. She felt confident that these new potential friends would be assets in fulfilling her need to find he who wounded her. Her confidence didn't come from her, but from Sam. And it was Sam not Jake, and definitely not Jameson. Sam frightened her for this reason. His motivation was greater than hers. That scared her. She had never met anyone that overcame her motivation.

The security, which had followed the 9/11 attacks, had been a skeleton of what it was. The barricades around the building were still in place, but manpower had been minimized. It used to be that a civilian couldn't get by a post to the parking area for agents. Today Sam parked next to Cooper. When she got out of the car she required a stretch. Sam however didn't seem to need one. He approached her as she relaxed.

"Not too bad of a ride?" Sam shook his head. "Actually Bina... it was kinda helpful."

Cooper raised her eyebrows unexpectedly. "Is that so?" Sam nodded. "Well Sam I'm glad about that for you." Sam smiled and said, "Thanks." Cooper had asked Sam if he wanted to come up with her. She hoped he would without explanation. She could use a hand with some of her stuff. It wasn't much but another set of hands would make it only one trip. Sam shrugged and said sure. He didn't much feel like hanging out in a FBI field office parking lot. She went to her trunk and opened it. She reached in and the computer responded to her manipulations. She inserted a disk and downloaded her programs and her personal data; stuff the FBI wouldn't be missing or even needing. She removed the CD and put it into her purse. She shut the trunk and indicated to Sam that he would need to follow her. He nodded as to suggest he understood. They proceeded through the building. As they walked through the office some of the Agents seemed to be otherwise occupied. It was hard for Sam to imagine that these people, who Cooper worked with, would have so little to say to her. He didn't give it too much thought. He just figured he would remain as innocuous as he could. Hopefully he could get out of here before there was a need to shake anybodies hand. They ended up at a desk that was separated from the rest. There were no closely placed desks towards hers as the others had been set up. She had some pictures of what he thought may be family. A couple of cactuses would need moving too. She mentioned to Sam, "You can wait here. I don't think I'll be too long." Sam said, "Okay, is there anything I can do while I wait?"

Cooper looked at her desk…. "Nope, I don't think so." She seemed to change her mind. "If you'd like, ya might want to take a look around for a couple of boxes. That would be helpful." Sam nodded, as she turned to leave. She was going to see whom she had to see. Sam glanced around the office. He noticed a water bubbler against the wall. It was situated near a common room, some room that resembled an office kitchen. He started towards the bubbler. He noticed a filler bottle on the floor next to the machine. A couple of extra empty bottles too. He got to the bubbler and noticed around the corner a room with a refrigerator and sink. There was a microwave on the counter. Sam moved to the lower cabinet door panels and opened them. He didn't need to look too much. When he opened the doors the contents spilled out. Pre measured coffee packets fell out of the counter revealing boxes of filters in plastic bags. Sam frowned. He could easily pilfer the boxes Bina needed. It would just require some attention to proper storage. He thought to himself…. *These folks might be in the business of managing The Nation's Safety and Civility, but they sure didn't know much about keeping house.* He got busy removing the coffee filters in the bags from one box. The stacking seemed more sensible than stuffing a box under the counter. Sam worked efficiently, and before long he was procuring a second box. As he was finishing up, an Agent had meandered into the kitchen area. He looked up and saw a curious Agent looking down at him. The Agent asked if he could help Sam. Sam had to laugh. "Nope I think I'm all set." The embarrassed Agent prompted a more direct question with more attitude. "Who are you, and what do you think you're doing?" Sam thought this Agent was one of the ones who might have disregarded Bina's entry to the office. Sam finished his packing and stood up. After he leveled off the coming conversation he found some attitude of himself. He was intending some sarcasm. Sam looked at the Agent. "Why I'm the organization fairy today, and I'm retrieving boxes for a departing Agent while she tells her boss to take this job and shove it." Sam smiled at his verbal response. He thought himself to be clever. The Agent didn't think much of it sarcasm. "An organization fairy", then he thought of the second part of Sam's response, "wait a second…is Cooper resigning?" Sam grinned some more, realizing this Agent was an idiot. Sam spoke again, "Cooper? Did I mention any name?" Sam thought about his previous response and repeated it. "Oh, now I get it… I said she! But that isn't a name now is it? It is a pronoun." The Agent was losing his humor steadily. Sam could see panic in the eyes of the Agent, and he understood it. Heck America was under attack, and unknowns in the office could be placing bombs in Federal Buildings. Sam figured he better help his case by limiting the sarcasm. "I am a friend of Bina's, she is tendering her resignation as we stare at each other, and she asked me to help out in procuring some boxes… I think for her personal things." The Agent had lost the panicked look. But Sam wasn't a *friendly;* he was a civilian. Somehow Sam thought he would be offered more disrespect because of the way he addressed an agent as a personal acquaintance. For all Sam knew this idiot probably thought Sam was Coopers' new boy toy. That was what Sam had assumed. And in assuming it Sam didn't make an ass out of himself. The Agent had reiterated, "Organization Fairy? Eh?" Sam wasn't sure if this guy thought he was gay, or just some stupid boy toy for Bina. It didn't matter one way, or another to Sam. He was glad he didn't have to think about his family, if only briefly. Or, even to have to think of having a thoughtful conversation with this Agent that he would never see again. At least he hoped he didn't have to. The Agent watched Sam collect the boxes and proceed towards Cooper's desk. He watched him sit in her chair and start to organize her personal things into the boxes. The Agent departed and Sam waited. Sure enough one at a time three other agents had to get an eyeful of Sam. The scuttlebutt of a resignation was more than they could manage. Sam grimaced each time a new one paraded by. He thought to himself, *If these guys can't pull off an inconspicuous pass by, how could they put a tail on anyone?* Sam was getting tired of this nonsense, and then Bina came back to her desk. Sam was relieved. Bina seemed to be as well. When she saw that Sam hadn't any difficulty getting boxes, she mentioned to him something along the lines of what he had just done as being the most cooperation she had ever gotten while she was there. She asked if he had any problems. He shook his head. "No, nothing to speak of."

"How did it go with the boss?" Sam asked her. She shrugged and looked to him suggesting she either didn't really know or care. "They are always pleasant, Sam. They act surprised instead of relieved." Sam nodded plainly. Bina was busy rifling her personal things, the things Sam had not known about. Before too long they were both on their way out, no other Agents had said anything to her as they left, they hadn't even come by to say goodbye. Sam was sure there was no loss here. He wondered about that.

They had got back to Sam's truck and put the two boxes in the payload part of the truck Sam produced a small tarp from the back of his seat and covered her belongings. They were leaving Hartford, and Bina had a smile on her face. Sam wondered about that smile as well. He wasn't going to be pushy about hearing any details. Patience was what Sam was focused on. Patience for most things was the rule Sam was living by. It was funny, before the murders Sam was patient but not like he was now. Sam was resigned to emptiness, one he had never known, and was loathing of accepting. He figured if Bina needed to say anything or vent she would when she was ready. For the moment she sat back and relaxed while Sam drove.

After a few minutes of driving Sam asked Bina a question. "Bina will you be going down to the farm with Jameson?" She remained in her relaxed position. "I don't think so Sam." "He'll need to go through the training I won't." "Knowing Nathan as I do, I would imagine he'll have an administration orientation for the three of us." She thought about it some more then added, "An abbreviated one I'm sure." Sam nodded and mentioned, "Well, whatever Nathan has in store for us is fine, anything to move closer to getting to the bottom of this." That did get Bina to move. She faced Sam and gazed at him. "Sam you are aware that employing the Feds can be problematic. And that getting to the bottom of circumstances is... well, not always as efficient as the taxpayer would like. I guess what I am trying to tell you is this, catching our guy might be secondary to the feds. In fact, we may come to know whom this individual is, and not be able to do anything until they are through with him. The powers that be may decide to leave him out there as bait." Sam listened as she said it. He didn't think much of what she was saying, but understood it. "Yeah, you said it might be a conspiracy." Sam knew that getting the guy who pulled the trigger wasn't what the CIA was thinking of as a priority. They were interested in where the capture of this guy would lead. This also meant he would have to be afforded liberty or protection for a time. He was also a bit unhappy about that, but patient too. Cooper watched Sam and tried to read him as she said her peace. He was difficult, that was for sure. He didn't seem to be intentionally withholding from her, but she had come to know Sam as quiet. "Sam, I've been after this guy for quite sometime, those idiots at the office were enthused about getting the shooter at first, but as time went on they lost interest." Sam glanced at Bina while he drove. "Bina I meant to ask you… How did you ever work with such apparent idiots?" Cooper laughed. "Are you calling my former work peers idiots?" Sam nodded and confirmed he was. "Yes I am Bina." She giggled again. "Well, Sam, they keep the white collar investigational agents in Hartford because there isn't too much violent crime in the region, or at least that was the previous thinking. Most of those guys don't know much about hunting down violent criminals, they are the corporate investigators, you know because of the Insurance Industry. That is one thing you can count on from the Feds, Sam. They always go after the money." Sam frowned, "Yes, the Martha Stewart's in the world are shaking in their boots." "Well Sam justice today is not so much in time served when there are fines that can be paid." Sam nodded. "Yep Federal Prosecutors seemingly want convictions that are handed to them." Cooper tried to get back to the subject of making Sam aware of the fact that justice of the Federal kind might not be the kind of justice Sam had been thinking about. He knew what she was trying to do, but she after all had the same motivation as Sam did, so he didn't sweat it. "Yeah Bina I get the message you were trying to get at.

By the way, I'm not the guy you need to be worrying about." Cooper had thought about it as being Jake, and told Sam that he was probably right. They kept driving. Sam wasn't looking forward to the business of getting back to Lyme. Erik has work that he finished up, which Sam was going to detest. He'd rather not talk of it before he had to. He would have to compartmentalize the ghastly business so that he could remain functional. Sam knew that at some point he would have to engage the business of grieving. He didn't know how, but he did know that it would happen. Right now, he thought the focus of finding out what had happened, would be a stress reliever that would draw him closer to engaging the grief. Sam thought it was hard to make any sense of the violence that was brought to him. So he didn't waist much time on it. He was doing what he could.

Cooper wanted to be sure that Sam hadn't any misconceptions about the result of the work. She thought about something else to say to Sam to convince him that this journey could be a long one, maybe even a dangerous one. After all these folks didn't want to be known and they would do most anything to remain anonymous. But as she tried to be more specific she came up blank. Sam wasn't interested in long range planning. He was immersed in dealing with getting his family buried, so she just let it be. Sam hadn't presented himself as a weak thinker. He was quick to understand the things she had already told him. These were the things her former employers scoffed at. Sam didn't. Sam thought greatly about that which Cooper had suggested. Truly, she was impressed with how much all of the guys were accepting of her ideas. It was refreshing even if the cost was so horrible. She knew that the CIA would be considering her victim profiling with more zeal than the DOJ. She finally thought that she was entering an atmosphere of inclusion as opposed to being left out of the loop. And, she was happy in that perspective. She was tired of selling her means of law enforcement strategy. She believed it, and now so did the man she was riding with, as well as Nathan. She was surprised at how good she felt. She figured she was closer to her own healing, she just wished she could have brought Sam to her revelation. Cooper asked Sam if he would mind if they listened to some news. He shook his head and said, "No." She reached over and turned on the radio. It had been tuned into the same station, which had informed Sam of his loss. Cooper watched Sam as the broadcast filled the cab of the truck and softened the whir of the tires meeting the road and the engine producing the power, which moved them. Much to her disappointment, Sam hadn't revealed any obvious sign of distress. They drove listening to the radio. Some mindless talk show was the program format and that was enough while she waited for a news report. Sam maintained his focus on the road while she gazed off at the passing roadside. She wondered how she would get Sam to open up… maybe he would as things progressed, maybe it would need some interceding? She didn't know but it had occurred to her. She couldn't recall anyone she knew who was like Sam. He was so private. She wondered what Monica was like, and if she dealt with the man in the same way, or if Sam had been less guarded around her. She figured, wondering about the past she didn't know wasn't productive and she tried to stop, but there was a hunger to know more about Sam. She knew he wasn't as voluntary with tendering information as Jake or Jameson had been. Maybe Sam in the past was Sam of today? She did know that the Sam of the past would have very little to do with her, as he would have been busy living his life as full as it was.

The news finally came on and her new boss was looking to be Porter Goss. President Bush nominated Goss after the Tennant resignation had occurred. All that was left was legislature approval. Cooper didn't know much about this fella, Goss or even much about Tennant. She knew the media was no friend to the Bush Administration or this war on terror. She thought generally anybody serving this President would be controversial. She was just interested in justice. She thought how she understood justice, before she was shot. She definitely had a personal interest in justice now. Before she was a victim, her duty was an oath to uphold justice for the sake of civility. Cooper still considered her oath, the one she was no longer responsible to. She wondered how it would change being involved with the company. Typical arrests, she felt wouldn't be happening as they had. Nathan was more interested in her victim profiling. She figured there were plenty of folks not too interested in losing their jobs, as did Tennant. It came to her... *Nathan was being offered a chance to be more creative about nailing bad guys...* She didn't make any noise... She didn't give Sam a reason to have a traffic accident by her surprising revelation... no she savored this alone. Something in her understanding occurred. A major cosmic aligning had revealed itself as an operations shuffling, which made sense as to why she was at bat. It all made sense to her now. And for this moment she relished the opportunity. Even more, she loved figuring Nathan's motivations out. She knew that was why he appreciated her capabilities. She figured things out that most others wouldn't pay any mind to.

To her surprise, Sam had noticed her smiling and looked at her with a curiosity. She finally noticed him stealing glances at her while he drove. When their eyes met on a stolen glance she smiled and Sam focused on his driving. He made mention to her smile. "Do you know Bina, you look like that cat Sylvester, ya know the one who eats Tweety Bird." Her smile grew larger as she heard Sam describe how she was feeling. She played with Sam a bit. She started looking up towards the roof of the truck cab. All around outside the windows... Sam watched her quizzically. "What are ya doing now?"

Bina giggled, "Why Sam I'm looking for the Little Old Lady's cane to slam down upon my head so I cough up Tweety-Bird." It was Sam's turn to smile and smile he did. As he did, Cooper knew that the Sam of the past was here. Maybe briefly but he was here. She was glad about that. Because knowing the Sam of old made her less fearful of his reticence to talk. She realized although Sam wasn't much of a conversationalist he was not impenetrable. He offered things about himself in interaction. She actually felt much better about Sam's potential as a revealing victim. And, this suited her fine. She was sure Nathan would be as excited as she was when he shared her revelation.

Cooper switched the radio to music and relaxed for the rest of the ride, the news hadn't had much else to interest her. Thankfully, nothing which would have robbed her of seeing Sam's smile over Tweety-Bird... that being nothing to report on the Murphy murder investigations. She lowered her head to the head support on the seat in Sam's truck and closed her eyes. She wanted to enjoy the cosmic aligning as much as she could.

Sam noticed her attempts to recline for the ride. He let himself focus on the road. However, her smile did warm him, at least briefly. For Sam, anything that proved to be a distraction to his loss was welcomed. So he savored her smile as he could. He wished he could express his gratitude, but he didn't want to become a blubbering idiot. There was time for that later, after the effort they were involved in had some resolve. Sam considered Bina's transfer from law enforcement to information gathering. He didn't care too much about law enforcement at this point. His law would be enforced. He would die seeing to it.

He thought about her being in the info end of the business, and how it would be more beneficial to getting to some resolution. Info was what they needed and as far as Sam knew The CIA was the best at tracking down information. At least that is what he understood before planes crashed into buildings here at home. The miles went by while Sam thought on such things and soon he needed to make a decision. He looked back at Bina; she appeared to be taking a power nap. He opted for the *Buried Treasure*. He wondered just what Jake was up to. As he got off Rte 95 and onto the exit ramp, Bina stirred but didn't show any signs of life. She had a small smile on her face… she was probably still feeling good about Tweety-Bird. Sam smiled again thinking of her antics looking for the old ladies cane. He was surprised she knew the cartoon. The smile dissipated as Sam drove through the once familiar place. He wasn't sure he was ready to go to Erik's. And, once that grim business was done, he wouldn't mind being somewhere else.

Chapter 14

Jake was below on the ***Buried Treasure.*** The sun had blazed his numbness into discomfort. He had found the heat disagreeable. He didn't see or hear Sam or Bina coming to roust him from his nap. He heard them come aboard as he woke with a part time hangover. They weren't noisy, and they didn't have cargo as so many other visitors might have coming for an afternoon sail. Sam waited for Bina in the cockpit area. He noticed Jake's figure bumbling towards the head. He suspected Jake may be loopy but decided to wait and see when Jake finished up.

Jake stood before the head and relieved himself. He was thankful for the ability to relieve the uncomfortable expansion of his bladder. His business was regularly celebrated with a badly sung song, or out of tune humming. Today however, Sam didn't notice any other noise besides the stream hitting the toilet. Jake seemed to be obligated to his business for quite some time. His bladder must have been quite full. Something in Sam's head made him think of watermelons… Cooper had noticed that Jake was having an unusually long urination. She looked at Sam with a quizzical look. Sam considered what she was considering. "Bina, did you know Jake is regularly called by the fire department to assist extinguishing fires?"

"So Jake has other talents?" They both laughed. Jake ascended to the cockpit of **The Buried Treasure.** The appearance Jake had said it all. He looked like hell. Jake spoke to the two is a scratchy voice. "That is they used to call me to fire scenes Sam." Cooper spoke up. "Why is it that they don't anymore Jake?" Jake ran his fingers through his bird's nest of a head of hair and blearily looked to Cooper. "Agent Cooper, or former Agent Cooper… The new chief must have been jealous. My hose is nicer than all of theirs." Sam expected it and smiled. It was an old joke they ran on the unsuspecting, Bina just happened to be available. She looked at Jake ready to say something, Jake interrupted. "Oh, yeah, my hose has more pressure too."

Cooper felt as though she was in some fraternal bragging contest. Her original thought was silenced and she started to formulate a comeback in her mind. She was a little groggy from her nap so it would have to be timed. She would wait, and let Jake have it at some point in the future. These two were pretty good with the set up and delivery of a punch line. Kind of like a Vaudeville Act. They just didn't know, that in their presence, was an expert heckler. "So you are no longer an employee of the DOJ?"

Cooper responded to affirm Jake's comment. "No, Jake, I am no longer an agent of the DOJ." Jake was comfortable with being foolish so he continued with the previous theme. "That reminds me, I need to get a help wanted sign on the dock." Sam just kept quiet. He wasn't sure where Jake was going with this last comment. Cooper walked right into it. "I am unemployed these days, what are ya hiring for?" Jake looked at Cooper and held out for a second. "Ah the position is… hose roller." She laughed, as did Sam. "I guess that isn't an hourly compensated job, eh Jake?" Sam was curious now he hadn't expected the redirect from Cooper. Jake was slow in his thinking, Cooper had taken him by surprise. "Yeah, Jake, rolling your hose takes all of what, a minute or two?" Sam laughed out loud while Jake panicked. Cooper just sat there waiting to see if Jake could outdo her ribbing. Jake was still too numb to figure a comeback so he remained silent, almost if he were chastised. After a couple of seconds, he rose to go to the galley. He was parched and needed to hydrate himself. He produced a tall glass of water and drank it. Once the water settled, he refilled the glass and joined the other two, topside.

Cooper couldn't resist. "Recharging the hose, Jake?" She just giggled. Jake retorted. "That is pretty good for someone who has no hose there Cooper." Sam shook his head, he sensed a verbal chess match developing and he knew that Jake didn't know he was in check. He just sat back and waited to see if Cooper was going to checkmate Jake. "That is right Jake, I have no hose of my own... but I know plenty of firemen and non firemen, and all of them bring theirs as you bring yours. And Jake, secretly I am a pyromaniac, so I could require the use of many hoses if I sought to, yours might be special to you, but to me it is just another hose."

Sam thoroughly enjoyed this banter. He enjoyed performing the jokes with Jake on the unsuspecting. But to see Jake getting worked over, with the tables turned, was delicious, especially by a woman he wanted to play on. Cooper had not only held her own she had laid it out to Jake. He was done, and when he lit a cigar Sam knew it. Cooper wasn't finished though. After Jake had a long drag on that cigar she timed it perfectly at his exhalation. "Yeah Jake there ya go, getting your fingers around something that's worth more than a minute or two, it must be nice to have a familiar substitute after the pumping is done?" Sam was beside himself. He couldn't bust out laughing so he went below to get a soda or something for himself. "Hey over-qualified hose roller, do you want something to wet your whistle?" Sam was being courteous. Cooper responded positively. "Sure Sam that would be refreshing thanks." When Sam was finished he came topside with the drinks. He offered Cooper a nice sparkling glass of ice water. She took her beverage and had a nice long slow sip. "Nothing like a little ice in the water, to cool it off eh Sam?" Sam nodded. "Yes ma'am." Jake sat with his glass of water without ice. He was lost. His water had no ice and his cigar had been compared to a size thing. Both Cooper and Sam looked at him and busted out laughing. Jake put his cigar into his mouth and smoked. "Ah, to the hell with both of ya. I'll find someone willing to roll my hose and appreciate my fine Cuban Cigars." Cooper was on a roll and kept going. "Well, Jake, it is a good thing I am no longer FBI." She waited for the response, and Jake was still not enjoying the numbness from earlier. "Okay Cooper, tell me why it is a good thing you aren't FBI?"

"Well Jake, if I was still FBI, I'd have to confiscate your fine Cuban Cigar's, then you'd be left with your flat hose." She busted out laughing. Sam had not ever seen Jake bested like this. He even thought about the *auxiliary power thing*. Nope, Bina had topped that one, Jake didn't have the sailing as a payback, to put those enjoying merriment at his expenses in their places. Sam had had enough and he was sure Jake did too. "Bina, would you be so kind as to find a fork?" She looked at Sam and understood. "You think he is done, is that your point Sam?" Sam nodded. Jake frowned.

Sam lit a cigarette and sipped his water. He sat back expecting to find out what Jake had to tell them. Cooper was snuggling up to Jake; she had let him have it but good and now she was trying to make him feel better about his flat hose and large Cuban Cigar. "Oh, Jake, I'm sure your hose is the best hose on the truck. If you would like I'll roll your hose for ya." Jake just sat back and said, "Nope, there will be no application taken from an over qualified hose roller, not here and not today." Cooper pouted. Sam watched her. He couldn't help to think, that is how Monica used to carry on with Jake. Monica was not as quick as Bina. Monica never competed with men in a professional setting like Bina had, so she couldn't have nailed Jake as Bina did.

As brilliant as Bina was, with working over Jake, she hadn't noticed what Sam had felt in comparison. Sam was drawn to the reality of why they were all together. That is to find out who did this. When she looked at Sam she noticed he wasn't enjoying the ribbing anymore. Something had changed. She wished she had been more aware of it, but neither she nor Jake knew it. And more than likely would never know. This was part of the silence that Cooper had been worried about thinking of Sam. One minute they were enjoying a laugh the next... well it was as if someone had died.

Jake had an idea about what Sam was thinking on, he wasn't sure as in knowing, but he did decide to change the subject quickly. He read the same thing as Cooper did about his friend. The deck of *The Buried Treasure* fell silent. Both Jake and Cooper were trying to think of what to say when Sam had spoken up. "I need to take care of some business." As Sam said business, both knew what he meant. Erik had his family. Jake again was surprised and begged Sam, "Give me a minute I'll be ready in the shake of a stick." Sam shook his head, "No, Jake, I think I got this one alone. I know they were important to you but I need this time for myself." Jake stopped trying to plead with Sam realizing that it was useless. "Okay Sam, you go tend to your business, we'll find something to do."

Cooper was shocked a bit as well.

She thought Sam might need some support. She followed Jake's lead and suggested hooking up with Jameson or Hendrick. She felt this acknowledged Sam's need to be alone. She didn't want to be intrusive. As soon as Sam had said it, he was disembarking *The Buried Treasure.* Both watched Sam as he walked down the dock silently.

Both of them, Jake and Cooper, sat silently for a spell. They each thought of the solemnity Sam left by. The shenanigans were over. Cooper wondered how Sam had such a change of heart, so quickly, and completely. Jake didn't think much about it because he knew that his friend was hurting. More than he ever knew Sam to hurt before.

"Well Cooper, I was trying to get sobered up for what I thought was gonna be a downer. That worked out real well for me." Cooper was still thinking on the abruptness by which Sam left. She simply said, "Sober is good." Jake heard what she said. He figured about as much. One minute she is ripping him apart, the next she can't even acknowledge a joke. "Jake… Why do you think Sam left so quickly?"

"Quickly, I didn't expect Sam to be here carrying on for so long. I'd have figured he would have collected me and went to Erik's." Cooper thought about what Jake had said. At first, she thought Jake might have offered her a personal insight about Sam. She thought some more to match her cosmic moment to Sam's perceived haste. *If it was as Jake had said, that Sam had spent time he otherwise wouldn't have here on the boat, just what was she missing? She was missing nothing.... Sam was being Sam as he had in the past like he was today.* "Jake I had seen it a different way. I didn't realize the time thing with Sam." Jake thought some about what Cooper was saying.

"Cooper you had mentioned victim profiling. And I believe it was to catch the perp?"

Cooper nodded affirming his query. "Well, Sam isn't looking to catch his perp. He is a survivor of many victims, namely his family, and he is off for a ghastly viewing. Something I don't think he ever contemplated. I imagine Sam could have seen himself laid out before his family, or even his wife Monica laid out before him and the kids." Cooper sat and listened; she knew Jake's point would be made. "But never as the only one left.... He is a Man Apart Cooper. He is a Man Apart. Until he puts some of himself together, you get pretty much what ya see." Cooper again thought on what Jake had said.

"I guess, Jake, I'm just wondering what Sam was like compared to who he is now." She paused. "And if that makes any sense?"

"Hmmmmm... makes perfect sense to me." After he said it, he

went down for some more water. He left Cooper a bit confused. He came back up top with water and no ice. Jake lounged; when he looked to Cooper she seemed troubled, maybe confused as far as Jake could see. He sipped his water. After that the cigar was placed back into his mouth. "Look here Cooper… what you seek I believe you will find. I just think you are working it too hard." She looked into Jakes eyes trying to understand what he was getting at. Jake sipped more of his water. "Alright let me try this way. Sam, that poor soul who you think left hastily, while we were goofing off, he got some chuckles in, mostly at my expense and your wit. He was taking a break from hurting, and enjoying it. Maybe something like a split second gave him a direct path to remembering the hurt. Something like you and me giving it to each other. Monica and I, we were royal ball busters… sometimes Sam would get up and walk away then. Whatever Sam's reasoning is, it has always been. Nobody ever asked, and he rarely told." Cooper seemed to lighten up a bit to Jake but this young one had something in her craw. Jake wasn't done explaining something to her. He wished he knew how to articulate it.

She changed the subject almost like Sam left. "Jake would you like to go see Jameson, I have a feeling he has some news…" Jake winked. "Sounds like a fine idea Cooper, guess you can drive my truck eh?" She nodded and they were off to see Jameson.

269

Chapter 15

Sam was driving in his truck. He passed Erik's several times. Sam knew well enough that he was expected. He did however lack some confidence. Confidence in being a man he was only getting to know in the short time since their murders. He knew Erik would be sensitive and willing to help out, hell he already did. He knew they were waiting for him. He just couldn't believe he had to do this. He didn't know how to do this. And, for the first time, all the things he had to know how to do, were motivated by what waited inside Erik's, for viewing. Of all the things Sam feared, he had never considered this as one of them. It was utterly inconceivable to him. Realizing that the inconceivable was a reality, Sam pulled over on a gravel shoulder wide enough for a large truck. Sam reached for his wallet... he flipped open the plastic picture holder and thumbed through the photos. He needed to remember how they looked to him. Somehow he knew that seeing them would be a difficult image to deal with for the rest of his days. He was thinking these photos he held, of them living, might minimize, in some manner, the nightmare of surviving them. When he thumbed to Monica, her picture affected him. All of them did, but Monica's was the most difficult. All the love he had for them was from her fertility. She was his life. Sam's eyes weld up. He blinked and breathed trying to control irrationality. A single tear fell off his eyelashes. The thud of the tear drove home the emptiness Sam was coming to know. What Sam couldn't say out loud he internalized. His teeth grinded, his face squinched. To anyone on the road Sam might have looked like he was in a serious regret. He folded up the wallet and checked the road behind him, it was clear. He began the drive again, this time he was sure he had the ability to turn into Erik's parking lot. This place, this town was all together too painful for him. He didn't want the charity people who knew him would afford him. He didn't want to be known as a widower, when he had been a husband and father. He didn't want to be a businessman here either. The love of his work soured. Sam realized they weren't here anymore, and life just couldn't go on with Sam surviving.

This thing needed righting. Sam was torn between paying respects to the dead and finding accountability. Not only accountability, but to find out who thought they had a right to leave him with so little. He wanted an explanation. He was certain that after burying his loved ones his only goal was to find the person so he could force an explanation. And, Sam was plum out of compassion. He hoped that once whoever was going to answer for this was completely clear about this explanation. Sam's determination was no longer being managed by the needs of a husband and father. He was single-minded about this for he had already accomplished more than most in his lifetime. Getting to those who were accountable was a certainty; time meant nothing.

Once again Sam approached Erik's. He turned on his blinker as he had the several times he attempted the turn and failed at today. He slowed down for the turn and willed his truck to turn right. He overcame his unwanted task as he parked. The ignition needed to be turned off before he could move to the entry and he needed to will his hand to the column. It responded and the trucks roar was silenced. Now the door needed opening. Sam had never thought about the details of driving or shutting a motor off like this before, it was frightening. Sam usually had a list of things, which needed doing while driving. He didn't know who he would be, he only knew how he would be, and his hand opened the truck door because getting past this was the first step in understanding who he would be. He slid off the seat and his feet took the load up underneath him. Another step, and his truck door became securely closed. Another step, and he was walking towards the entry to his nightmare. Sams' rectum and scrotum were tightening up; his chest was heavy, every step… agonizing. He thought going to the gallows might be easier than this. Sam was losing patience with his fear. He hoped Erik wouldn't be a victim of him losing control of his loathing of this. He found his hand on the door. Erik had been at the reception area directly behind the door, when he saw Sam he hurried towards the entry. Sam wasn't waiting for the door to be opened by Erik; he was just contemplating the entry. Erik seemed to notice this as he slowed his pace down. Sam had opened the door as Erik had gotten to the entry. Erik extended his hand to greet Sam through the door. The men's hands clasped and Erik guided Sam into the reception area. Eriks' grasp was pacifying to Sam.

He didn't know how, but he figured he had his practice. Erik didn't let go until Sam looked into his eyes. And then, his grip was released only after he mentioned some simple words. "Sam, greeting people I know, is always unpleasant. Even those I don't know are difficult." He released Sams' hand as his other hand rose to the back of Sams' shoulder. He somehow knew Sam's having difficulty in proceeding forward. He escorted him so that Sam felt himself floating effortlessly to where the tides of life left the debris exquisitely presented in a peaceful end, like deadwood cast upon a storm's high tide line. Sam might have tried to hesitate, but Erik had an overwhelming and calming grace as he moved Sam forward. Sam had survived the storm his family had not and without a possibility to stop, he came upon them. Thoughtfully, Erik had a chair at the end of the walk directly in front of them. Sam put the chair to his advantage. He was experiencing a loss of equilibrium. The feet that took up the load from sliding off his truck seat were failing him now. Once Sam was seated Erik sat next to him in another chair.

Both men sat in silence. Sam tried to say something and Erik raised his index finger to his lips. "My experience Sam is to just sit at the start, accept the reality and deal with it as only you can." Sam listened to him intently as though every word counted, because it did. Sam knew one thing about sitting here... he must be honorable, not for them but for himself, because he would be doing the living. Sam nodded towards Erik, and he responded by excusing himself with a promise to be back directly. He also said Sam's legs might be better suited to carry the load ahead after a short sit. And then Erik was gone. Sam sat in his newest friend's presence while his past loves' lie in front of him. This new friend was silence... No more bickering between the kids. No more favors for Monica, and no more surprises. All of the things, which made the comfortable noise of his family alive, were here. They however were not, and maybe that is what Erik had meant. Maybe what Erik had meant was recalling the noise of his family in silence. Sam's trepidation in getting here was long forgotten. He was now grateful. He was at home. Sam suddenly felt as though allowing some tears to flow could be a survivable thing. His eyes started a consistent but impatient flowing, and to Sam it felt good. Sam realized his runny nose would be in need of attention; his intention was to maintain some composure. He scanned the area and there were tissue supplies everywhere. Sam could wait to move. He sized up his legs and feet. They had felt like they had strengthened, more to what he expected. He shifted his cheeks on the chair and separated his feet.

His hands reached for the other chair back, he used it to support his rising. One step and another and Sam's nose was being dried by a facial tissue. He always thought these things could have more to them. It always-seemed one was never enough so he took a handful of them. Maybe they were a security for Sam? He now had the ability to gaze upon them. His crying ceased, and his sniffling abated, they were here. They were beautiful, each one of them. He was stilled at their radiance. They looked as they did when he saw them sleeping peacefully. Erik was a master of his work. Sam walked by each of them. He touched his children on the faces and felt cold softness. They were never supposed to be here like this for him.... Never.

He swallowed his hurt of all the impossible possibilities these children of his would never experience. He was robbed of seeing them through all the future good and bad times. Of all the heartthrobs and heartbreaks they would share with him and their mother. All silenced. His rage was compressed in this room of silence, hardened and hidden away from his being. His memories of this time needed clarity. Rage was not needed, love was. And Sam's love for them, even here, was observable.

Erik had rejoined Sam without him knowing. And Erik saw a healthy interaction. He knew although Sam's road was a very tough one, he would make it through. Erik had seen people wail and carry on as a display of uncontrollable emotion, which was later regretted. The degree of regret was heightened by Erik's reuniting of the survivors of loved ones. Some never got over it, and they came back as parcels. Erik didn't see this in Sam and he was pleased. He left Sam to take his steps.

Sam had finished doting on his children. He was brief, but not hasty. His wife was waiting, as she had in life. She knew where Sams' heart ended, it was with her. Sams' throat tightened. If Monica could see Sam, her heart would burst for him. He gazed upon his beloved. She was beautiful, not a nightmare. He felt foolish thinking so. She would understand if she could. He rested his head upon her chest as he had during the more difficult times they had experienced. She never doubted Sam in his thinking... sometimes she offered him sight that only gave him a greater determination to accomplish what he thought would make them happy. And, that he did. She afforded Sam that of a King, and it was only a Queen's ability to do so. Sam worshipped her, because she was a large part of him. He apologized softly to her. His lips touched hers only to find saddened loss. Like he realized on that terrible night, she would never again touch his flesh. But here, in this silence, his heart closed. Like it had with the rage, it was hidden; put away. He touched her face once more and stood up. He returned to the seat he had before. He sat for a bit, letting a stream of thoughts plague him. They were sorrowful, sad and sometimes happy. His mind embraced these things with a thirst he had never known before and would likely never experience later.

Erik had rejoined him. "I was here earlier Sam, you were in a moment of silence." Sam looked at Erik and nodded. Sam wanted to express to Erik how foolish he felt but didn't. He wanted to say that before being here, he thought this was his worst nightmare, but didn't. He wanted to tell Erik how much he appreciated his professionalism but didn't. He just gazed at them Erik sat next to Sam for a time without saying a word... after a reasonable amount of time Erik had spoken to Sam as he did seating him here. "Sam you have overcome the most difficult part of this journey... you have faced it and reckoned with it. There is nothing more to do here except welcome those who shared their love and thank them... and I have taken the liberty of making the announcements. Sam...it doesn't get any easier." Erik stood up holding Sam's arm, lifting him out of the chair. "We must leave them now Sam, being here too long is not good for the healing. You'll see them once more, and you'll also see how many others loved them or just thought highly of them." Sam didn't want to leave but Erik urged him and Erik allowed this to be less than a nightmare so Sam listened. He rose and left them. Erik had them safe. He would also be back for them as Erik had said. Sam and Erik's hands met once again and while the clasp was the same as before it wasn't a guiding hand, but a releasing hand that Sam felt. And, release was good.

Sam walked to his truck and got into it. He started driving towards nowhere. He tried to think of what to do. He drew a blank. This was more of the new silence he would use to remember the noisy past. The silence wasn't bad while he was remembering the noise. Sam remembered for several miles before he found himself pulling up to *The Buried Treasure.* The memories were better than the silence, but both needed to end. Sam was overwhelmed. He knew that upon *The Buried Treasure* memories could be silenced with the amply supplied bar on board. Maybe he would be lulled to peace, thinking of the loving he and Monica shared upon this vessel. Sam thought of the irony, his treasure would be buried soon while he sat on *The Buried Treasure* trying to forget. Sam got on the boat and turned on a small light. It was just enough light to select his poison. He shook his head and poured himself a glass of Bourbon, a tall glass. He raised the glass to his mouth and accepted the biting warmth. His body quivered after ingesting a healthy gulp. He lowered the glass to the center table and lit a smoke. There he began his treatment of ending the battle raging in his head. Soon it would be quiet; soon he wouldn't care. The booze was serving its purpose. Sam finished his drink about the same time he finished the smoke. He got up repeating the dosage again, and again until he could do so no longer.

Chapter 16

Jake and Cooper saw Hendrick at the Lyme Police Station. They hadn't realized that Jameson was expeditiously excused from the building and the job. Hendrick couldn't offer too much as to how the meeting with the Chief had gone. Jameson simply stated that he was to be in Washington tomorrow. Neither Jake nor Cooper were surprised at the news, but they were surprised that he wasn't here. Hendrick showed Cooper the DOT report, she looked it over and seemed satisfied. Hendrick followed up on his progress after Cooper was finished.

"I made some calls in Northern New York, I have a friend working with border patrol. He said the info was already posted and most had their eyes peeled for Jackson." Cooper was impressed, not that she had to be, she knew the reach of info from a Federal All Points Bulletin was as effective, if not more so than the new Amber Alerts. "Good work Hendrick." Cooper gave credit when it was due. "You're thinking

Jackson is on a northern evasion pattern?" Hendrick nodded. Jake asked the obvious question. "Why north?" Hendrick sighed; he was expecting to have to answer for his reasoning. He himself wasn't sure but the likelihood was north.

"Well, Jake, Northward evasion just makes more sense. It is an educated guess at best, but considering the theory of the crime, the fact that it may be a conspiracy, and the notion that terrorism may be behind it... leaves me to think the mastermind of this would likely be in a non-friendly country. Canada and her population have many gripes against us here in the states, and their policy allowed the 9/11 terrorists entry into this country. The odds are Jackson is being told how to move, so he must have a handler. You know him better than anyone else here. Is he smart enough to pull this off without some kind of help?" Jake thought of the question... he figured Hendrick's reasoning was solid enough, but he wasn't betting on anything until Jackson was securely confined, and available for questioning. Hendrick knew that Jake still had a sense of skepticism. He also knew it was a valid concern. "Jake, I understand you need to see to believe... however, an all points bulletin notifies all those responsible. There will be eyes looking for him at every conceivable exit point of the country." Cooper had some input as well. "Jake they are not only covering exit points, they are thinking of how he may be trying to deceive them. There is a slim chance that he may get away, but doubtful. After all this fella is a material witness of the killing of a family... that tends to motivate people to the core beliefs many have. That is how they do their job, and how they make a difference. Nobody will ever tell you this, but more attention is paid to the circumstances of the crime, and this is one of those crimes that sticks in all guts."

Jake seemed to understand just what was being said. His mouth watered at the possibility of knowing Jackson wasn't going to see it coming. "Do you both think he has any idea of how small his world has become?" Both Cooper and Hendrick paused to consider their answers. Hendrick needed less time to formulate his answer. "I don't think it is likely Jackson knows his peril." "I think the people who are directing Jackson know his peril or at least the possibilities of their own if he gets grabbed." Cooper nodded in agreement. "It is imperative that we get him first... if these folks know we are close, Jackson will turn up as remains. Killing the loose end is the easiest manner to avoid being known."

They sat considering all the posturing. Hendrick spoke up as an after thought. "By the way, Keniestyosky, the patrolman Jameson seemed to be so fond of is now questioning all of the women Jackson knew. I have a feeling we will be getting some direction from those results." Cooper seemed to be hopeful by that news. "Yes, I didn't want to become lead on this one, but it was out of my hands. Jameson is off to greener pastures."

"All Keniestyosky needed was some refined motivation. Come to think of it, Jameson had exhibited an exceptional means of choosing the right man for the job." Hendrick wondered aloud. "I guess I never saw him with that ability. I am sure he will do well in the CIA."

Cooper was relieved to here Hendrick was the lead locally. Although they had gotten off on the wrong foot, Hendrick was redeeming himself with a welcomed professionalism.

Jake forever the wise guy stated the obvious. "So the retirement is on hold?" Hendrick actually welcomed the comment. It just wasn't going to be Jake's day for being class clown. "Yes, Jake, my retirement has been delayed. Not indefinitely, there is only so much the locals can do when the perpetrator has entered the jurisdiction of the Feds. Unlike other cops, I welcome the help. Turf wars only impede the seeking of justice. So, while you are all chasing down this known bad guy and unknown other bad guys, I'll be the donut eating liaison from where it all started, and getting paid for it."

Cooper laughed out loud. She shook her head and told Jake that he might have wanted to stay at *The Buried Treasure.* He wouldn't have been able to be so cute from his deck, and would have certainly had less abuse from the Sea Gulls. Jake understood her point. "Geez I knew I forgot to turn on the abuse clock, I usually get double time for abuse and taking it." "Maybe the Chief could put in some expense paperwork for you to be compensated?" It was Hendricks chance to laugh. "Hell, Jake, the only thing the Chief is doing is letting folks go, cutting his expenses for the fine taxpayers of Lyme. I'd be surprised if he would appreciate having to pay for your just deserts." Jake frowned, "Well, all a guy can do is try."

Cooper had enough of this. "Detective, can you point us in the direction of Jameson's last known where-abouts? Sure I can Cooper, he is at his house packing I suppose. That is where Keniestyosky was delivering him." She nodded, and thanked Hendricks for the 411. "Let's go find the young detective, Jake." And they were off. Hendrick put his face back into some paperwork.

Cooper liked the fact that this area was not far from anything; a short car drive and they would be knocking on Jameson's door. She did have an affinity for his home. She felt good there. Jake was thinking of something, she could feel it. "What are you thinking of Jake?" Jake wasn't sure about much, but he was thinking about how all of this would be behind them here shortly. Things were moving relatively fast and planning wasn't part of it. "I'm not sure of what it is I'm thinking Cooper. I sense that we won't be here for much longer. This investigation is being realigned before our very eyes. The geographical implications are vast." She nodded as she listened. "I guess I was wondering how I would be outfitting *The Buried Treasure.*" This planning by Jake had taken her by surprise. Once she heard it she knew what he meant.

There were difficulties to contend with if Jake wanted to use *The Buried Treasure* as a home base, so to speak. Nothing unmanageable, just more details, details that Nathan could have covered if she had known to tell him. She figured there would be plenty of time to talk with Nathan after a conversation with Jameson. And, the more she thought of it, the better it sounded using *The Buried Treasure* as a home base. She filed it for later reference, another mental note. They were coming to Jameson's home. She wondered if he was frantic or calm, cool and collected. They would soon find out. They parked in his driveway and exited the car. Jake seemed to be impressed. He hadn't imagined Jameson to have such taste. Then again why would he? Jake didn't know that Jameson's fiancée had been killed on 9/11, and that she was also a very big part of his life. She, like Monica, had a major unseen part in developing the man. And without her being there it was easy to make such a mistake. Jake wasn't aware of such things, the women he knew were for lesser purposes. Not that anything was wrong about that fact, just different. Cooper thought Jake may have known how women of his friends were a huge part of their lives, but she wondered if Jake had ever known how it was to be a part of something like that. It was one thing to have married friends as a bachelor, and to even be a part of the friends' family, but it could never replace having a family for oneself.

The door was open as they approached Jameson's entry. They peered into the doorway to see if Jameson was readily available. Cooper rang the doorbell and from the back of the house Jameson yelled out that it was open. The two entered and Jameson met them. Jameson stated that he had been packing some things, and that he was glad to see that his guests included Cooper. "I was wondering if you had any advice as to what I should be packing for The Farm." Cooper shook her head. "No, Jameson, I'm sorry I don't, however I need to talk with Nathan and I'll inquire for you." A smile appeared on Jamesons' face he looked towards Jake and asked how he was doing since this morning. Jake responded, "I'm not sure Jameson, things appear to be very fluid. Heck Cooper and Sam came to wake me up, then, Cooper here, had her share of busting my backside." "Then Sam headed off to see his family at Erik's." This tidbit caught Jameson's attention. "You mean he went alone?" They both nodded. Jameson seemed to be dismayed at the fact that Sam had went alone. "Geez, I would think he could have used some support. I was sure Sam would have taken you Jake, at the very least." Jake just shrugged. Cooper didn't say anything to respond. "Well, do you know where he is now?" Both of them shook their heads. Jameson was at a loss. He wasn't sure about leaving Sam alone with such a difficult thing to face. Jake realized that maybe Jameson was questioning their neglect of his friend. He put an end to Jamesons' worry. "Look here young Jameson, Sam is a man who does what he wants to do. He didn't ask us to go, he simply said that he had some unwanted business to take care of, then, he left." Cooper confirmed all that Jake had said with a nod. Jameson processed the information and asked them if they had a thirst or if they wanted a bite. They both passed. Cooper looked at her watch, she wondered if Nathan would still be at the office, she figured he might be and excused herself to use Jameson's phone. She used the phone in the kitchen and left the two men alone.

"Jake do you think Sam is okay?"

"I don't know Jameson. I imagine he is alright. We'll find out before too long."

"I guess it seems unorthodox for me to see you not with Sam. It's probably silly to think of you two in such a way, but we have come to know you together. Where one of you was, the other was close by." Jake thought on all that was said to him and about the fact that Sam and Jake had been paling around. Jake wondered why people thought that they were inseparable. He didn't think that these new compadres knew Sam and him so well, only as they could observe the recent past as the norm. Jake accepted this because it was reasonable while incorrect. Jake took a seat in the room; he was tired. After he did, he spoke to Jameson. "I don't think you should concern yourself with packing too much Jameson, I have a feeling most of what you need will be there." Jameson simply offered, "You're probably right about that Jake."

"Let me ask you something Jameson…. Do ya think you're ready for this?" Jameson took a seat across from Jake. After he sat down he tried to focus. "Jake… I'm not sure about too much of anything. The new position is more than I could ever have imagined for myself, I am extremely excited about it. I think you asked if I was ready for it?" Jake nodded. "I sure hope so. But for right now, the priority is getting these bastards who made Sam's life so difficult. I'm hopeful that this transfer will be play a more positive role in that respect." Jake smiled. "Don't worry about that Jameson, from what I know about the CIA, they are the cats meow in uncovering information that is meant to be secret." Jameson seemed to be enjoying that very thought. He knew that being a detective in a local law enforcement community would be nothing in comparison to the expanse of The CIA.

As the men were sitting contemplating the possibilities of what was coming, Cooper returned to the room. Jake smiled; he was dying to hear all that she had to say. "Did you get through to your friend Nathan Cooper?" Cooper found a seat next to Jameson. "I sure did Jake." She stretched her arms. She knew the guys were waiting to hear what the conversation was about. She enjoyed the little game, even though Jake wasn't taking the bait. His sobering up represented a lost opportunity she enjoyed earlier. She couldn't keep Jameson waiting though. "Jake Nathan can't wait to meet you so he can tell you what you need to do." Jake laughed. "I hope he thinks saying things, which don't matter is standard business." She frowned at Jake. "Jameson, Nathan said to come packed for a long weekend; he said most of what you will need will be there." Jake puffed himself up a bit Cooper was unsure as to why. She ignored it.

"He also said there is a plane ticket waiting for you at T.F. Green airport in RI. You will need to be there for 6am. He also said be punctual with an ID, the flight leaves as soon as you get there." Jake found this to be delicious. "Well, Jameson, I guess you weren't ready for that." Jake remained silent, and waited for a response. Jameson cleared his throat with an "*ahem.*" "Jake I didn't expect that at all, quite honestly, I don't think the departure time clears any of it up for me either." Cooper nudged Jameson, "That is a good plan Jameson." Jake smiled he offered Jameson advice directly. "Yeah, Jameson, stay honest and remain confused… Haha look how far it has gotten ya. No, wait, departures, on Corporate Jets." Cooper smiled at Jakes remarks, as did Jameson. "Yep, Young Jameson you hit the lottery." Jake was genuinely happy for Jameson. He was celebratory for the time, it was expected. He was tired too. He wished he could sit here and feel good with these two who were departing in the morning, but there were a couple of things Jake needed to do. He let out a grumble. "Why don't you two kids get your day straight, and that would be tomorrow. There are a few things I need to do before the real celebrating can begin. I'll stop back when I'm done." He stood up and suggested some dinner after he got back. Everyone was agreeable and he took his leave. Cooper and Jameson didn't see it coming before Jake excused himself, but they did understand when he let them know that he needed to leave. They did need to spend time to have a mutual strategy for tomorrow so they did.

Jake got into his truck and started it. He put one of his cigars into his mouth and lit it. After he enjoyed a long puff of it he put the truck into gear and made his way to Eriks. He hoped Sam was all right. And Erik was the last guy to see Sam.

Chapter 17

Jake didn't have the issues which Sam did turning into Eriks'. Jake didn't see Sams' truck but went to the door anyway. He entered to an empty reception area. Jake knew he would be seeing Erik soon; his door tripped a building wide notification that guests were in the reception area. A sign indicated a dedicated portion of the funeral home to The Murphy Family. Another sign directed other funeral parties elsewhere. Jake wouldn't be waiting on Erik too long. He hated the thought of interrupting Eric preparing a body. To Jake, the whole process burying someone was morbid, and excessively costly. Dying for Jake was just another part of life. He had trouble with being killed. And, as far as burial preparation, Jake wouldn't mind being cremated. To him, burying a corpse was ineffective land management. Tributes to the dead after they were dead sure never helped anyone out, except of course the gravedigger. Jake started in the direction of Monica and the kids.

Hell, Erik could find him. He found himself where Sam needed the seat, and moved to the caskets. Unlike Sam he visited Monica first…. Jake looked at Monica softly. His eyes welled up as he said hello. "I never thought this was possible Monica…. Both me and Sam are in shock Hun." He let the back of his hand brush against her forehead, and cheekbone. He sniffled some. "I'm looking out for him the best I can but you know Sam. Monica… we are mad. Hell, I'm mad. We're working on it, we are gonna find them bad folks. I don't know how it will be except to say that you are a huge void in our lives now. And that void needs some filling to be as whole as it can be again. Oh Monica…. Sam misses ya something awful. He misses the kids. Don't worry Monica, I'll be there as much as I can for him." Jake got up and went to the kids…

Erik had gone to the reception area only to hear Jake talking. He followed the voice and came upon Jake telling Monica he'd be taking care of Sam. Erik watched Jake move to the children. He spoke to each of them as he had with Monica. Erik waited for Jake to finish up. He would rather let Jake turn to see him, rather than sneak up on him. Jake made Erik weary.

Jake saw Erik and held his hand out. "Hello Eric, ya caught me having a word, did ya?" Erik nodded towards Jakes question. He spoke to Jake without explanation. "Sorry for the loss Jake. Sam was here about an hour ago." Jake looked at Erik. "Thanks on both accounts

Erik." Erik nodded. "How was Sam, when ya saw him?"

"The whole experience will be very difficult for him, but I think he'll be okay." Erik wasn't sure if what he said should have been worded differently. He waited for Jake to continue. "I think that is accurate Erik. Do you have any idea of Sam's direction?"

Erik thought of departure and said, "No, Jake, I sure don't. He left in command of himself, if that helps."

"Yeah, it does, thanks again Erik, I guess I'll be seeing ya later on. By the way, nice work on them." Jake smiled. "Thanks Jake, that helps me out." Jake winked on his way out the door. Erik was glad Jake was on his way.

Jake got back into his truck without haste. He was thinking Sam might have found himself at **The Buried Treasure.** He re-ignited his cigar as he started his truck. He couldn't help but think how Erik saw things. Always seeing people at their worst, he knew he couldn't do it. Jake always thought folks who made their living with the dead were plain old weird anyways. He started his search again by driving off towards his last hunch. It wouldn't be long until he would need more thinking on finding Sam. Jake thought sincerely that Erik did do a nice job with them. He also thought Erik tried hard to answer considerately. He didn't know if Erik spoke to him as he did with others. He didn't think so. The business of displaying the dead was something Jake involved himself with rarely. He was the kind of guy who remembered the living. He was anxious to know the condition of Sam, hell he knew where his family was and it sucked.

Jake pulled up to the marina; he eased his concern seeing Sam's truck there. He noticed the lights were low; maybe Sam was just relaxing? Jake loved walking up to *The Buried Treasure.* He never missed an opportunity to enjoy her beauty. He hoped Sam was finding some peace on board. As Jake approached, he was glad not to hear wailing. He hated men crying. He hated it when he did it. He didn't know why, and he didn't care. He boarded and worked his way down to the cabin. Jake had apprehension briefly before he located Sam. Sam's efforts were that which Jake might expect. Jake leaned over and got the ashtray Sam had been using. He picked up the bottle Sam almost emptied. Jake spoke out even though nobody would hear. "It figures." He looked at Sam breathing; stone drunk. He threw a blanket on him, and left Sam were he found him. Sam checked the rest of his love… everything seemed ship shape. He worried about the armaments on board and Sam not having any idea. Jake went back up top and looked about *The Buried Treasure.* Nobody was really around except the usual. That was a good thing.

Jake thought of what he might want to pick up for an extended sail or for just porting about. He felt as though Mid-Atlantic waters might be their new home for a bit. Sam thought about Jameson down at the Farm and wondered if they would be ready for him? He laughed to himself. He produced a fresh cigar and lit it up. Jameson at the Farm, the thought of it was humorous to Jake. Somehow he thought Cooper was finally going to the place, which would be most advantageous for her. Wherever the investigation led is where he and Sam would call home. He felt as though tonight would be a great time to sail a bit. He liked night sailing. But Sam needed the rest without motion. And, he had intended on rejoining Cooper and Jameson. He scanned the surrounding area again as he disembarked his love. All seemed to be normal. He made his way back to the truck. Then back to Jameson's. He sucked on his cigar as he always did. Most of what he needed to see to would happen tomorrow or the following day. He knew Sam was looking forward to some different scenery. Sam was facing memories he wanted to hold back. Maybe it wasn't holding the memories back? Maybe familiar things were just not assaulting him. Whatever it was to Sam, he was on his way to find out just what that meant for them. He made his way back to Jameson's.

Jake drove along while he formulated the coming day. He would need to talk to Stephan and George or Stan. There were things Stephan was going to need to know and he would need access to cash. So would Sam. Stephan was going to earn his pay here shortly, dealing with George and Stan. The business monies would also need to be managed without oversight. He was pretty sure this was already set up. He just wanted to make sure.

Jake wondered some more. He thought Sams' in laws would be getting to town tomorrow. Sam had better be ready for them. Jake knew they weren't really friendly, so he hoped that would work out for Sam. Jake had seen the surviving in laws hold the victim accountable before. He wondered how they would be to Sam. His bet would be, that they might hold Sam accountable. And, if they did, it didn't really matter to either Sam or him. Heck, Jake remembered all the reasons why they disliked Sam. Sam told him. They thought Sam took her away from them. That was one of many. Hell, even Monica felt sorry for Sam concerning her parents. Sam was always a good sport. Jake thought Sam was that way, for the lesson it taught the kids.

Jake finally pulled up to Jameson's house. He sat in the truck for a bit. He watched the house, and he wondered... What would it be like tomorrow with Jameson gone, and maybe Cooper? He was sure Sam would be interested.... Jake checked that, he hoped Sam would be interested. He got out of the truck thinking of Sam all boozed up. He wished Sam had the sense to have him there when he saw them. Jake figured Sam needed no one to go see them, otherwise Sam would have asked. He considered this while walking up to Jameson's entryway. The door was open, only the screen door barred the entry. Jake rang the bell. Jameson hollered from the kitchen, "Its open!" Jake entered and made his way to what smelled exquisite. When he entered the kitchen he saw Cooper relaxing and Jameson in an apron, working his kitchen.

Jake shook his head as they both looked at him. "Hello Jake." Cooper said. Jameson added a working greeting. "Holly Jesus! What the hell is going on?" They both looked at Jake with some silliness. Jake made one of his disbelief faces... "Jameson? What the hell? Is Cooper not doing the cooking?" Cooper returned her focus to her paper work and flipped the bird towards Jake. Jake watched Cooper extend her finger with further disbelief. He pointed to her and said, "See Jameson, only the FBI teaches those gesticulations, be very thankful." Jameson turned to Jake. "Thankful Jake?" Jake nodded, "Yep, professionalism, which offers the bird in response to an observable question, is only taught in the FBI, and not where you're going. See, at the CIA, I wouldn't have been greeted in such a way. I would have been greeted with a sexual complaint. Just think of all that paperwork..." "Yeah Jake I guess I'm lucky...." Jake went back to cooking. "Oh yeah, Jameson, don't be offering to cook at The Farm." "Why's that Jake?" "Cause they'll fail ya to get a cook." Cooper giggled. "I don't think so Jake." "Jameson, no offense, Jake's got a point. You are one hell of a cook. And Jake, the answer to your first question is easy enough." Jake waited to hear. "I like eating." "So do I, how much longer?" "Not much longer Jake, get a drink for yourself." Jake did so while they settled in for a delectable sitting. "Oh Jake, apparently I won't be here for the burial... Would you extend my wishes to Sam?" "Sure I will Jameson, sure I will." "Thanks Jake, I sure hope he is alright." "Right now, at this moment Jameson,

Sam is feeling no pain. Tomorrow might be a different story, but right now Sam is in La-La Land." That pretty much silenced everyone. Jameson was making noise getting the food to the table. He was a one-man show and Cooper seemed to be enjoying it thoroughly, Jake figured he could follow suit.

The meal hit the table. Jake whistled. "Damn Jameson, This looks like it is worth coming back for." Cooper agreed and said to Jake, "Jake, you wouldn't know it by knowing Jameson as a law man, eh?" Jake shook his head. "Nope, Bina, you sure wouldn't." They all enjoyed Jameson's effort. They sat and spoke of The Farm and what Jameson might be expecting and even what Cooper might be expecting in her journeys of Transfer.

There wasn't much cleanup. Jake rounded out as a portion cook. Not much waste. Jake spoke to Jameson… "It is a good thing you don't have a dog Jameson… He'd be a thin bastard by the way you cook." Jameson looked at Jake. "I thought you liked it Jake???" "Oh, Jameson, I did, but there isn't enough left to fill a dog bowl now think about how sad a pooch would be." Cooper snorted. "Screw the mutt, with food this good." Jake looked at Jameson. "Guess the folks at the FBI never heard of A.S.P.C.A." Jameson didn't have much to say about Jake's comment. But, Cooper sure did. "Look here Jake, DOJ has investigated many animal cruelty cases." Jake looked at her wanting an explanation. "Well it is like this, when the elephants are in the house, the donkeys get investigated, just as it is the other way around." Jake laughed. "It wasn't that funny, Jake. By the time we got there they needed putting down. Those herds of elephants and donkeys sure get stubborn about things."

Jake stood up after the meal and collected his dinnerware. Jameson said to Jake that he didn't need to bother himself. "Well Jameson I figured with the way you grew that woman, without womanly duties to her mind, I would just be helping out." Cooper had such fun before she extended the finger again. Jake saw her gesticulation… "See that Jameson, you might want to tell her that guests don't get the finger at the end of a meal." "Especially not a praised meal" Jameson got into the banter. "Cooper, are you giving the guests the bird?" Cooper looked innocently up at Jameson. "Not me, we ate the birds last week." After a pause, she filled them in. "You remember, they too enjoyed the parrot under glass, and at the end of the meal, instead of giving them the finger, I kicked their asses." Jameson laughed, "Yes, now I remember, I think I told you then the same type of rules." Jameson looked at Jake. "You know Jake, I only spent short money on the woman fixture, guess I'll be telling her what to do a week late." Both Jake and Cooper laughed, but Jameson didn't get the bird. Cooper took over the clean up routine leaving Jake standing, wondering what to do. Jameson just told him to relax with his drink. Jake thought about another drink but passed. "I got one on board who has drank enough for the both of us.

He probably is fine, but tomorrow is going to be difficult. I had better be on my best behavior."

Jake looked at Jameson. "I'd offer you the same advice, except your mentor is former FBI trash with no manners. Hell, you two will show up in two days clothes, smelling like sin." Cooper laughed. "How else did ya think a chosen detective would be dressed for the Farm?" Jake thought about this day. He remembered how, as of late, Cooper was killing him in cut ups. It was a little disheartening for Jake because he was usually the one letting them roll. He thought about how Cooper could mix it up. He was smiling.

"Besides, Jake, you aren't finished with me yet. Jameson takes his cooking alone tomorrow. I'll be here for a few days more. Ya know the best for last, Jameson here is just the warm up." Jakes' smile widened some more. He got up and walked to the porch out back and lit a cigar.

Jameson followed him out. Cooper finished up inside. "Jake I did want a word with you." Jake stood inhaling a puff, listening. "You two, you and Sam, aren't gonna be crazy after I leave are ya?" Jake shook his head. "Good, I just wanted to speak on Hendriks' behalf. The guy is covering me, you know, short term? Jake nodded. Jameson thought about some of the other things he thought he needed to say. The thoughts vanished. Jake looked at Jameson as he exhaled a large and unbelievable puff with no cough. "Jameson, I got it covered. Go to the Farm in peace and learn them a thing or two. Just don't enjoy the cooking like you do, some stuffed shirt would railroad your ass right into his personal kitchen." Jake thought a minute. "These days, Maybe a she stuffed shirt." Jameson laughed and Cooper joined them.

Jake was enjoying the smoke for a bit. He had a sensation that he needed to leave. He wasn't sure, but it was something he couldn't avoid or compartmentalize. He looked at both of them, and stated he needed to leave. They both were a little surprised, but not enough to stop or make an inquiry of Jake. Jake looked at Jameson. "Young Jameson, have a splendid time down on the farm." Jake extended his hand. So did Jameson. They shook and Jake had said that he and Sam would be seeing him before he saw them. He looked at Cooper. "Listen you foul former FBI… you let that boy get his sleep tonight."

Cooper glared back at Jake. "That's a likely thing to say for an old man looking out for himself rather than a buddy." Jake felt like an all day loser with Bina's jibes. He just shook his head. "Alright guys I'll see ya." Jake excused himself.

Jake was feeling a bit uneasy. He thought of why and couldn't fathom it. He got into his truck and drove towards the job sight. Something pulled him there.

Jameson and Cooper were looking across the sound. Jameson felt good. He did seem to be missing his fiancée, since he found out of his departure this AM. They had put both of themselves into this house. Jameson thought he might do like Sam and just sell the house. "Hey Cooper do ya think I should sell this house?" "Huh?" Cooper verbalized. "Why not rent it Jameson? This really is a beautiful home." She paused a bit. "Think of retirement Jameson…. Where do you want to be?" He just said to Cooper, "I don't know Cooper, I don't know. I know I don't want to be stuck like Jake or even Sam. You know it is easy to find sympathy for Sam, but Jake, he's got no excuse." Cooper laughed at Jameson's comment. "You have a point Jameson."

Jameson begged a pardon from Cooper. He needed to get some things straight. Like what he was packing. She gave her pardon and looked at the night sky. She wondered about Nathan and his new bunch of friends. She found a chair and seated herself, and enjoyed the quiet.

Chapter 18

Jake hadn't been unsettled like this recently. He was thinking back to when he might have felt this way. He wasn't sure, but he thought it must have been a lifetime ago. The feeling was absent; Jake couldn't put an emotion to it. However, it was strong enough to motivate him towards action. To ask Jake why he was driving to the job site would have provided a simple answer. He would have said that he didn't know. Jake would have normally driven right up to the job sight entry. He would have parked his truck and stepped through the gates. This time, however, Jake drove around the backside of the job and around the project. He felt the need to park mid trip. He just stopped the truck; only partially to the shoulder. Jake didn't understand the need to stop, or the need to shut off the lights. But he did. He did nothing except sit there. Jake was getting somewhat concerned with his obedience to irrationality. He decided a cigar to chew on wouldn't violate the light rule. He popped one into his mouth and chewed on it. The glands under his tongue felt sour and started producing the saliva needed in the first stages of digestion. Jake wondered about how the system could anticipate one thing and be fooled by another. It was almost as if the enzymes in the saliva came out to start digesting bread and were tricked by the tobacco. He wondered why the enzymes didn't revolt. Why they didn't say, "This isn't carbohydrate work! Call us back when we are required for the essential need we were designed for." Jake wondered why he was revisiting grammar school science. He wasn't sure.

Just as Jake was about fed up with sitting there something happened. He noticed lights in the work sight. They seemed to be coming from the side he would have entered had he not obliged his psychic awareness. He studied the lights. They seemed to be held by hand, like a flashlight. Jake got out of his truck with his .45. He walked ahead of the truck trying to be silent. As he made progress to a place along the fence where he wanted to be, the flashlight activity seemed to be the same. He found a birm with low scrub.

The position gave an advantage of the machinery from a distance. Jake slowly approached his perch to examine what he considered as suspicious activity. He looked upon the machinery and didn't see anything except for the light flashing behind the machines. Jake thought about the Colt .45 in his pocket. He doubted that he could get a clean shot off even if it were daytime. He thought about scaling the fence, but that would give away his surprise. He looked to the left & to the right. If he got in his truck to drive around to the front, he might never know what or who was behind all this. Whoever these idiots were, they might have an escape route planned. They seemed to know there way around the place pretty well to Jake.

Jake grew frustrated with his less than dependable psychic ability. It got him here to see this, but gave him no resolution. Jake felt like going in there a gun's blazing. Asking only after these fools knew he had the drop on them. He felt a need to do something. Just as he was ready to scale the fence one word came to his focus.... *Stealth*. And then Jake was calm. Strangely so, a minute ago he was the cavalry, now he was the stillness of patience. He looked to the right again needing to make a move. He crept to his right slowly not to create any noise from negotiating the scrub. He stayed low. And before he knew it a fold in the chain link revealed itself. He looked at it, and couldn't believe it. The fold was an unsecured end of the chain link. This was confusing to Jake because this was one of his pet peeves with the fence contractors. He thought he had it worked out, but thankfully not this evening. Jake sized up the fold. It looked big enough for him to slip through. He reached up and grabbed the fence. The bottom was snagging, but a slow tug ripped the grass growth from the fence. Jake was careful not to shake the fence so as to make noise. Once he pulled the link back to what he thought was wide enough, he passed through it. He peeked up to where the activity was before and looked for a path to get closer. The lights were apparently in the same area. He still had the urgency to remain stealthy. Jake looked to the cement blocks used in the sewer construction. They didn't provide a screen of cover. But if he could move from one to the next, he would feel comfortable about being in range of the suspicious nocturnal events. Jake thought about noise. Namely the noise he could make during his anticipated movement. His keys were in his truck, no change to speak of. There was something else he needed to realize before he left. Jake started patting himself down. *It* wasn't long before Jake realized *it* was a cell phone, which had been newly acquired. Jake was relieved as he turned the phone to off. Then it seemed as though Jake could move. And move he did. He made it to the first block without giving himself up. He continued to the next, and the next block. While Jake was peeking at the unknown flashlight holders something changed. The flashlights had moved to another machine. Away from where he approached. Jake watched for another moment. He noticed a figure looking back to where they had vacated. To Jake it looked as though someone might have been bringing up the rear. When the focus of the figure switched back to the group's activities, Jake moved again. He looked to see what was going on and had determined that there were three beams of light, 3 people? Jake thought of his .45, the Colt had 7 rounds. The way Jake was situated was lucky. He was on the other side of the group. They would need x-ray vision to see him through the machine if they were going to make out Jake's approach. He figured stealth wasn't getting any better than this. He pulled out the .45 and moved to the machine they had been at first. He stepped softly, but quickly. Jake could hear muffled voices. He couldn't make out what they were saying but something sounded unfamiliar. Jake decided to go around the front of the tractor shovel. If he needed some cover the bucket would be the place for him. As he came around the front of the machine he realized how close they were. The unfamiliarity from before was now an accent, which he couldn't place. They weren't Americans though. Jake saw the beams of light flashing through the articulation part of the machine. They were on the other side. Someone was giving orders, and a series of sounds followed them.

To Jake it sounded like tools being moved. Then a distinct sound became heard. Somebody had put down a gun. Jake's motivation halted. Three unknowns armed were too much for him and his Colt. One thing kept coming back to Jake. Stealth. He decided not to proceed any further. He decided to make his way back to the entry point and find their vehicle. He retraced his steps back past the blocks of cement. Then back through the fold of the fence and back to his truck. Jake's sense of stealth slipped away as he moved away. He climbed up onto the payload of the pick up truck to see the lights once again. They were there. Jake got ready to open his truck door. Something stopped him.

Stealth stopped him. He realized if he opened his truck from this side the key in the ignition would activate the dash alarm. He crept around the front of his truck, to the passenger side, to open the door. Now it made sense to him as to why he didn't park further into the shoulder of the road. He wouldn't have been able to open his door. He reached inside to behind the seat and came out with the 9mm Beretta. He pocketed the added weapon and shut the truck door.

Jake took off at a joggers pace to make it around to the front entry of the job sight. As he labored through the jog, he felt every Cigar he ever smoked. His lungs burned. He maintained a flow of breathing as he remembered from his athletic days. In through the nose out through the mouth, he repeated it in his mind until he came to the entry area. Stealth was still on his mind. As he viewed what might be there, he did so from a protected area. He moved to gain a better field of view. And there it was. A dark panel van was parked off to the side of the main gate. The windshield was towards him. Stealth was obviously not part of the others consideration as the person behind the wheel was smoking a cigarette. Jake could see the glare of the cigarettes head. Jake wondered if he could manage to slide down the side of the fence and shrubbery without being made by the driver. He looked down the fence. If he stayed low and moved consistently, he thought he could make it. He began to moving. He knew the driver was smoking, so his full attention might not be what Jake was up against. He moved slowly trying to keep an eye on the driver, and an ear for those inside. He had determined four people were involved. He thought about employing his cell phone but the need to be stealthy wouldn't let him. While he crept slowly closer, he noticed the flick of the butt out the window. Then the door opened. The driver got out and moved to the back of the van. Jake didn't figure that the driver needed to relieve himself, he just moved when the driver removed his focus from being an observer. Jake moved to the gate rapidly and looked to where the others were located. They were still doing whatever it was that they were doing. Jake took advantage of the driver's need to be indisposed. He could approach the van from the passenger side. He didn't notice the tag on the truck because it was in the shadows. He reached for his 9 mm. He heard the guy finishing up his relief. It sounded as though the guy was shaking extra long. Jake crept to see in the opposite side view mirror. He looked to see a silhouette facing away from the truck. He waited and watched. The figure made a motion to turn towards the front and Jake dropped, he snuck down the passenger side of the van and around the back. He rose and stepped to the last corner of the van. His 9mm came up as he turned the corner. The man who was just raising the water level tried to get to the horn on the steering wheel. Jake said, "Freeze!" He moved closer to him. Jake didn't waste a motion. He was holding the gun to the unknown mans head. His left hand reached out to pat down the driver. The driver turned suddenly, and Jake pistol-whipped the guy. The gun caught the man in the temple region and sent him to the ground. He remained still. Jake looked at the gate; nobody was there yet. The guy on the ground moaned, Jake moved to him. When the man started to move Jake hit him again. Jake thought that ought to do it. Jake looked at the guy. His nose was now bleeding profusely. Something had told Jake time was limited. He didn't question it. He knew he had one down. He moved to the body at his feet and felt around. This fella wasn't nice. He packed a knife and a pistol. Sam tossed the pistol to the bushes and took the knife.

On further investigation Jake found nothing. Jake sensed he violated his need for stealth. He was no longer an observer he was involved. Whoever was in the yard was expecting a ride out of here. The driver was down. His realization of limited time had become a reality. He saw the flashlights moving back toward the entry. He felt the pockets of the guy. There it was a package of cigarettes. He grabbed them and placed them in his pocket, which held the .45. The driver had seemed like he was coming around again. This time Jake had enough. He grabbed the barrel of the 9 mm. He raised the gun back in hammer fashion and delivered a blow, which drew a shadow over the man's consciousness. Jake slid the man off the side of the road into some grassy brush. He went back to the van and assumed the driver's position. He fumbled for one of the drivers' smokes as to create a subterfuge and waited. He noticed the flashlights being flipped off. They were close. He hoped they had not been under an expectation of predetermined action. An action, which if performed incorrectly, would blow his advantage of remaining stealthy. He thought it and they appeared at the gate. He started the truck and put it into gear. He didn't turn on the lights... that would be too obvious. The feeling that drew him from Jameson and Bina took hold of him again. He waited until the men moved closer as he let the van roll forward. They seemed to expect nothing other than their intentions, and that same feeling from before took hold of him. He floored the accelerator driving straight for the men. He smiled in satisfaction as he did. They were without expectation as the van proceeded to hit all of them even the guy who had the best chance of getting away. When Jake hit them, they became projectiles. They flew through the air hitting the ground hard. By the time they had stopped rolling Jake had stopped the truck and was out pointing both guns across and covering the scattered men. He watched them all as he moved to one. With the .45 he clubbed the first man somewhere in the neck region. He lay limp while Jake moved to the next. Jake saw the guy reaching for something and let a round off from the 9mm. The guy stopped moving during Jakes rush at him. He too got a pistol whip. Jake moved to the third man. Nothing. He moved closer noticing that man was still. Once Jake was close enough he saw the man's head in a very unnatural position. That man was dead. Jake was pretty sure his neck was broken. Jake turned to the newly injured and moved to them.

They were satisfactorily incapacitated.

He checked the guy who moved last, the gun he had had a shoulder strap. Jake knew these were bad guys. He removed it from the body and tossed it some distance away. Jake thought about using his cell phone, if the gun report didn't produce law enforcement he most certainly would. Meanwhile he wanted to rest. Something wouldn't let him rest; he was tired of this something, but remained its servant. He went to the first man he struck and found similar weapons on that body. Again he removed the weapon and tossed it to where the first lie. He moved to the front of the van and parked himself against the hood of the truck. He groped a cigarette out of the stolen pack and lit one. In the distance, he thought he heard a yelp from a siren.

He did. Law Enforcement pulled up to the area. The lights were flashing but the Lyme cops practiced noise stealth. A couple of young guys got out of the car; weapons drawn. Jake made no sudden moves. Right behind them was a Ct. State Trooper. Jake smoked his cigarette as the cops told him to raise his hands above his head. He did as he was told.

Jake knew the State Trooper by past business. He couldn't recall the guy's name, but he had given Jake some grief once for an overweight violation. Jake had no permit. Jake got a $1,500 fine. The state trooper was being kind. He could have pinched Jake for a lot more, and Jake knew it. As the Lyme police were formulating what to do, the State

Trooper spoke up. "Hey guys," he proceeded only after he had their attention. "If you ask me, I think the shooting is done, we can holster our firearms." After a slight unwillingness they did holster the weapons. "You might also want to get some detention medical assistance." The taller of the two nodded in the others direction, then to the radio.

The trooper walked over to where Jake was. His flashlight found each man except for the driver. The shorter cop spoke into the handset transmitter from the dash of the squad. "Three to transport." Jake spoke loudly "Better make it four." The officer corrected himself. "Make that four down." The trooper was a big fella. Jake didn't like this guy, but all considered Jake had had enough of the hand- play and games for the night. The last thing he wanted was to deal with two guns pointing at him, especially with four bodies scattered about. All on a reported gunfire call.

Jake took a last drag and flipped the cigarette. "Hello trooper it is nice to see you again."

The trooper flashed the light into Jake's face. "Mister Blaques, it will only be nice to have seen you again, if I can avoid the paperwork on this mess." Jake tried to look past the flashlight and laughed. "I know just the guy to make that happen." The trooper said, "Yes, I bet you do."

The dispatcher who took the call must have been on the ball. Another car had arrived with the flashers on. When the doors opened both Jameson and Cooper had gotten out of the car. "We got a call from the dispatcher. He said Hendrik couldn't be reached."

Cooper moved to the bodies and then to the trooper and Jake. Her disbelief was very apparent. Jameson was wondering what to make of all of this as he explained their reason for being there. Jake spoke to the trooper. "These folks there are your pass on your paperwork, trooper." He asked for identification of both. They complied in offering who they were. The trooper was satisfied for the moment. Cooper looked at Jake. "What happened here Jake?"

"Well, not that much Bina. I had left Jamesons' house because of an unexplained need. I came here and parked behind the job sight. At first I didn't know what for, but then I saw the two living here and the dead one over there, fooling with the machines. I thought Stealth and came back out to the front of the job jogging the whole way. I saw this truck parked over on the other side of the gate and the fool in the bushes back there smoking. I moved closer and snuck up on this idiot when he was taking some relief, and brained him and then again. I removed his weapon and tossed it in the bushes and then, assumed his position in the truck. After a couple of seconds these guys moved to be picked up, and got ran over. I brained that guy first, and then noticed this guy moving and let off a shot. He remained still and then I brained him. I moved to this guy and he was dead. I wanted to rest, but I moved to disarm these guys and found those." Jake pointed to the semi-automatic weapons in front of the van. "Then I lit a smoke, and waited for you all."

Cooper had heard Jake. He spoke clearly and reasonably. The trooper started laughing. "I think I'll hang around for this one." Cooper looked at him. "I think that is a good idea." As Cooper looked on, Jameson was busy telling the patrolman to go investigate the interest of the machines. They got into their car and drove through the gate.

The trooper gave Jameson his set of handcuffs. He told Jake to follow him. Cooper tagged along. "Mister Blaques, why don't you point out the driver to us?" They walked to match Jakes description and found the guy. When the trooper pointed his light at the man, there was a huge puddle of blood under the man's face. "This guy gets the first medical care." Cooper looked for the weapon and located it just as Jake had said.

Cooper was obviously thinking on something. "Jake everything checks out as you told us." The trooper nodded, as he looked at Cooper. "This is the kind of stuff you see on T.V. movies... one guy taking out four men." Cooper added, "four armed men."

Jameson joined them and looked at the 4th guy.

When he saw the blood under the guys face he felt for a pulse. The guy was alive. "Hey Cooper would ya mind getting the first aid kit." Jake didn't let her get a chance in. "I do mind." Jameson looked up and shrugged painfully. "Hell, Jameson, he'll survive."

The trooper asked Jake if he was stilled armed. Jake nodded. The trooper kept a stare on Jake waiting for him to produce his weapon. Jake's left hand reached into the pocket holding the .45. He removed it slowly. He dropped the clip so it hit the ground and opened the chamber dispensing the chambered round. The gun was empty. He put it on the ground near the clip. The trooper recognized the gun as a Colt .45 caliber semi- automatic. Jake reached into his right pocket and removed the Beretta 9mm. He repeated the steps as he used on the .45. The trooper was afraid to ask. He had his hand on his side arm. "Any other surprises?" Jake thought a moment and remembered the knife. "Oh yeah, here ya go." Jake tossed the knife on to the gun pile. While the group was considering all that happened, the patrol car returned. Jake thought the looks on the faces of the officers returning were more revealing. Those guys were panicked. Jake noticed that they needed to interrupt the interest of Jake's weapons. Jake broke the ice.

"What did you two find out?" "There are some irregular wires on those machines." That is all that the tall one could manage to say. The trooper was off to his car, just like that. Cooper and Jameson seemed to snap right into another line of thinking. Cooper went to the bags dropped when the suspects were struck by the van. They opened them. Cooper had opened the bag she found. "I hope that trooper is calling for a bomb squad." Jake figured as much. Jameson looked in one bag and then another. He rifled paperwork that he found. The State Trooper yelled across his car. "The medics are here. Probably the press guys too." He knew that the information of the press needed to be said. Jameson told the patrolman to set up a roadblock once the ambulance had gotten through. The guys nodded. Before they could leave he caught them.

"Tell the Press we'll have a statement in a ½ hour, don't let them in here." The guys looked back confused. "Them?" "Well our local guy will be first, but the bomb squad doesn't roll without those listening responding." The guys nodded and got in the car to set up the blockade. Sgt. Gunn also showed up to help out. He indicated a message had been left with Hendrick. All four of them, Jake, Jameson, Cooper and the State Trooper huddled. Jameson was the first to say what direction the group must follow. "We need a story for them." Cooper nodded. The trooper listened and Jake lit a cigarette.

Cooper spoke through her thinking. "A jogger reported suspicious activity on a cell phone. The Emergency Dispatcher put a call to investigate a report of suspicious activity." Jake interrupted. "Where or who is the jogger?" He understood the need to have the cover, but it had to hold up.

Cooper stopped her speaking through thinking. She looked at Jameson, he returned the look and they both smiled. Jake didn't know what to make of it. Neither did the Trooper. Cooper looked at the trooper and asked his name. The trooper responded. "My name is Don Henry." Jameson said, "Nice to meet you Trooper Henry."

Jake caught on quickly. "Trooper Henry, I know you asked to get out of paperwork on this one, but it looks like you just single handedly or with cooperation from Lymes' finest apprehended four suspects thought to be material witnesses in the Murphy Family Murders." Jake paused a bit. "I told you I could get you off of that detail." The trooper laughed. He looked at Cooper and Jameson. "This is subterfuge so those who are really behind it aren't the wiser?" They both nodded. He shook his head. "I could use the accommodation come review time." "Okay then, that is the story?" They all nodded. The trooper looked at Jake. "Mr. Blaques, no fine this time. You are free to go after you collect your guns." He flicked his smoke, and nodded at the trooper. "It was sure nice running into you again officer." Jake collected his guns. He took the knife even though it wasn't his. He pocketed it and told Jameson and Cooper where he'd be. He congratulated the State Trooper and left through the work site. He went by the machines but he didn't investigate. He climbed over the fence and walked himself to the truck and got in. He reached for another stolen cigarette and lit it. He took a breath after a drag. He put the truck into gear and followed his new feeling.

Cooper and Jameson left in his car. Jameson looked at Sgt. Gunn and The State Trooper as they left. He couldn't help to think how this case affected so many in so many different ways. Cooper saw the same men and scene but thought of it differently. Jameson could only think of what had transpired as a new detective; she thought of it as vindication of her theory of victim profiling. She was unnerved and excited. She couldn't wait to tell Nathan of the developments. The two made it back to Jameson's house. They sat in the car for a moment. Jameson was thinking to say something. Cooper finally did. "Here we were wondering why Jake left a little suddenly, thinking it was cause of Sam." Jameson agreed as he heard it being said. "Yeah, what a break, huh?" "You know Jameson? You get to listening to old guys like Jake and Sam. Ya hear them talking and making like they're tough." Jameson was smiling as she said it. "Then you meet one! Do you believe that Jake took those four guys out?" Jameson nodded thinking on the implications of what Cooper had said. "Cooper??? Do you remember what Jake had said about Sam?" She shook her head. "Hmmmm, maybe I didn't tell you." She waited for enlightenment. "Oh, Jake was telling me about a guy Sam was tuning up for vandalizing his machine. He said, he had to call Sam off of the guy, he thought Sam was gonna kill him with his bare hands. I guess I thought maybe they were both talking some shit. Guess not now." Cooper agreed. "Yep Jameson, these men are capable and motivated." They got out of the car. Jameson said to Cooper "I don't know about you, but I'm ready for a drink." Cooper thought Jameson was reading her mind.

Chapter 19

Jake found himself at a place he frequented. He sat in the truck for a second wondering about his psychic abilities. If they even were psychic. He didn't know why he ended up here. He figured it didn't much matter. He stowed the weapons under the seat, grabbed a cigar and headed into the establishment. Upon entering Jake took a seat near the T.V. but not under it. He looked about and surveyed the bar area. Some of the folks he knew nodded. A couple of the girls he knew smiled. He waited for the bar keep. She came over, as soon as possible. She had been helping another customer to a beverage. She asked Jake how he was doing, fully aware of Sam's loss. He looked at her and forced a smile. "I am doing like I feel a double coming on, How are ya Susie?" She smiled slightly. "I'm fine Jake, double of the good stuff?" He nodded. She tended to her duty and returned to Jake with a triple and some peanuts. Jake took the drink she placed before him and downed it. She raised her eyebrows watching Jake do so. He nodded indicating the need for another drink. She obliged and told him to take it easy. He waited for the first to warm him up. He reached for the stolen cigarette pack. Susie had noticed the smokes. She knew Jake to be a cigar smoker, and she made a note of it. Jake lit the cigarette and exhaled an ignition drag. Blue smoke pushed its way forcefully across the bar. Susie noticed her other customers were in need of her attention. She saw to their needs and moved her work towards Jake. He seemed to be contemplating something. Susie figured it had to do with Sam's family. Jake noticed Susie moving back up to him. He asked her to put on the local station. She looked at Jake for a moment. She knew that he was asking her to do something that would be seen as unfavorable, she wanted to know if he knew how the others would react. Jake reached into his pocket and threw a wad of cash down. "Buy the whole house a round."

She winked and did so. "A request has just been made to switch the T.V. channel people." Everyone harangued about it. "Mister Blaques wants to buy the house a round for the inconvenience."

The room applauded. She satisfied the channel switching and then the patrons. Channel 8 had a Live Broadcast of a 2nd rate news reporter who just happened to be on call. "She was reporting that the state bomb squad had been deployed to a site which has a connection to The Murphy Family Murders. She had said that The Connecticut State Troopers and Lyme Police Detectives were on the seen and were planning a news conference 18 minutes from now. The network apologized for the need to depart from live coverage. The anchor said they would be reporting live when the conference between both agencies began. Jake thought that even the networks were slaves. The remote switched to the other local affiliate and the last bit of a special bulletin was ending. A couple of folks had the great idea of leaving the bar to go see what all of the hubbub was about. Then one of the bar elders asked how it was that they would explain to officers why they shouldn't be arrested for driving drunk. The room laughed in response and the idiots just shut up. Susie snuck up to Jake. "How was this not surprising to me after you came in?"

Jake sipped part of his second drink. He put the glass down, and leaned over the bar. "Susie, do you know any psychics?" The conversation happening in the bar seemed to quiet down when some folks took notice of Jake leaning towards Susie. They were wondering kinda like Susie was. When Susie had realized the shifting of the focus to them, she replied to Jake. "Well, Jake, I don't know how they would feel about such a thing. Let's find out. Okay folks, Jake Blaques was wondering if anyone would take offense to him buying another round for The House?" After a second, when folks had realized that another free drink was being offered, another cheer had replaced the interest.

Jake loved Susie's professionalism. His only thoughts were total stealth. He smiled at Susie and she poured those who needed another and cupped those waiting to drink the first.

She came back to Jake and started counting his money. It was a subterfuge she understood. Jake had a need unlike any other in here, and it was a unique need for this crowd. "Jake, Hun, I know a little about psychics, I know some stronger ones than myself." Jake finished his drink. She poured another. She finished counting off his debt in clear view of all the other patrons. She knew people watched these money transactions in bars, even though they would never claim to do so. When she returned Jake asked her a question. "Who can you get to replace you tonight?" She frowned trying to think of who the regulars might not want to see replace her. Jake watched a light bulb go off in her head. She went to the phone. She called Colleen. When Colleen answered she spoke into the handset of the phone. "Colleen? Hi it is Susie from the bar." She waited for Colleen to respond. "Say listen Colleen, do you think you could cover my shift for the rest of the night?" Jake followed the phone call and pointed to the money, and then rubbed his fingers together. "Yeah, I know it is a slow night... Hold on Colleen, this is important Hun. Yeah, Jake Blaques needs some help. Yes, that's him." Her facial picture released its stress. "Okay then I'll see you here in.... 15mins, fine, thanks Colleen." When Susie had hung up the phone she went to her customers to serve more beverages to them. "Alright everyone... Mister Blaques has requested my psychic help for the evening. His suggestion to me was to find a fill in you could all appreciate. Colleen is on her way in." The Bar seemed agreeable to the substitution. Somebody hollered, "Psychic Help, Huh?"

There was a minority laugh throughout. It simmered down when Jake hadn't shown appreciation for the laugh. Jake held his finger up and whirled it signaling to Susie to get them another round. This time she only cupped the patrons. Nobody was ready for another. In fact, by the time everyone would be recalling this whole evening, they would be doing so on a Jake Blaques hangover. The news came back on, but this time there was a whole lot more news. There was a live feed of the scene from a helicopter. The State Bomb Disposal was on the scene and working around machines Jake owned. There were bodies being loaded into Department of Corrections Ambulances. The reporter said that of 4 suspects 3 were being treated for wounds and one was a fatality. The incident resulted in a single gunshot. Nothing more was said that was pertinent. The rest was media hype. Jake, like many others, heard four men down with one dead, at the site of a bomb scene. Back to regularly scheduled programming. The bar was silent.

Jake had left before any of them save Susie knew it. Jake waited for Colleen to arrive.

She did so with her boyfriend driving her. He walked over to the car before she could get out. He knocked on the window and she rolled it down. He spoke into the car. "Thanks for coming down folks. I needed to talk with Susie right away." Jake extended his hand with two crisp hundreds between his fingers. "I hope this compensates ya for any inconvenience." Colleen took the money and handed it to her boyfriend. A voice in the dark spoke out. "Mister Blaques, your kind of inconvenience is welcome anytime." Jake didn't give a shit that he had just bought an evening with a girl from her boyfriend. He didn't even give a shit that she didn't know any better. She leaned across the seat and kissed the voice, he told her he'd see her at closing time. She leaned to open the door and Jake had it for her smoothly. She got out of the car and leaned down to say goodbye again. The car's engine revved a bit as the car moved forward. It was gone before she could get into the bar. Colleen was a looker. Jake thought it too bad that her wits didn't match her looks.

She looked up at Jake, and he knew as she did, she would do anything for him. He again said thanks for coming on such short notice. She said it was better than sitting around watching cartoons. He feigned agreement and she giggled. They moved towards the door of the Bar. "Mister Blaques.... if you want, I could give you my number... You might think of calling during the day when Jimmy is working." Jake tilted his head to the side and raised an eyebrow, which caused Colleen to giggle once more. "I'll tell ya what Colleen, things are pretty hectic right about now, would it be alright if I got your number from Susie and called ya here in a few days?" She smiled nodding seductively. Jake opened the door for her and the bar welcomed her. He didn't follow her in, but waited on Susie outside. She didn't keep him waiting. It was only a couple of minutes and she was out the door. She and Jake spoke for a bit. They agreed to drive to Susie's house and continue the conversation. Jake hoped he could keep it brief. He was wondering about Sam. Susie actually lived in the next town over. Closer to the Fox wood's Casino. The drive took a bit of time. Jake followed her to her house although he knew the way for they had a history. Jake wondered why he never took the time to know her as being a psychic. He thought about their past and the shortness of it. Jake could fathom a simultaneous need for some sex as the reason; that had to be it. By memory, it seemed to be the reason to why these two had a past.

Jakes mind wandered a bit. He wondered what the extent of the bombs would be. He wondered about how Jameson and Cooper had been so surprised by what had happened. And, Trooper Henry, Jake broke a smile thinking of him. Jake spoke out loud, "Paperwork." Then he laughed.

They had pulled into Susie's driveway. She lived in a house, which needed repair. Her ex, who was now gone, was a widely known scumbag. Susie had seen her share of tough living. They parked their vehicles and got out of them. Susie waited on Jake to join her. It wasn't much of a house and she knew it, but she had no pretense of apology. She was a straight shooter. As he joined her, she grabbed his arm with both of hers. "So what is the new interest Jake? Psychics?" Jake nodded as his loose hand covered hers. They walked up the path familiarly. She said, "Come in and tell me all about it." Jake looked at her like she was crazy. "Weren't you the one with psychic ability?" She giggled nodding. "Jake, how do you think it is that I was motivated to have you come home with me, another roll in the hay?" Jake said, "Touché." They entered her home. "Have a seat Jake, take a load off."

Susie went to the cabinet, which held the booze. She grabbed a less expensive whiskey Jake could make due with. She poured two. She let the drinks sit as she squared herself away. She grabbed the drinks and returned to Jake. Susie sat on the floor sideways to Jakes knee. She held his drink to him and he grabbed it. He said, "Thanks." She nodded and held her own to toast. She rested her elbow on Jakes knee and used it as a support for herself while she faced Jake. "Jake, tell me what you need to say." She sipped her drink, and watched Jake try to formulate some words. She sensed his frustration. "Jake, take a sip of your drink and stop thinking for a second." Jake had a sip, the thinking didn't stop, try as he might. After trying to cease the thinking, Jake had a realization. He looked at Susie and smiled. "How did you know that I couldn't stop thinking?" Susie smiled at Jake she put her drink down and placed her hands on Jake's knees. She turned herself to face Jake. Jake watched her move. He decided she was up to no good. He let her proceed. Her hands slid up his legs slowly. "Jake did you know that psychic ability is available to more of us than actually know it?" Her hands seem to move by the pull of her fingers. She used them as tools. Jakes' thinking was slowed down. He knew that she knew this. Jake might have been otherwise distracted, but her touching him was settling if not arousing. "Honey, did you also realize that when men are highly psychic, it presents itself when they are under tremendous stress and pressure?" Jake shook his head. She looked into his eyes softly as though she were a fantasy revealing a special secret. "Jake, not many women know that the easiest way to get a man to stop thinking is only after he cums." Jake didn't laugh although he may have at some other time. Her hands slid past Jake's package. Close enough to get him hardening. Her fingers got under his belt and pulled him to a stand. She pushed up off her knees and put her head near him. She grabbed his ass and moved her mouth open to cover part of his developing erection. She looked into his eyes. "Jake, aren't you only thinking about one thing now?" Jake offered her an "mmmhmmm" and she could feel him smile. Her fingers unbuttoned his pants as she still moved her face over his package; looking up at him. Her fingers negotiated the zipper downward. Her hands rubbed inside his pants down and away. The waist of his pants was down around his knees. Jake didn't have underwear on, but Susie knew that about him. Her cheekbone rubbed against his erect manhood. She turned and licked it down his shaft. Her hands grabbed his cheeks as she kissed him. Jake groaned. She grabbed him and stroked him smoothly a few times; her lick lubricated him nicely. She lowered herself on her knees again and took another sip of her drink. After she put it down she removed her own top, then the bra.

Jake couldn't remember this Susie from before. If he had he may have never left. He sat down and removed his shirt, then his shoes and pants. Susie approached him on her knees. Her eyes were intoxicating Jake watched her as she watched him. She employed her mouth, hands and eyes to silence Jake's thinking like he had never known. He knew with certainty, this was not the same Susie. Something was different. The difference was the reaction to her psychic power as a lover. When Jake started to get close to his time his hips started to move. Susie knew her efforts needed only a few more seconds. She responded to Jake taking him deeper into her mouth. Her hand busied itself squeezing his scrotum and contents enough to feel his release. Her other hand slid back to his rectum one of her fingers applied pressure to it as she accepted his load. She took his energy in the mouth, and let it fall to her breasts. She rubbed his love over her breasts and stroked his member as it softened. She finally kissed him, and took another sip of her drink. Jake collapsed from her doings. After she finished her drink, she got up for another. She found Jake a cigarette, lit it and put it into Jakes slightly opened mouth and sat where she had performed her silencing therapy. "Jake, have your thoughts been quieted?"

He nodded with a beaming smile. After a drag on the cigarette, Jake told her everything that happened since dinner. Susie looked at Jake knowing he was pumped about finding those guys in the yard. She also knew Jake needed more silencing; therefore she led him by the hand to her bedroom. They worked at silencing each other for the next couple of hours.

Jake and Susie spent time talking of psychic ability. Susie answered most of the questions Jake had but he had a couple she couldn't answer. She did promise to ask for Jake. She had some reading she lent to Jake after their lovemaking. Jake seemed to understand that even those with psychic abilities couldn't really explain them. For all that Susie could tell Jake, most gifted psychics spent huge and inordinate amounts of time trying to manage their abilities. Some were downright miserable with them. Jake was thankful that he had not endured the slave-like bondage some psychics experienced.

Susie explained it like this: "Jake to a certain extent, all of us are psychic. Some go through life never becoming aware of their abilities. Others get the power from existing in stressful environs." Susie smiled at Jake. "That is likely your reason for this sudden awareness, but Jake it wasn't sudden." Jake looked at her and wanted an explanation.

"Jake, when we first got together, did you think there was psychic energy flowing?"

Jake volleyed an honest answer. "No, I thought it was a mutual need for love." Susie smiled. "Yes Jake, a need for love. Psychic ability is surrounded by love. When we first hooked up, I saw your ability." He raised his eyebrows. "You had it Jake but you didn't need it." Jake thought about the time shared with Susie earlier and compared it to this most recent time. "Don't even go there Jake, it is like mixing apples and oranges. Our love making just now was so much better because your psychic energy was strong." Jake smiled at Susie. "Honestly Susie, I liked this last meeting much more than before."

Susie just smiled. "So did I Jake. So did I. Jake, I know you are impatient to go and see Sam, but I beg you to stay just a bit longer." Jake didn't argue. He obliged Susie. "There are other things you need to know." Jake listened to Susie with a grim ear, the way she said it gave him a cold shudder. "Jake part of the reason we spent so much time connected... was so that I could share your energy." She smiled with her seductive face. "Touch, works for me well, it clears things up for me. Some say that touch is the strongest prompt. I never agreed with that though. I know touch is a great prompt, but the truly great psychics know before that, they can simply sense it, like you did here earlier." Jake was flabbergasted by what she had told him. How could he be great? He just became aware of a need and followed it. "I don't follow you Susie. You said I was a great psychic?" She nodded. "Greatness, Jake, is not always recognized as greatness by those who are." He listened to her some more for clarification.

She hated this, trying to discuss how it works with someone so skeptical. "Jake, how is it that you picked the bar I was working at to let off steam?" She knew the answer before she asked the question, but she asked it so Jake could contemplate the question. Jake simply said, "I don't know." She just shook her head. "Isn't that just like a man? He holds an answer most other struggle to understand their entire lives and answers with such a simplistic view. Jake the point is you did know, forget about how you knew, and just understand that you do know." Jake made the connection. He smiled with a touch of naughtiness. "Susie, I am not one to question things endlessly, so it is easy for me to trust what you say as being truthful." Jake lit a cigarette, exhaled then continued. "It is just such a new thing for me." Susie looked at him and said, "No it is not new, you are just more aware. Jake most of the time when folks get the ability, they spend their entire existence denying themselves the ability because they think there is something wrong about it. I have seen it destroy psychics, they simply shut down and die." She thought some more. "The denial becomes an addiction, one they never overcome."

"Jake, this ability will grow in you. You will need to manage it. There will be times when you think you may be crazy. The reality you will come to know will leave you at a loss." Jake face grew tense. Susie could see the change occurring in Jake. "Don't fret Jake." She hugged him and pressed herself against his body. He appreciated Susie's soft side and caring more than she could know. "Jake living life is learning new things and saying goodbye to things known. Living life is steeped in loss. If you can remember one thing about all that you have experienced here tonight, remember that. Living Life is steeped in loss." Susie continued, "Jake this thing you are in is dark, it is of the worst evil, men conspire. Your battle of today won't be the last you face, there are many yet to come." Jake somehow knew what she meant. He looked at her and said, "That which is yet to come requires more loss though, isn't that right?" She nodded.

Jake hugged Susie. He thanked her for all her help and got up to get dressed. Susie got out of bed naked. She went to her closet and retrieved a box. She brought the box back to Jake and opened it. Jake watched Susie standing before him naked. She was beautiful to him. She lifted out of the box a necklace. It had a charm on it. "Jake I bought this after we first got together, I knew you'd be coming to collect it, just not when." She put it around Jake's neck. "This amulet is feminine, and for a good reason." Jake listened as she explained. "This will temper your ability as I did in quieting you down." She looked into Jake's eyes. Her other hand moved to his groin and touched him. "Do you remember that?" Jake nodded with a smile. "Just use this as a substitute for quieting yourself down, focus on its ability to calm you." Jake didn't like the way she said it. She knew, but there was nothing she could do. "Living life is steeped in loss Jake." She released him from her embrace.

Jake knew he had to go, so did she.

Jake was in his truck starting it. Sam wasn't awake yet but he probably would be before Jake could get there. Jake left Susie's and motored his way to the marina. He still hadn't thought much about the past few hours. He recalled Susie saying that it was just like a man to know that others struggled for their whole existence. Jake was still unsure about this psychic thing, and he wasn't sure about how it happened, probably just as Susie said 'it just never happened', it just was, an unknown. Jake wondered about the past. He wondered why it was that he and Sam had so much fortune. Could this psychic ability be an attribute? And, was Jake alone in having it? Might it be that Sam had it and was simply still in the dark? There was more Jake could ask Susie, now that he thought of these things. He thought about Susie and how he thought had known her. He shook his head. Thinking on it presented more questions than he could possibly answer. Jake was approaching the marina. He saw that Sam's truck was parked in the same place he saw it earlier. Jake guessed that Sam might be stumbling around *The Buried Treasure.* He got out of his truck and walked to his love. As he thought of *The Buried Treasure* and how he called it his love, he suddenly knew, she wasn't his love. He enjoyed her immensely. He struggled for her. Most of his earning days could be attributed to financing *The Buried Treasure.* Jake eyed her, she was beautiful, and he liked her, but he realized he didn't love her. The *Love* word had new meaning. Jake knew there was a lot of catching up to do in understanding Love. He was sure he had the basics down. He boarded his enjoyment. Jake had noticed the light was still on. He moved to the cabin entry and descended.

Sam wasn't in the bunk. Jake spoke through the head door. "How are ya feeling in there Sam?" "Hey Jake, I'm feeling a little rough right now." Jake nodded to that.

"Yep, you're lucky you're feeling anything." Sam opened the door and stepped out of the head. "Jake old pal. I wish I didn't feel anything." "Yeah, well you would be wrong about feeling that way." Sam shrugged and went to the overhead storage and grabbed some Alka-Seltzer for his condition. He fumbled with the box and retrieved an envelope containing the remedy he needed. Jake already had a glass of water ready. He placed it on the galley counter space. Sam's fingers shook a bit as he opened the envelope. Jake waited for Sam to take his first bit of his medicine. He watched Sam swallow it down. Jake noticed Sam differently since he had left him earlier yesterday. He couldn't put his thumb on it, but it was different. Sam finished off the concoction. He placed the glass down almost where he had picked it up from and sat back down in his bunk. He waited for the physiological effects to occur.

Jake angled his questions after Sam was mending. "Sam, did you just wake up?" Sam nodded his eyes remained closed. "So you have been out since you started yesterday?"

Sam summoned his focus. "Jake, God Damn it... what is your point? Yes I have been out since I passed out." Sam obviously needed some more time so Jake remained silent. He took a seat across from Sam and fired up two cigarettes. He gave one to Sam who took it and choked a drag down. He coughed his exhalation.

Sam finally opened his eyes to interact with Jake. Sam noticed there was something different about his friend. The hangover he was experiencing prevented any further thought on as to why he thought so. Jake said to Sam, "Things have changed big time Sam, while you were passed out." Sam could only expect bad news. It is all his head could imagine, as the pounding slowly subsided. The Alka-Seltzer was working. Sam took another drag. "How so Jake?"

"I'll tell ya, but you're never gonna believe it." Jake stood up and started a pot of coffee. Sam looked at Jake and said, "I'm not ready for coffee yet Jake." Jake didn't stop doing what he was doing; he simply spoke through the motions. "Well Sam, you'll be ready before this story is over." Jake finished up and sat back down across from Sam. "After I left you here thoroughly polluted, I made my way to see off Jameson. Cooper was with him. Let me tell ya Sam, that man can cook." Sam rolled his fingers as if to beg without speaking to keep going. "Well, about the end of the dinner, I had a sudden awareness that left me feeling a need to leave. I got into my truck and followed this awareness to the job sight. Sam I have no explanation for the feeling motivating me to do what I did. I usually drive right into the yard... not this time. I drove around the perimeter and parked in the middle of the access road; I wondered why I didn't park off the shoulder, Sam I was literally talking to myself. It was the craziest thing." Sam bore up through the details of Jakes story. What else was he gonna do?

"So Sam, I'm sitting there wondering why I'm there and I notice flashlights in the yard. I walk to the front of the truck towards the low scrub on the birm. I sneak up on the birm and investigate. There are several flashlights in between the machines. It is dark and I get a feeling to move to the right." Sam asked, "A feeling, a feeling like before?" Jake modded and continued. "I'm slinking down the fence and I find a fold in the chain link... two ends not attached, I'm thinking how likely is this? Ya know after, I chewed the fence guys out?" Sam seemed to be paying more attention. "Anyways, I move to the sewer blocks along the roadway. I see a bit of motion and sit tight. One of the figures is bringing up the rear. All this time Sam, I'm thinking stealth. When the figures move to the next machine, I move to the opposite side of where they just were. I'm listening and I hear a gun being placed down. I had the .45 in my pocket, but these accent speaking bastards number three, I got seven rounds. I didn't like the odds, so I retrace my steps up to the fence and the truck. I'm about to open the door to get the 9mm and I stop, realizing if I open the door, the ignition buzzer goes off. I walk around to the passenger side open the door and get the 9. If I had parked on the shoulder I couldn't have opened the door." Sam was very interested in Jake's story now. He shook his head, the pain slipping away to the effects of the Alka-Seltzer and interest in Jake's story.

The coffee was finishing up so Jake stood up to prepare two cups of the brew. "Anyways, I got the gun, and I'm thinking these guys have an escape route. I go back up to the birm the flashlights are still there, then, it comes to me. I ought to double around the front on foot cause if I start the truck these guys are gone." Sam followed Jake's logic. He sipped his coffee and said thanks to Jake. Jake took a sip and continued. "So here I am jogging to the front of the yard, my lungs are killing me, all I can do is think to breathe in through the nose and out through the mouth. I finally get to the front and the same feeling puts me on caution. I get to the corner and peek around the fence, to see that there is a dark panel van parked at the entry. I can see some guy smoking in the driver seat, the dumb bastard gave himself up with his smoke. I'm standing there wondering if I can slink down the fence and avoid being seen; all of a sudden the prick gets out of the truck to take a leak." Sam is now enthralled. He is waiting on every word Jake spoke. "The guy is off to the back of the van so I run up to the passenger side of the van, and look through the cab to pick him off in the side view mirror. I see him shake it and turn to face the cab. I drop out of his possible line of sight. I move down the side and around the back of the van. I raise the

9 and face him. He makes a move to get to the horn and I pistol whip him." Sam is listening in disbelief. "The guy starts moving I let him have it again, oh yeah, he had a gun and a knife on him." Sam was like a kid listening to a ghost story.

"I see the flashlights are headed back this way, and I'm starting to panic, I think stealth. The driver moves again and I really let him have it, this time with the butt of the gun. I drag the poor bastard off to the brush and dump him there; I steal these cigarettes from him and get in the truck. I light one up trying to maintain my stealth and subterfuge so that everything appears A-Okay. The flashlights go off. Something tells me to start the truck and they appear at the gate. Sam, I didn't have a clue as to what it was I was gonna do, then it came to me, I let the truck roll ahead in gear, they seemed to get ready to get into the truck and I floored it. I ran the pricks over and jumped out of the van. I moved to the first guy and hammered him with the 9, the second guy was making a move so I let off a round; he stopped and I clubbed him. The third guy was dead, his neck got broke." Sam was looking at Jake like he was pulling his leg, his mouth was open and his hands were trembling.

"Sam, I wanted to sit so badly, but I checked these guys out, they had semi-automatic shoulder arms. I cleared the weapons and had a smoke. By the time everyone had gotten there, a need for a bomb disposal unit had been determined. They decided that for a public announcement it would be better to suggest that the Trooper had investigated suspicious activity and a reported gunshot. Jake turned on the radio so Sam could validate all that was told to him. "I got three of them alive Sam." He had listened to it all, he hadn't said a thing.

Sam rose and went atop. He moved to the open edge of the slip and dove into the water. The cool water seemed to ease Sam's discomfort. He let the force of the dive take him well below water's level. After his downward motion stopped Sam floated to the top. His head broke the surface and he took a deep breath. He swam in circles for a bit and dipped back under. He forced air to pass through his nostrils and shook his head. His swim was done. He moved towards the other side of the boat and climbed up on the dock. He walked down along the side of **The Buried Treasure.** Jake was waiting for him. Sam was surprised to see him. He figured Jake might be in the head.

"There is more Sam." Jake handed a towel to Sam. As he took it from Jake he wasn't sure he wanted to hear it. "More than what you just told me?" Jake nodded. Sam sat in the cockpit. He looked towards the east. "Daylight is coming Jake." "Yeah, Sam, it sure is coming." Sam dragged the towel across his head and sat back. "Shit, Jake, what more could you possibly provide?" Jake went below and brought up two more coffees. "Sam do you remember that girl I frolicked with, her name is Susie." Sam thought about Jake's frolicking, "I don't think so Jake. Well, when they cut me loose from the scene, I thought about coming here to check on you. The feeling I had directed me to one of my watering holes. I'm sitting out in the truck in front of the joint wondering what the hell I'm doing and I go in. Susie is behind the bar. I pick my seat and get to asking her about anything she might know about psychics. I buy the bar a few rounds, one to get the channel switched to the news, and the second because they needed a distraction after seeing the news, and three for having Susie get Colleen in there to cover her shift.

We depart to her house over near Fox woods. I'm thinking she is gonna tell me something I have questions for. We get into her house she pours a couple of drinks and blows me. She said she knew how to quiet down my thoughts. And then I get to asking questions about these feelings I have." Sam is beside himself listening to this part, of more. Jake saw the skepticism on Sams' face. "No, Sam this is nothing but the reliable truth." I ask her about this psychic stuff and she tells me she knew I was psychic when I knew her before. Sam looked at Jake. "Jake, every time you get with these women you're half-cocked on booze, who are you kidding?" Jake heard what Sam said and understood him. He didn't blame Sam for his thinking because he was correct. Jake also knew that Sam would be hard pressed to believe him. "Sam, she gave me this amulet." He reached in his shirt and showed it to him. Sam inspected it and shrugged. "She bought it for me years ago, she said it was to remind me of calming and quieting myself. She also said that loss was a part of living life, and that I should expect more. She said 'What has fallen upon us is dark and is the worst evil men can conspire'. She said 'many battles were to come and there would be loss in them'."

"Jake I know you are repeating the story, believe me I do, but I don't want to hear about more loss right now." "Yeah Sam, I'm sorry about that but the story needed to be told as one story not two."

Sam asked Jake, "How many guys did you take out?" Jake answered, "Four, Sam." "Did you say these guys had accents?" Jake nodded. "Cooper must be pretty happy about all of this... Kind of validates her victim profiling theory, eh?" Jake nodded in agreement. The men sat silently. Jake was silent, Sam was suffering in silence.

"Oh shit! I missed seeing Jameson off." Jake spoke up to Sams' exclamation. "No ya didn't, he wished you well last night at dinner." Sam nodded, "Cool. How was he doing Jake?" "He seemed to have his eyes wide open last night Sam. I think he'll do fine."

Jake took notice of something. "Sam I tell you this shit kicking story, and well you're hung-over, but I thought you would have been more surprised." Jake thought to put his point of reference right out in front. "Jake, I'm glad this psychic thing worked out for you and us last evening, really I am. However, these aren't the guys who are responsible. They are simply the idiots working for the one responsible, right?" Jake nodded, "I guess so Sam." "Well, until I have that prick answering my question as to why it was done, I don't see a need to celebrate just yet."

Jake spoke to Sam's reference. "I suppose you're right Sam, but I got to tell ya, I think it is a huge step in the progression of the case. Shit, it takes some of the questions out of it if nothing else."

Sam finally acknowledged the point. "Yes Jake, you are right, and I am glad that you are okay too. But, Jake they aren't in the ground yet." Jake could only say, "I know."

"And, Jake do ya know something else?" Jake shook his head while he listened.

"I think, I'm gonna let Monica's parents take them home." Jake was taken back a bit. He hadn't considered that choice of action, but when he heard it, his heart agreed. "Sam I think that will make it much easier on them, it is a good choice." "Yeah, well, Jake I wish it wasn't mine to have to make." "Wise choices are usually like that Sam, they are made alone."

Sam had another realization. "Have you talked to George or Stan?" "Nope." Sam stood up and went below. "Jesus, Jake ,what are they going to be thinking when they show up to work?" Jake let out a laugh. "I don't know Sam, they'll probably want to know if it is a paid day off." Jake cackled again. He found his own response amusing. Sam didn't. Sam jumped into the head and showered off the morning's swim. He got out as fast as he got in and dressed. "Hey Sam are you sober enough to drive?" Sam just looked at Jake and said, "I guess I'll have to be, I'm heading over there Jake, I'll see ya later." Jake watched him leave. "Okay Sam, I'll be here."

Chapter 20

Sam was in his truck speeding to the job sight. As he drew close he saw the emergency beacons flashing. He pulled up to the roadblock keeping the general public and press away from the investigation. He identified himself as the business owner. The cops already knew who he was, and they allowed him to pass. He drove up to the area where the authorities had been congregating, and he pulled his truck into an area abruptly. He got out of the truck and headed to the group of law enforcement and emergency responders.

Hendrik was there and Sam thought he recognized some of the uniforms. Hendrik saw Sam and moved close to him. As he did, he motioned Sam over to his area. "Good morning Sam, if ya can call it that." Sam nodded. "What do you have Detective Hendrik?" "Apparently Sam we have bombs. The Disposal Team is working on the last one." Sam nodded, "Have any of your guys seen the guys who work for me and Jake?" Hendrik shook his head, "I don't think so Sam. Maybe they saw it on the news last night?" Sam hadn't thought of that. He looked at his watch and noticed that they would be pulling up any time. "Tell me Hendrik, will they be able to work today?" Hendrik looked at Sam and said, "Nothing doing Sam, not for quite sometime." Sam looked at Hendrik. "Do you need anything from me Hendrik?" Hendrik just shook his head. "No, I can't thing of what I would need from you yet." Sam nodded, "Okay, I'm going to get back to the blockade and wait for them." "Okay Sam, I'll send someone for ya if I need anything." Sam got back into his truck and drove down to the blockade. He parked on the protected side of the barrier and waited. He rested his head, which was still pounding slightly from last night. His eyes closed and he fell off.

Sometime later, Sam didn't know how long, an officer knocked on Sam's door. Sam looked at him thinking this bad dream was coming to an end. The patrolman pointed to a fella wanting to get to work. Sam looked to see that it was George. He got out of his truck and went to let George know what was up. George already knew. George saw Sam for the first time since the murders. He offered his condolences. Then he mentioned, "That all of the guys felt about the same." Sam thanked George. "George, I guess this is gonna be a crime scene for some time." George realized Sam wasn't thinking straight about things. "Sam, you and Jake have been very good to all of us. We knew there would be no work today. Everyone decided that after last nights news." Sam listened to George obviously he and Stan were working well together. "I have already been in touch with the state authorities, so we are up to speed with the delays. We notified the customer as to the production shortage and Sgt. Gunn in Lyme P.D validated it. We're okay Sam, don't fret about any of this. The good thing is the fact that that trooper had done some great investigating... we still have the machines." Sam had forgotten that these guys were waiting on a day to come where they would be the bosses. George asked Sam "Is that why you are here, because you thought, you needed to tell us?" Sam just looked at George. "Yeah, I guess so George." "Well Sam, I'm glad you care so much, and it is helpful, but we are on the job, or were on it." Sam realized again they had told George and Stan that they were the new owners of the business. "Yeah, you're right George and you seem to have it all together." "Well, Sam, you and Jake had set some great rules for running a business." George looked at Sam. "Do you need anything from me or the others?" Sam shook his head. "No, no thanks George."

"Okay Sam, I need to go look at another bid, maybe I'll see ya later?" Sam nodded. "Okay George."

George waited another second or two. He seemed to be waiting on a response from Sam. Sam never offered what George was looking for. George turned his truck around and waved at Sam. George had left.

Sam suddenly thought of what Jake had said about more loss and dealing with it. Sam no longer found himself as a vital part of the business. Sam thought the loss of his family sucked, and he was beginning to see how others things had a portion of sucking in loss.

The day had come; it started without Sam being needed. He was off taking a vacation. He grew a bit upset with himself and needed some quieting down. He was on a rip from last night and slightly out of his mind. There was no context Sam could figure. He hadn't been apart of the past hours. He thought back to Jake saying, "A lot more loss to come." Sam wondered how much more loss he could reasonably put up with. How much more did he have to lose? He was fit to be tied. He visualized the day when he had a faceless person in his grasp. He tried to funnel it into some sort of control. He walked back to his truck and got in. He didn't know where he wanted to go. He didn't know what he wanted to do. That was a lie, he did know, he just couldn't have it. Emptiness cursed him. Sam isolated this feeling, as emptiness and he knew it would be a companion for some time. He started his truck and went back to *The Buried Treasure.*

When Sam returned to the marina there was a car next to Jake's truck he didn't know. Sam grumbled to himself, *the psychic hadn't had enough of Jake.* Sam wondered if he should leave and go elsewhere. He was feeling too poorly. He made his way to the slip. To his surprise it wasn't any psychic who was at the boat, it was Bina. Sam had a difficult time understanding. When he got back to the boat Jake and Bina greeted him.

"How goes the job Sam?" Sam looked at Jake. "It doesn't and it won't, not for some time." Cooper perked up seeing Sam. "I heard you were taking some time for yourself last night." Sam half-heartedly smiled. "I feel like hell. I don't know what to do or where to go."

Jake knew this was coming. "Well Sam it is a good thing you came back." "We were just talking about that." Cooper chimed in, "Yep we were wondering how you felt about heading down to D.C. waters?" Sam listened but had no response. Jake said to Sam, "There is only one Potomac River Sam, and it is a beauty." Sam finally got around to asking a question. "Why D.C.?" "Well Sam, Jameson left for the area this morning, Cooper is going in a day or two, and we are just plum out of things to do here in Lyme." Cooper qualified the need to go. "The guys who met Jake last night are being extradited to the Federal System, they will be local to us from D.C., pretty much the whole investigation happens south of here after I go."

Sam sat with them in the cockpit. He put his face in his hands. He separated his hands and rubbed his temple region. Cooper and Jake where waiting on Sam's agreement to the south. He looked up at them. "I guess D.C. is as good a place as any." Jakes' heart swelled seeing his friend Sam so torn up. "'Ya know Jake, this morning when I jumped out of here to see what was going on after you told your tale...

I don't know what I was thinking... George had conversations last night with the guys after he talked to the State Authorities. Cooper here has received some validation of her theory on Victim Insight, and you my friend... you have found something you always had, but never knew. Shit, even Hendrik and The State Trooper have enjoyed some success over the single event, which has left me with only one dreadful thing to contemplate. My family is even in better hands with Monica's parents."

Cooper watched Sam close chapters on his life... in her experience Sam was ahead of any normal part of grieving. Months ahead, Sam had described himself void of everything that was important to him, and brilliantly. Nobody hearing what Sam had just uttered would have any confusion. Her eyes swelled with tears, her heart choked her throat. Looking at Sam wrecked from the effects of the self-inflicted poison, only taken as a self-medication, she decided to give him a hug and cry on him. Sam resisted at first, but Cooper was like a kitten wanting a pet, having realized that mommy was no longer around. She broke Sam down. He yielded and it was as if Coopers' crying did something for Sam, like an unknown release, Sam felt Coopers' sympathy and somehow found it within himself to release some of his pain. He joined her crying.

Jake sat motionless watching his two friends, and he was cool with it. He knew in his heart and mind that these two would yield to each other in the future. He knew both of them had enough pain to share. Enough pain shared so as to stumble upon some happiness. They didn't know it yet because they were both too miserable. Jake could see the rage behind the soft and caring embraces they offered to each. And Jake knew that after today, tomorrow would have a new direction to it. Jake knew he had to go to Eriks'. Sam was in no shape to visit his in-laws.

Jake would get an early start. Arrangements needed to be made, Erik would need to know about the shipping of The Murphy Family, and Monica's family needed a friendly face. Jake left *The Buried Treasure;* he went to his truck and drove to Erik's.

About the author

Martin H. Petry is a 42 year old man living in Woonsocket RI.

He supports himself as a route driver in the medical waste industry and is employed at Stericyle.

Formerly and in younger days, he was an arborist for a period of 20 years.

Martin graduated from Bryant College in 1986 with a BS in Business Administration.

Martin's writing began after a car accident, which later proved to be the end of his climbing days as an arborist.

During the time of rehabilitation, Martin began a determined period of writing poetry, essays and a few other manuscripts.

He has a few lyrics in the mix as well.

You can view Martin's work at

http://usamutt.journalspace.com/

Martin would like the reader to understand that this book Hard Justice

The Violation

is the first of a trilogy, and he hopes the writing of the first would

offer any reader a desire to look forward to reading the 2nd, which is being written.

Printed in the United States
67267LVS00003B/79-120